WINYAH BAY

By

DAVID MARING

ISBN: 1484882601
ISBN 13: 9781484882603

Library of Congress Control Number: 2013908866
CreateSpace Independent Publishing Platform, North Charleston, South Carolina

PROLOGUE

The ancient sea receded over a hundred miles and left an imprint upon the land in the form of a bay fed by numerous rivers. Into this land came a Pre-Clovis people who arrived by trekking along the ice bridge that connected Europe and the North American continent. Even after the ice melted and the land bridge disappeared, their kindred continued to follow the footsteps of their predecessors using primitive watercrafts. Finally, the contact between Europe and North America was broken by the vast expanse of the sea and climate change.

At a later time people from Asia crossed the Bering Strait and spread across the American continent until they also reached the bay. They were stronger than the original inhabitants, and soon displaced them as the region's inhabitants. For countless years they were the sole occupiers of the area. Then Vikings from the island of Greenland arrived in North America and established a base in Newfoundland. Their settlements in the North lasted over two hundred years. The Vikings were people of the sea, and eventually had contact with the culture around the bay. Later, others from the great powers of Europe were drawn to this body of water. Each group thought it belonged to them. But the bay belongs to no one. Even the present inhabitants will one day disappear, but the bay will remain and always be a magnet to the human species.

THE ARCHEOLOGIST

The light from the morning sun reflected off an object protruding from a layer of pluff mud in the excavation pit. Karen reached down and with great difficulty freed the item from the embrace of the earth. After removing the debris, she studied the large silver pendant in the palm of her hand and was impressed by engravings on the object. The symbols were definitely of Viking origin. Karen had seen similar inscriptions while working in Norway. Placing her find to one side, she probed further into the mud.

As Karen lay in her tent near the excavation site that evening, she pondered her discovery. How did a Viking artifact find its way to this bluff on the Waccamaw, a river that flowed into Winyah Bay. While her knowledge of Viking history initially rejected the idea of a settlement this far south, she could not dispute the silver pendant's existents. She had found it below the layer of earth that held Winyah Indian artifacts and Spanish coins. This could be the link that would confirm reports from

Spanish explorers that a white tribe resided on the South Carolina coast in 1521.

Two days later another remarkable discovery was unearthed—a collection of charred bones and a skull that appeared to be human. Among the bones was a golden necklace that she suspected predated even the Viking artifact. Using caution, Karen removed the items from the earth that had kept its secrets hidden from the eyes of man for centuries. She decided to have the bones and skull delivered to the lab at Massachusetts Institute of Technology in Cambridge where her former fiancé was department head. Though they were no longer personally involved, she trusted him when it came to performing a DNA analysis. A second package containing the necklace and pendant would be sent to the controversial archeologist Stephen Camp. His recent book had propounded the theory of a Pre-Clovis people in North America. Camp believed that at the time Indians crossed the Bering Strait, a more ancient people from Europe already inhabited the eastern seaboard. This Pre-Clovis group had arrived during an ice age, which provided them access from the European continent. Recent discoveries in places like Aiken seemed to give credence to his theory. Camp's view was a minority one and not widely accepted in academic circles. But Karen felt the mounting evidence would soon shift the tide in favor of a European presence prior to the Clovis migration from the Asian continent.

THE
FISH PEOPLE

By the time the year one thousand arrived, the group was less than a hundred individuals. It had not always been this way; once their villages had spread across the landscape near rivers that flowed into a bay. But over the years a new race, whose skin resembled the color of clay pottery, had moved in from the interior. They forcibly seized the best hunting grounds, looted the villages, killed men, and carried off the women and children as slaves. Now the sole remnants of the Fish People, who arrived in this land eons ago when ice still hugged the continent, were restricted to a sliver of land infested with mosquitoes, snakes, and alligators. A dangerous place, but one that yielded a bountiful harvest from waters that fed the marsh along the bay.

In the beginning their ancestors lived on a diet composed almost entirely of fish. When the ice age ended, their supply of fish was greatly diminished. Many died because they failed to adapt. But in human history there are always those individuals who change their lifestyle and survive. These survivors became land meat-eaters because of the numerous buffalo that inhabited the region. But this supply was diminished as the climate changed. In order to continue to exist, they turned to other avenues to find sustenance. As wild animals of the forest multiplied when trees replaced the grasslands, the people became adept in hunting them. To this source of meat was added domesticated plants from seeds purchased in trade from a civilization that flourished in a land far to the south. This added source of food sustained the people when animals were scarce during the cold season.

The Fish People were secure by their inhospitable location from the other tribes during heat of summer. However, when the cold winds blew and biting insects retreated for the winter, others could be seen hunting in the region. Any encounter with those who wore different moccasins meant death or enslavement, for the clay-colored ones excelled at the bow and tomahawk.

* * *

In a village erected on a bluff upriver from where the bay led to the sea, Kote, the village's priestess, waited for Kei. She had not wanted her daughter-in-law to go into the forest that hugged the riverbank. Strangers had been spotted two moons ago at a creek a day's distance from the village. This news had kept even the men in camp. Despite Kote's warnings, Kei had gone to the sacred burial ground determined to bury the bones of her man who was killed by a black bear while hunting thirty moons ago. There she would bury him as tradition required, now that a funeral pyre had blazed, and his remains were dried by the sun.

Kote mourned the death of her only child, Fahe. But she took comfort knowing that before the bear attack, her son's seed had sprung forth in the body of Kei, a woman everyone in the village thought was barren. She had not borne a child, although she had lived in the lodge with Fahe through five maize harvests. Now everyone knew the gods had smiled upon her because Kei's body showed a new life pushing through the thin animal skins that covered her tall, slender, white body.

* * *

Kei's feet made a crushing sound as she stepped from the heavy foliage of the forest onto the cleared plot of land near a bluff on the Big River. There the plants of late autumn lay frozen in heavy dew. They had turned to ice as the temperature plummeted after the light rose in the heavens that morning. She stepped carefully across the cleared land until she reached a grove of pine trees where her ancestors' remains were buried. There she laid the charred bones of her mate in a deep pit, one she had dug the day after his death. She removed a golden necklace from around her neck and placed it in the grave. The necklace had been passed down for generations and originally was brought by the first settlers from a land across the sea. Before she completed the burial, her ears picked up a sound from the forest. For a moment her hands stopped pulling dirt into the pit. Her eyes strained to see through the foliage. She saw nothing that gave her alarm. A moment later she returned to her goal. Afterwards, she placed several dead tree limbs across the mound of dirt that now covered her mate's bones. She looked down with satisfaction. The pit was deep enough to prevent wild animals from picking up the scent and digging until their jaws could retrieve the remains and crush them for the marrow.

Kei stepped to the edge of the forest, sat down along the riverbank and placed her back against the trunk of a large oak tree covered with moss. Soon her eyelids grew heavy, and her alertness gave way to a peaceful sleep. She dreamed of a happier time when her man had returned from the hunt with the carcass of an animal slung across his broad shoulders. It was a day when he was greeted with cries of joy from the inhabitants who appreciated the fresh meat, which added variety to their daily course of corn, shellfish, squash, and sweet potatoes.

* * *

The Winyah braves slipped quietly through the trees. The forward movements of their moccasins were not impeded by brush, for the forest grew so thick along the riverbank that the trees' branches denied sunlight to nature's floor. The warriors were from a village that lay to the north of the bay on a river whose color was black from the organic matter that washed from its bank every time it rained. The target of these warriors was a village of Fish People, a group whose characteristics were distinct from those of the surrounding tribes. They were taller, and some of these strange ones had eyes that were blue; hair grew upon the faces of their men. The color of the hair on their heads was also different, a variety of brown and red. But the most striking characteristic was the skin.

In the settlement of the hairy ones, the Winyahs expected to find stores of food to feed their families through the cold winter months. These strange people had learned the art of taking the seeds of wild plants and bringing them to fruition on plots of land they cleared in the forest. In the spring their fields were ripe with a variety of edibles, and in the fall, squash grew in abundance in their fields. Some of the magical ways of these strange ones had been adopted by the Winyahs whose women had learned the art of agriculture from females taken as slaves in prior battles. Because of this knowledge, the tribe did not suffer as their ancestors had when the cold wind swept across the land, nor were they as dependent upon the buffalo which were fast disappearing as the climate change led to less grassland and more forest. The Fish People had also affected their culture in other ways. Some Winyahs now built lodges from trees and plastered them with a combination of cracked sea shells, mud, and moss.

Coan, the leader of the raiding party, was surprised to find the village stood alert to their presence. He thought of turning back but then saw storehouses built with sturdy pieces of wood and thatched with the heavy grasses that grew in abundance in the marsh. They must be full of things the Fish People had stored to get them through the winter. It was too much temptation for him to resist. He observed the village had few strong warriors. Most were old men and young boys. Perhaps, the best fighters had already been killed defending their village from earlier attacks.

Thirty warriors gripped the handles of their tomahawks with excitement as they waited for the signal. Coan raised his tomahawk in the air and let out a war cry; the feet of his warriors moved swiftly through the forest toward the village.

The Fish People fought valiantly, but in a few minutes their village was overrun. After the battle, the warriors searched every structure. The wails of the women and children filled the air, as they were dragged toward a collection point beside a storage hut. Coan looked on with pleasure. There were twenty healthy females that could be bred. The old ones his warriors would kill by a blow to the head. The children would be incorporated into the tribe.

Kote looked into the eyes of the warrior who had just entered her hut. His intent was clear. She knew old women would be viewed as having no value, which meant certain death. Before his weapon could strike a blow to her head, she began to utter a loud chant and threw pieces of silver and bright colored stones into the air, items that had been brought by her ancestors to the shores of this land. The warrior, observing her action, realized this was a holy woman, and that he should bring this creature before the chief. He lowered his tomahawk and grabbed her by the long red hair that sprouted from her head, then dragged her through the hut's opening. She didn't resist as the heels of her feet broke the soft ground. A moment later she was deposited in front of the man who was responsible for her village's destruction.

She listened carefully to the words spoken by the warrior to his leader. She knew that her actions in the hut had made an impression upon her captor. He believed she was a shaman, a person whose life was respected even by the most barbaric tribes. Before the first words fell from the leader's lips, she knew her life would be spared.

"Do you speak our language?"

"Yes, I learned it from a woman of your tribe who was one of our slaves."

"You possess magical powers?"

"I can speak to the gods, and I know the art of healing."

"Your powers will be tested, and if you fail, you will be killed."

"That is as it should be."

"Go back to your hut and retrieve the things on which you depend to cast your spells and heal the sick."

"I have one favor to ask before I serve you."

"Old woman, wasn't saving your life enough?"

"My life is nearly spent, but I have a young woman that I am teaching the ways of the gods. When I am no longer, you will need her to speak to the heavens for you."

"Where is this woman?"

"At the burial ground of our ancestors," she said, pointing in its direction.

"You shall have this favor from me. Do not ask for another, for it shall not be granted."

The leader turned and spoke to his men. After the words fell from his lips, two warriors ran in the direction the old woman had pointed.

Kote felt no guilt in disclosing the location of Kei. The young woman could not survive in the forest alone. It would be better for Kei to be a slave in the camp of the Winyah than to die of starvation.

* * *

Kei awoke from a deep sleep. This restful respite, after the physical labor earlier performed in her pregnant state, left her refreshed. I must return to the village, she thought. Kote will be worried. She rose to her feet and began the short walk along the path that led home. The first indication that she was not alone was a sudden flight of birds through the trees. She quickly slipped into some undergrowth. She lay quietly, hoping that the two warriors coming down the path had not seen her. Her hope was dashed when they came straight to her hiding place. She understood their language and knew they did not intend to harm her. Her wrists were tied with a strip of vine, and then she was led back to her village.

Kei's eyes filled with tears. The bodies of the slain lay on the ground. She knew the life she had known was now a thing of the past. She would have to build a new life among these strange, primitive people. She must survive for the sake of her child.

Coan looked down at the two women he had spared. The old one's red hair was sprinkled with gray, and her blue eyes were surrounded by skin wrinkled by the sun. Several of her teeth were missing, and the remaining ones were darkened by rot. The other woman had the same characteristics of red hair and blue eyes, but her other features contained the vitality of youth. He saw that she was with child and this pleased him. *If it is a male child, I will add him as a warrior in fourteen springs. And if it is a female, she will breed with one of my warriors and produce many offspring.*

The Winyah were a small tribe and in constant danger of being decimated by larger groups that lived nearby. Their only hope of survival was to incorporate others into their tribe at every opportunity. The Fish people were one of those opportunities.

Coan gave orders to load the canoes with the captives and the booty taken from the village. The canoes were made from tree trunks that had a span of thirty feet; the inside of each had been hollowed out by fire and stone tools. Each canoe could carry up to ten passengers.

Kei helped Kote load a heavy wooden box that contained items she used to communicate with the gods. These items were ancient artifacts brought to this land by her ancestors.

"We must protect this with our very lives," Kote said to her daughter-in-law as the trunk was placed into the canoe. "It is the only physical evidence that we are not of this land. One day our people will come from across the sea and find us."

Kei did not believe the old woman. Too many generations had passed, and she felt certain that those to whom they claimed kinship now had no memory of them. But she would not utter these words, for she knew Kote carried in her heart the belief of those generations who had gone before her, a belief their people would come. But the earlier inhabitants of Europe that existed when the ice age connected the two continents had been overwhelmed by others and no memory existed of them, nor of those who had migrated to the North American shore.

THE
VIKINGS

In the year 1200, Ingri watched with interest as two men bartered over her value. They did not take notice of her presence. It was as if her small body crouched in the corner of the room did not exist. She listened closely to the conversation, afraid her father's price would be too high. He had turned down offers on previous occasions. The others had been older–some even older than her father. Until this day, no young men had entered negotiation for her because they were still under the direction of their families and had no independent source of income. The man now bartering for her was no more than twenty, but he had assets. She was impressed by his physical appearance. He was taller than other men in the village. She had seen him strutting about the streets as if he were a member of the ruling family. But he wasn't. Ingri knew the descendants of Leif Ericksson, and he did not belong to that clan, though he did come from a line of merchants.

Vangard looked at the Norseman that sat across from him on a pile of skins thrown on the floor by Ingri. Even in his drunken state he could see from Baldar's chiseled face that this was a man whose body contained the prowess and physical strength to make the journey across the sea and bring back riches from which he could make the payment necessary for Ingri. Besides, Baldar already owned a merchant ship; one inherited upon the death of his father last year. As the only surviving child, he had also inherited personal goods and a small house that lay a short distance from the harbor. It would be a good match. In his old age Vangard would have grandchildren to listen to his tales of plundering the land of Wales and of the walrus hunts. These tales would be told as he sat by a warm fire in a house that Baldar planned to build on a farm in the western province. He would give serious consideration to this young Viking's proposal, but he would act disinterested for a few months. It would be good to let the man who sat across from him have his appetite grow for the tasty morsel that he knew his daughter presented.

* * *

Weeks after summer disappeared and when ice began to form a thin crust upon the harbor, Ingri sleep was disturbed by the sound of laughter in the big room. She crept from her bed of furs, which lay upon a stone floor of the small room attached to the main structure. The words from her father's mouth stunned her.

"Yes, she would make you a good wife," he said to Bortz.

This man was not a stranger to her home. He had been a frequent visitor since his wife died in childbirth five years ago. This was not the old man's only tragedy. His sons had been lost at sea during a walrus hunt, and the same year his only daughter had died from a plague that swept Greenland, taking many in its wake.

"Thank you, Vangard," Bortz said. "I must have a woman to give me an heir before next spring, for I am the last of my line, and my days upon this earth are numbered. Your daughter will no doubt outlive me and have the opportunity to wed another while she is still young enough to birth many children. I just need to survive long enough to have my seed take root in her womb. As agreed, you shall have all my possessions upon my death, but the payment of silver, I will have my thane deliver to you within three days."

"So let it be, and may Thor bless this union. Come, let us go to the town lodge and spend this night drinking with the sailors who came into the harbor today on that merchant ship from Iceland."

After the two men departed, Ingri could not return to her sleep. Her thoughts traveled back to a time when the home was filled with laughter between the two older brothers and her. But that cheerfulness had left when the two were killed over a dispute with others about possession of Welsh women taken as slaves during a raid. And now her mother was dead, and her father was in the constant company of Bortz. They were in a drunken state most evenings as they shared their sorrows.

As the two old men walked down the street, Vangard caught a glimpse of Baldar, as the young captain hurried toward his ship at the dock. He did not feel guilty about the situation, although he had promised to give the young Viking an answer on his proposal for Ingri before he set sail. But things had changed since their meeting months ago. Silver in his pocket and possession of his friend's assets in the near future was a better deal than Balder could offer at the moment, for no one knew what might lie ahead. Balder might never return. His ship like many others could be lost at sea. Besides, his friend was old and in poor health. By the time Baldar's ship had time to make the return voyage to Greenland, Ingri might be a widow and perhaps even a tastier morsel with her body developed from motherhood. Virginity was not something upon which Viking men placed great value.

* * *

Baldar observed the last of the furs and walrus ivory being loaded on board his ship. This cargo vessel, a knar christened the *Fallehal* in memory of his deceased mother, had been inherited upon his father's death. As his feet paced back and forth upon the wooden deck, he pondered the fact that the season was growing short to set sail from Greenland. Soon the coming winter would make travel upon the high seas impossible. Already a thin layer of ice clung to the land along the fjords in the northern parts of the island; even the farmers in the western provinces had begun to retreat into their longhouses for the coming winter. Feeling the chill of the morning air, Baldar pulled a hood made from bear skin over his head, then turned and directed his men to bring the last barrel of pickled fish aboard.

"We are ready to sail," said a deep voice from behind Baldar. His large-framed body turned to face Nor, the first mate, a man whose height reached only five feet. But it would be a mistake to underestimate this red-headed Norseman who, despite his lack of height, was not a man to cross. His sword had taken the life of many strangers who failed to understand that size was not a proper measurement of skill or courage. The other members of the crew also knew the thrill of taking a life. They had whetted their articles of death upon unsuspecting souls during raids upon the Welsh coast last spring while seeking slaves, a trade that Viking ships engaged in at every opportunity. For trafficking in human beings was profitable. Thanes were always in demand in the ports of every country but especially female slaves in the province of Greenland. With the eastern portion of this island now settled by 5,000 souls, the greatest need after lumber was women. The men so greatly outnumbered the opposite sex that fights over the few available women on the island had reached a boiling point that threatened the political stability of the colony. But while the prices for female thanes were high on the island, they brought an even greater price in Vineland, a Norse region that lay two weeks' journey to the west. This trade area, founded by Leif Eriksson generations earlier, had grown to a population of nine hundred permanent settlers, spread out over three settlements. The land was rich in hides and furs, but the most important item not obtainable in Greenland was lumber. Greenland trees not already harvested were too small to be of any use, except keeping the hearths burning for warmth and cooking. This state of affairs made lumber always a commodity in great demand for shipbuilding, the making of shields, and other instruments of war.

Baldar watched with pride as his men hoisted the sail on his knar. Movement across the sea would depend on this square-rigged sail because, unlike a warship, his merchant ship carried no oars and was solely dependent upon the wind for propulsion. His crew of eleven was less than the number a trading ship of this size normally carried. But he knew additional sailors would take up valuable space needed for the goods he was carrying to the Norwegian coast. The vessel would be even more crowded on the return voyage, for he planned to bring as many female thanes back as he could fit on his ship's deck. He kept this plan secret. If word of such a cargo was dispersed to the Viking community in the North Atlantic, it might encourage other ships in the area to seize it. His planned destination on the return voyage was also a closely guarded secret. He did not intend to sell the thanes in Greenland but planned a voyage to the settlement of Hop in Vineland where they would fetch a better price. This journey to the Norse settlement would also give him the opportunity to stack the deck of his knar with lumber. Such a cargo would provide him with enough profit on his return to Greenland to purchase a farm in the western province. He had visited the region once with his uncle. He still remembered a beautiful valley in which grew a thick carpet of grass. The volcanic soil that lay beneath it was fertile and would grow wheat from which he could sustain a farm with sheep, pigs, and perhaps a few of the thick-haired ponies from Iceland.

As Baldar waited for the men to remove the gangplank, his thoughts turned to Ingri, the beautiful daughter of Vangard, whom he first noticed last spring while walking down the street in Brattahlio. Her arms that day were filled with birch wood for her father's hearth. The load looked heavy for such a young maiden, and he had taken the bundle from her arms and carried it into her home. There she had offered him a wooden cup filled with sheep's milk. As he gulped it down, his eyes had filled with amusement as he saw the red flow from her neck to her face, when she caught his eyes admiring the developing young breasts that pressed against the thin skin of her blouse. At the time he estimated her age to be fifteen. No article upon her person gave evidence she had a husband, though it was unusual for one at her age not to be married. The shortage of women caused girls in the colony to be betrothed as soon as they budded into womanhood. Sea life formed a major portion of their diet, and this source of food brought puberty early to girls on the island.

The father, Vangard, had entered the dwelling before Baldar finished drinking the milk poured by Ingri. The daughter quickly explained his presence inside the family lodge, and her father's fingers released the grip on the handle of his sword. Then an invitation to dine that evening was forthcoming from the old man.

That evening, as the sun set, Vangard and Baldar finished their meal of bread, mutton, and cheese before they sat down on the stone floor before the fire. As the fire crackled in the background, the men consumed a large quantity of beer made from barley. The fermented drink removed Baldar's inhibitions and soon he cautiously raised the issue of marriage. Since that event, several months had passed without a response from Vangard. Then last evening as the moon rose in the heavens, the father had sent him a brief message by a male thane. A decision on the issue of a marriage must wait until his return from the voyage.

* * *

Ingri was viewed by the community to be her father's child. It was true she had exhibited a partiality towards him instead of her mother, a woman who died during the same plague that took Bortz's daughter. And it was also true she rejected her mother's attempts to convert her to a new faith called Christianity. Like her father, she had clung to the worship of the Norse gods. Now for the first time in her life, she was contemplating actions in defiance of her father's wishes, and she had time to put these thoughts into action. Her father would spend the night drinking and not return until late morning to their lodge.

The last items loaded, Baldar was about to order the crew to lift anchor when he saw a person with furs strapped to her back and carrying a small trunk approaching. The figure walked at a brisk pace toward the ship. For a moment he did not recognize her, for the facial features were hidden by the fur pulled tightly over her head. But when she reached the gangplank and looked up toward the deck, he immediately recognized the person who stood upon the wharf. She was the same maiden for whom he had negotiated last summer.

Ingri saw the look of surprise on Baldar's face. But this did not deter her. With the firm determination of a Viking woman who knew the course she had chosen, she placed her feet upon the gangplank and walked onto the ship.

"I've come to sail with you and become your wife," she said.

Baldar was taken aback by such bold words spoken by a person he met only once several months ago before he left the port to spend time at sea seeking walrus ivory.

"Has your father consented?"

"No. He agreed last night that I should become the wife of old Bortz who promised him great wealth in return for me."

"Are you sure that you want to take this dangerous voyage with me?"

"My actions have Thor's blessing. Last night while I prayed to him, he sent a star streaking across the heavens."

"A good sign he has smiled upon your request. We shall sail immediately before your father discovers you are missing. We must catch the morning wind and travel far this day lest your father send a ship to reclaim you."

"In this chest are my mother's valuables which I inherited, and the furs upon my back are from animals that I skinned last winter. The furs I bring to you as a gift. Besides this gift, I promise to bear many children who will care for you in your old age when you are no longer able to sail the sea in search of profits."

"Come quickly. We shall store these items among the cargo."

* * *

Ingri stood on the bow of the ship as it left the harbor and sailed through the Eriksfjord, her eyes focused on the open sea ahead. Not once did she turn to look back at her home in the settlement, nor at the surrounding open fields, which were filled with livestock munching on the wild grass that grew abundantly on the rich volcanic soil that lay beneath.

In the days that followed they shared the deck with the crew, and at night everyone huddled together beneath a thick sheet of canvas made from animal skins. Body heat from the group provided the necessary warmth to get through the cold nights. The days were awkward. No private conversation existed on board this ship. One thing of a positive nature that the difficulties of the trip produced was that it forced Baldar and Ingri to read each other's thoughts through body language, something that would later prove of benefit when they were in the company of others.

On the third day of the voyage a bad storm developed. Ingri feared the men would blame her, for many sailors on ships in the North Atlantic believed it was bad luck to have a woman on board. She had heard stories of crews throwing women overboard to appease the gods. But after a few hours the storm abated, and her fears subsided. Later Ingri stood on the bow of the ship and kept a sharp lookout for land. Baldar had predicted that with favorable winds they would sight civilization soon.

When we get to Iceland, Ingri thought, I will go ashore and enjoy the hot spring I have heard about and clean my body. She could not abide the days of stale sweat which made her stink like Baldar and his crew. At home the town's people often commented on her obsession for cleanliness. Her mind soon turned from matters of personal hygiene to Baldar. We must be married before we sail to Maleyfjord in Norway. Perhaps Snorr, my mother's uncle, will perform the ceremony. After all, he was the head of the church in Iceland. And nowadays no marriage was recognized by law in this part of the world until sanctioned by the church. Ingri would secretly ask Thor's forgiveness, for she knew he would be angry with her for engaging in a Christian ceremony.

It had been a long time since Ingri had seen her great-uncle. In fact, her contact with Snorr had been limited to one summer when he stayed with her family in Greenland. Only six at the time, her memory of that event was dim. But she did recall some of the stories told by her mother in later years as they sat by the fire—how her great-uncle was the first

Viking born in Vineland where his parents had resided for three years trading with primitive tribes. They had returned with enough trade goods to make them one of the wealthiest families in Iceland. Snorr had converted to Christianity as a young man and later served as a missionary to the Norse pagans on the surrounding islands. Now the new faith had established its roots, and the pagan ways of the Vikings were fast disappearing.

The storm now a distant memory, the ship entered the port of Reyoarfjall under a sunny sky. Since it was just the beginning of the winter season in Iceland, the ice had yet to appear at this latitude, and the terrain was still a mixture of green pastures intermingled with beautiful layers of wild flowers that bloomed among the crevices of surrounding boulders. In the cliffs above nestled a multitude of wild birds who constantly took flight, gliding over the ship. The Vikings on board took this as a good sign from the gods, for to a man they still followed the old religion.

When the ship reached the wharf and was secured, Baldar and Ingri were the first to depart. The trusted Nor remained behind to protect the trade goods, while the other sailors went ashore to enjoy the life that surrounded the local taverns; beer, food, and sex were always available there.

Ingri followed Baldar down the street to a public lodge where he paid for her stay during the period his ship was expected to be in port. He would spend the nights on the knar until arrangements were made for the marriage ceremony. Ingri would have time to refresh herself, and then she would shop with the handful of silver coins in a leather bag he had placed in her hand. Plans were made to meet the next morning for breakfast at the lodge. In the meantime, Baldar would go and see the local authority and then pay a visit to other merchants in town.

Baldar entered the large stone building that served as Iceland's commerce hall. From this building, *Althingi*, Iceland's governing body raised tariffs for operating the existing governmental structure on the island by taxing a portion of every item sold in the course of commerce. Baldar resented this tax as much as he resented the tax levied in Greenland on goods by the descendants of Eric the Red. A tax that during this famous

Viking's life had made him the wealthiest person on Greenland and now kept his descendants on the top of the social heap on that distant outpost of civilization.

"Baldar, it has been a long time since your last visit," said the plump bureaucrat from behind a desk covered with long slips of paper filled with notations on ships and the goods on board them.

"Nomer, it has indeed been a long time."

"Where is your destination this time?"

"Taking trade goods to the Norwegian coast. I plan to set sail for Maleyfjord in a few days."

"It is a bad time to go there. Terrible word reached us yesterday from sailors on a Norwegian ship that's now tied up at the wharf. There is a plague about in that land."

"There are always plagues in any port that has traffic between the east and west. But we on the outer island must trade or starve. Only Thor knows the time and place of one's death, and man cannot change that."

"You best be careful using the name of the old god for things have changed since your last visit. The *Althingi* is no longer satisfied with levying a small fine. It has discussed banishment for those who speak of the Norse Gods. I suspect burning at the stake will not be far behind." Then, changing the subject, he asked, "Would tomorrow morning be a good time for me to come and inspect your ship and do an accounting of the merchandise you have on board?"

"Yes."

Then the bureaucrat lowered his voice and whispered, "The same arrangement as before."

"I have reserved space on my ship."

A smile spread across the fat round face of the man behind the desk.

"I will come at noon, but my thanes will bring my goods on board during the early morning darkness. Try and get a good price for me from those merchants in Norway."

* * *

The public lodge was operated by an old woman whose face was wrinkled like an old piece of fruit and whose breasts had shrunk to the size of two walnuts. Her red hair, once thick, was reduced to a few strands. But this woman whose body had lost all its feminity still retained a sparkle in her blue eyes and a radiant smile.

The woman led Ingri to a room and promised to return later with hot water for the tin tub that stood in the corner. After the woman departed, Ingri observed her accommodations. The lodging was approximately eight feet wide and ten feet long. Within this small space stood a fireplace that emitted warmth into the room from burning birch logs. A small cot was pressed against the wall.

The innkeeper re-entered without knocking, followed by three male thanes carrying buckets of hot water, which they placed next to the hearth.

"Here is some soap," the innkeeper said, handing her a large bar made from animal fat and ash. "Strip off those clothes, and I'll wash them. In the meantime I'll loan you something to wear until your clothes are dry."

A few minutes later, she reappeared with a gray cotton dress and heavy wool coat.

After soaking in hot soapy water and washing the grime from her body with a sponge, Ingri stepped out upon the cold stone floor and dried herself in front of the hearth. The task completed, she turned and looked into a mirror attached to the wall on the opposite side of the room. For the first time in her life she observed the full image of her body, for no large mirrors existed in the settlement she called home. Her calculating mind immediately took note of her attributes. Her body was trim. Not an ounce of fat appeared on her five-foot frame. Her erect nipples pointed forward, and were perched upon perfectly round mounds of flesh. The abundant growth of hair that surrounded her womanhood reflected the same bright red hair that sprouted from her head and fell to her waist. She knew her body was ready for a man, a moment anticipated since puberty. She was confident Baldar would be pleased on the first night they slept together as husband and wife; during the voyage no opportunity existed for him to take her virginity. Now under the rules of the new faith, he must wait until the Christian marriage ceremony was performed.

* * *

As the sun rose in the azure sky, Baldar was busy supervising the construction of a small cabin on the knar. As captain of his own boat, he intended to have some privacy with his new bride as they journeyed upon the sea. He had seen cabins built on other merchant ships, and he calculated that the length and width of his boat was sufficient to allow a small room for the evenings. No longer would Ingri have to sleep with the crew beneath a canvas on the hard wooden deck. He sent one of his sailors to tell her that he would not be able to meet for the morning meal at the public lodge, but would sup with her that evening. He ordered the man to say nothing about the cabin, for he wanted to surprise Ingri.

Ingri was not disappointed when a sailor delivered the message from Baldar, for the delay in their meeting that day would give her an opportunity to visit the baths. There hot water bubbled forth from the bowels of the earth, and brought with it a mixture of brown liquid sediments full of minerals that invigorated the body and strengthened one's immunity from disease.

That morning Ingri wore a loose-fitting garment made from the skin of a caribou and because of the damp cold weather, she slipped on a bear coat. These items she had purchased yesterday from a trader on the wharf. Before leaving her room, she braided her long hair into a round bun, which she attached to the top of her head with several small forked goose bones. Later, after having a bite to eat in the main room of the lodge, she walked in the direction of the public springs that lay on the edge of town. On the outskirts of the settlement, she removed her new leather shoes to protect them from the volcanic mud that had washed from the surrounding fields and now lay an inch deep on the road.

She had no problem finding her destination from the instructions given by the innkeeper. The springs lay a mile from the lodge and a short distance off the road. It was distinguished from the landscape by a stone hut that was enclosed by a fenced area, which also surrounded several warm springs. An old woman stepped from the hut and greeted Ingri with a toothless smile. She held out her hand for payment, and Ingri dropped one silver coin into her palm and then followed her into the hut. The room was sparsely furnished with a double bed, small table, and two chairs. It had a large hearth from which hung a contraption that held an iron pot filled with water kept at a steady boil by the fire beneath it. In the corner were several buckets used to pour clean water over patrons to wash away mineral mud that clung to their bodies when they finished soaking in the springs. The old woman instructed her to remove her garments and when they had dropped to the floor, she handed her a large sheepskin to cover her body during the walk to the springs.

There weren't other patrons that morning so Ingri had the springs to herself. She chose a pool whose width and length was large enough to completely stretch out her body. Just as she stepped into the bubbling spring, she removed the sheepskin and threw it on the dark gravel that surrounded the water. Soon her naked body was submerged until all that remained in the open air was her head.

Through an opening in the wall, the woman saw Ingri remove the sheepskin. Jealousy flooded her soul as she stared at the naked body and then watched it sink into the soothing hot water. She remembered long ago when her body had been young, filled with vitality and a sexual craving that no man could satisfy. Forcing these thoughts from her mind for a moment, she turned and walked over to where Ingri's clothing lay. Her old but still nimble fingers searched the pockets. A smile spread over her face when her boney hand touched a small leather bag with a pull string cord. She loosened the cord and gazed at the small silver coins it contained. She removed several from the pouch, then pulled the drawstring tight and placed it back in the pocket of the garment. After hiding the stolen coins beneath a loose stone in the corner of the hut, she returned to watch. While she waited for the young woman to finish her bath, her hands caressed her own body trying to create the thrill she had once known in her youth.

Ingri stood up and reached for the sheepskin. Although the bath had a wonderful effect on her, the innkeeper had warned her of the danger of soaking in the miracle water for too long. She looked up and saw the old woman come out of the hut with two buckets of water and with a long piece of drying cloth.

"Come here," the old woman called out with impatience in her voice.

When Ingri reached the hut, the woman snatched the sheepskin from her body and proceeded to empty the warm water over her shoulders. After the second bucket the woman dried her with the piece of cloth despite Ingri's protest. When the woman's fingers took liberties with her naked body, Ingrid fled from her reach into the stone hut. Before the old woman could enter, she grabbed her clothes off the wooden chair that stood in the corner of the room and quickly slipped into them.

Despite the look of excitement that filled the woman's features when she entered the hut, Ingri noticed the glance toward the bulge in her pocket that contained the silver coins. A disturbing thought crossed her mind. Before the woman could utter a word, Ingri ran from the hut and stopped only when her feet hit the mud of the nearby road. There she paused and removed the purse. Counting the coins only confirmed her suspicions. Several coins were missing. She marched back to the hut. The old woman stood at the entrance holding a heavy wooden staff in her hand. Confronting this woman would be futile. They both understood a theft had taken place, and that the thief was willing with the deadly staff in her hand to fight to retain her ill-gotten gain.

* * *

Baldar felt refreshed after the hot bath. While standing beside a blazing fire, he dried his body with a soft piece of bear fur before putting on fresh clothing purchased from a merchant whose ship was tied to the wharf a few yards from his knar. He glanced into a mirror hanging on the wall and was pleased with his appearance. He hoped Ingri would recognize him with his long black hair now cut short and his beard shaved, the effect of which had given him a less-fierce appearance. Dropping two coins into the custodian's hand at the front door of the public bathhouse, he left the establishment and took a right onto a street that passed in front of the public lodge where Ingri was staying. On the way to the lodge he was suddenly filled with an overwhelming desire to see her. Until this moment he had not realized how close they had become during the voyage where she had been his constant companion. A long time had passed since he had held a woman beneath him. It had taken all his self-control during the trip not to be physically intimate with Ingri during those cold nights when her body was pressed tightly against him beneath the waterproof canvas made of seal skins.

Opening the wooden window of her room to catch the rays of the noon sun, Ingri glanced down the street which led to the wharf. She saw a clean-shaven young man making his way slowly up the street. Something about him looked familiar to her—the way he strode with an air of confidence and held his head slightly to the left. As he drew near, she studied his features more closely. He was almost to the front door before she recognized him. A moment of panic ensued as she quickly brushed her hair with an instrument that had an ivory handle. After pinching her cheeks to give them a rosy look, she hurried downstairs to greet him.

An awkward moment ensued as they stood in the doorway facing each other. He smelled of harsh soap. And he had a strange new look in his eyes. She could feel his desire through those blue eyes, and though no words had yet been spoken, she knew a change had occurred in their relationship. For a minute Baldar hesitated, then he reached out and took Ingri into his arms.

"I missed you," he said.

For the first time his lips pressed upon hers. It was a slow and consuming kiss. All the passions of a young Viking male surged at this first moment of intimate contact.

Ingri felt strange as emotions that she never felt before flowed through her body. The fear she once had about the first time, a terror induced into her mind from old women who spoke of the horrible pain on their wedding night, disappeared. She knew this man would be gentle, and the thoughts of being intimate with him washed away all fears.

* * *

In his flowing white robe Bishop Snorr lit the candles in the Church of the Apostle John before kneeling in prayer before an altar covered in walrus ivory. After finishing his prayers for the heathen souls of his region, his eyes surveyed the interior of the sanctuary. His heart swelled with pride at its beauty, for he had directed the construction of this house of worship.

The design was as sturdy as the old Bishop who turned eighty last week—an age that was unprecedented in this part of the world where most men died before forty. Although crude when compared to the cathedrals of Europe, the sanctuary was the envy of other churches in the surrounding islands. Its spiral bell tower stood higher than other structures in Iceland, and it could be seen on a fair day by ships miles from shore.

Returning to his study, Snorr sat down to a meal prepared by his wife and delivered to the church by her thane. After he devoured the pickled fish, along with a small loaf of bread, he made plans for a wedding that would take place tomorrow afternoon. An event he should have looked forward to performing. After all it was his kin, a young maiden who he had not seen in years. But something was troubling him. At their meeting that morning, he inquired if she accepted the Christian faith. Her answers seemed evasive. He had a policy of not marrying a couple if either party was a pagan, considering any such ceremony performed in the sanctuary to be a sacrilege. He had directed her to return tomorrow with the man she planned to marry so that he could examine the prospective groom on his faith.

The stolen oak table from Ireland filled the floor space in the dining room. Several guests in the public lodge were already eating when the young couple took the last remaining seats. An old thane with a scarred face and missing teeth placed two wooden bowls before them filled with a soup made from a thin broth filled with pieces of fish. A moment later he returned with a loaf of bread and two mugs of wheat beer. When Baldar placed a silver coin in the palm of his hand, the thane gave him a thankful grunt, then dragging his bad leg, entered the kitchen adjacent to the dining room.

Hindered from a private conversation, Baldar and Ingri focused their attention on consuming the food that lay before them. Soon the table became vacant as the other patrons finished their meal and departed.

"I went to see my great-uncle this morning," Ingri said.

"Did you make the arrangement for our marriage?" Baldar asked.

"He wants to examine you on your faith."

"You know I am a follower of the old gods," he said, lowering his voice so as not to be overheard.

"The stubborn old man will never grant permission for us to marry once he finds out that you are not of his faith."

"Then we must be married by one of Thor's priests."

"Where will we find one on this island? The prosecutions by the authorities have driven them into exile or underground."

"I will ask Nomer. He will know what to do."

"Can we trust him?"

"Whether for friendship or the lucrative profits he receives when I sell his furs in Norway, he will help us. But we must be careful. If the authorities find out our lives could be in danger."

After leaving Ingri at the lodge, Baldar returned to his ship. He was pleased to see that the cabin had been completed in his absence. Though small, the room contained a bed with a mattress filled with bird feathers, and there was shelving built into one side of the wall. A small double shutter opposite the entranceway allowed the occupants to have a look at the sea, while on the outside a ladder would allow a seaman to climb onto the flat top of the cabin for a view.

"Nor," Baldar called to his first mate. "Go to the customs house and speak privately to Nomer. I need to see him before the sun sets this evening."

He watched as the small-framed sailor walked down the gangplank and started down the wharf toward his destination. He was a good man and one on whom Baldar could rely. The man had served his father faithfully since he had been taken from Wales as a boy. Baldar's father on his death bed had rewarded the man for his loyalty by granting him a writ of emancipation.

As the sun was descending, Nomer arrived at the knar. When Baldar explained his dilemma, Nomer calculated the danger involved in helping this pagan and decided the risk was slight. An hour after he departed, a thane arrived with word that a priest of the old gods would arrive before daybreak. After the thane left, Baldar gave orders to his crew to prepare to sail the next morning. It would not be wise to linger in the harbor after the ceremony. Then he sent one of the crew to tell Ingri to pack her things. A crewman would come the next morning before daybreak to help her bring them to the knar.

While the crew slept that evening, Baldar removed his sword from beneath the bed in his cabin and slipped over the side of the ship in the darkness onto the wharf. A short time later his feet were on the way to the hot springs on the outskirts of town. When Ingri had disclosed to him what happened that morning, he had formed a plan that he kept to himself. As he approached the stone hut, he noticed through the cracks in the wooden shutter that a light burned from within. Quietly he approached and peered through the crack. An old woman was lying in a cot in the corner of the room, another body intertwined with hers. From the candle light beside the cot, the image appeared to be that of a young woman. He applied pressure to the front door and felt it move forward. Finding it was not bolted, he gave it a hard shove with his right shoulder and charged into the room with his sword in hand.

"Where are the silver coins you stole this morning," he shouted.

The two occupants of the cot stared back for a moment with a bewildered look. The younger woman cursed him as she jumped up and charged at him, her face contorted in an angry frenzy. With one swift blow the blade in his hand cut through the neck, and the head flew across the room where it bounced off the wall and rolled across the floor until it finally lay still in the corner. The eyes stared up at Baldar and held his attention briefly in a hypnotic trance until the force of a staff hit him between the shoulder blades. The impact caused him to lose his balance and fall to the floor beside the severed head. He looked up just in time to fend off with his sword another blow from the old woman. As another strike came toward his head, he rolled over, and the blow fell harmlessly on the dirt floor. He quickly rose to his feet and shoved the blade straight through her chest. An old rib cracked as the point of the blade brushed past it and went straight to the heart. As she fell, the swinging sword in his hand severed her head. A massive amount of blood sprayed the wall as her headless corpse fell to the floor.

Baldar looked about the room and saw a jug of wheat beer on the wooden table. He put his hands around the vessel and turned it up to his lips. After quenching his thirst, he began to search. It did not take long to discover the items he was seeking. Ingri's coins were hidden under a flat stone with eighty others. The old hag had collected quite a treasure trove from her thefts over the years. Now the fruits of her labor would be of no benefit to her. But it would provide Ingri and him with funds to start their new life together. Without remorse Balder stepped into the darkness of the night. An hour later he was back in his cabin on the knar asleep on the soft feather bed.

* * *

The old thane, Beawolf, packed his few personal items in a trunk. He did not plan to return to his owner once the marriage ceremony was performed. Thoughts of burning at the stake for his pagan activities were enough to terrify him into leaving Iceland. In between his clothing in the trunk, he placed the small stone figures of Freya, the goddess of love, and her twin brother Frey, a Norseman's defender in battle. These were the only possessions left from his father. A man who was a giant among his people, before he was beheaded by the swift sword of a rival Norseman. The attack, which came unexpectedly from the sea, left Beawolf an orphan at the age of twelve. On that day, which was imprinted into his memory, he clutched in his hands the stone gods his father had worshipped. The failure of the statues to protect his family did not diminish his faith in them. Besides, they were all he possessed that connected him with his past. A month later he had been sold by his captors into slavery to Thor's high priest in Norway. He led a secure life until the king converted to Christianity and required his subjects to do the same. His master refused and continued to perform the sacred rituals until the king burned him at the stake. Not long afterwards all the possessions of his master's estate were auctioned. He was purchased by a merchant from Iceland who put him to work in one of the public lodges. There he remained for the past ten years. When the authorities commenced persecution in Iceland of those who worshipped the Norse gods, he secretly became a priest and conducted pagan rituals at night. The religious authorities had no idea until recently of the vast underground network of pagan believers that existed on the island. But last week a member of his flock converted. Now it was only a matter of time before his activities would come to the attention of Bishop Snorr.

Rising early that morning, Ingri waited impatiently until Nor finally arrived and knocked on the door of her room. After a gruff good morning to her, he swung the small trunk at her feet across his shoulder and without a further word started walking toward the wharf where Baldar's ship lay anchored.

Nor did not like her. But then he did not like any woman. It didn't help that he felt some jealousy. Before she had come aboard the knar that first morning back in Greenland, he had been Baldar's only close companion. Now he was forced to share him with this woman.

When they reached the wharf and stepped aboard the knar, Ingri sensed immediately that Baldar was disturbed. It took only a moment for her to understand the reason. The priest had not arrived. Just as she started to speak a word of comfort to him, Nor shouted from the bow of the ship.

"He comes now."

Everyone on board looked down the wharf and saw an old scared-faced man with a limp, dragging a cart in which set a battered wooden trunk. Baldar recognized the man as the thane that had served their meal at the lodge.

"Good morning Master," the thane called out as he pulled the cart up to where the knar lay anchored. "If your men will help me with my trunk, I will come aboard."

Nor and another sailor went forward to help him.

"Wait a second," Baldar said to his men. "You're here to perform a wedding, not to sail with us," he said to the priest.

"I cannot stay in Iceland any longer. I must seek refuge elsewhere. Passage on your ship will be my condition for performing the sacred ceremony."

Baldar looked around at Ingri who stood slightly behind him. He saw the pleading in her eyes to let the priest on board.

"Help the priest with his trunk," he ordered Nor and the sailor standing beside the cart on the wharf.

Once he was on board, the thane announced he would not perform the ceremony until the knar was at sea. Inside Baldar smiled at the thane's declaration. Balder knew the priest was afraid that once the ceremony was performed, he would have his men toss him back on the wharf. And that was exactly what Baldar had in mind. But once they were at sea, if anything bad happened to the priest, it would be considered a bad omen. The suspicious crew would believe that the wrath of the Norse gods was directed upon the knar and all those who sailed upon her.

It was a beautiful cold day as they set sail from the harbor. The deck was packed with trade goods for the merchants in Norway. In exchange for these goods, Baldar would receive some payment in silver. However, most of his wares would be exchanged for items that would bring a great price in Iceland and Greenland, such as merchandise made of iron and steel, which was always in short supply in those colonies.

As the land mass disappeared over the horizon, the thane opened his trunk and brought forth his two stone idols. He also retrieved a robe which was embroidered with the names of the Norse gods and a diagram of the heavenly bodies.

Baldar stood before the priest with the sun at his back. He turned twice to look toward the cabin door, for Ingri, who had disappeared behind it. After a few moments, he told Nor to go find out what was keeping her. Before the crewman could deliver the message, the door of the cabin swung open. Ingri appeared in a one-piece loose-fitting wedding dress made of a rare white doe skin, and around her neck hung a silver pendant. These were some of the valuables she had inherited from her mother. On her head was a crown made from holly, and it was filled with numerous red berries. Her hair was combed straight, and its length fell to her waist. Everyone stood quietly and stared at her beauty as she approached Baldar and the priest. Before the ceremony began, a flock of birds flew over the ship, a sign to the suspicious crew on board that the gods blessed this union.

That evening Ingri opened the wooden shutter and stared out at the sky. The sun had disappeared some hours ago, and now the heavens were filled with a vast array of stars. She wondered how much longer before Baldar would come to her. Hopefully, the celebration outside on the deck would end soon. From an opened beer barrel the crew had been toasting their captain since sunset. She had cracked open the door of the cabin several times and looked out upon the scene. Baldar seemed to be enjoying himself. Once when he caught her eye, he gave her a look of distress, frustrated that he could not come and join her.

Except for a ray of light that streamed though the open shutter and fell upon the face of his bride, the cabin was dark when Baldar entered. He stood in the darkness for a moment and observed Ingri's chest rise and fall as she slept. He was not experienced at lovemaking. His previous sexual encounters were with female thanes captured in raids along the Welsh coast. Most had offered their bodies willingly, others had not. Either way it had been a matter of lust and power. He wanted it to be different with Ingri. A feeling of tenderness swept over him as he approached where she lay. He removed his clothes and placed them in a chair nearby, then slipped beneath the heavy animal furs that covered the bed.

Ingri had her eyes closed, but she was not asleep. She had heard him come through the cabin door and felt his eyes upon her even before he came to lie beside her. Now she turned in the bed and pressed her naked body against him. His lips found hers in the dark. Her hand reached down and firmly gripped his manhood. The size of it terrified her at first. She had a sudden flashback of what the old women said about pain the first time. Then she remembered the preparation made from melted fat she had used to moisten herself. Her legs parted, and she guided him toward the sacred place. When he entered, a small cry of pain escaped her lips. Ignoring the initial discomfort, she wrapped her legs around him as her arms clung to his neck. Moments later she heard a shout of joy escape from his lips as his seed was planted deep within her. Although they did not make love again that night, each held the other in a tender embrace until the sun came up the next morning.

While sitting between two crates, Beawolf observed the newlyweds as they wandered about the deck. Last night in the marital bed must have gone well for both parties, he thought. The captain strutted about with a continuous smile upon his face, while his wife leaned against the rail and looked out across the vast expanse of ocean. She looked poised, and her body language carried a confidence that had not existed there before.

Seeing the priest observing her movements did not make Ingri uncomfortable. It could do no harm to have her god's spokesman on earth take a personal interest in her. When he approached the ship yesterday morning, she was not impressed by his appearance. And she was not impressed by the fact that at their first meeting he was a mere thane serving food at the lodge. In her world this type of situation simply did not exist. For despite the appearance of Christianity, the priests of Thor were still held in high esteem in Greenland, and those around them were careful not to give offense lest the Norse gods be angry and strike them with misfortune

"Good morning," Ingri said, as she approached the priest. "Could I impose upon you to bless this voyage?" she asked. "Baldar said I could seek this favor from you."

"I usually require blood from a freshly slaughtered goat. There are none on this ship."

He saw the downtrodden look on her face from his response and relented.

"I must at least have some type of fresh blood for the gods."

At that moment a school of large fish engulfed the boat.

"It must be a sign from heaven," Beawolf said. "Hurry, we shall have the crew harpoon some of them."

For the next week the boat stunk from the slaughter of the numerous fish harpooned and brought on board the knar. Not only did the priest have his fresh blood for sacrifice, but everyone ate fish for several days. One evening after the supply was finally exhausted, a heavy rainstorm blew across the knar's bow and washed the deck clean. The next morning the ship was once again free of every offensive odor, since even the foul-smelling crewmen had been washed clean by the storm.

* * *

Maleyfjord was a flourishing port on the shore of the Norwegian coast. This thriving center of commerce contained a permanent population of five thousand souls. Another thousand temporary residents from other parts of the world could be found upon its streets at any given time. The local population of the town was Christian, as was the entire region since the conversion of its king. Recently a fiery bishop, who believed he was a prophet of God, had come as a special envoy from the pope to enforce discipline among the lax clergy of the area. And that was not the only change that was to come in the kingdom. Rumors abounded that an edict would soon issue abolishing slavery, an edict that the power brokers were not happy about. But the king was too strong to resist at the moment. So those who would suffer economic loss from freeing their thanes would hold their tongues and wait for a more opportune time to express their opposition to the crown.

Ailish was cleaning vegetables for the evening meal when she looked out the glassless window of a dwelling that rested on a hill and saw a knar entering the harbor. This was not an unusual event, so it sparked no particular interest in her. She returned to the task at hand. The priest would return soon, and he could be cruel if the evening meal was not prepared before the sun set.

Up the narrow path toward his lodging, the priest, Rhone, made his way slowed by the bag of goods he carried across his shoulder. The other hand held tightly to a live chicken that a peasant in town had given him in payment for a prayer of mercy for the man's dying daughter. The peasant had been sworn to secrecy, for the new bishop forbade the taking of reward for the granting of a prayer. Rhone was an impatient little man whose soul had been scarred by life's bruises. Abandoned at the age of four, he had been taken in by the head of the local abbey. Food and shelter were provided, along with severe physical punishment until he was sixteen. On his death bed the monk, who had served as his guardian, made a dying request that he be sent for further religious instructions at the Munkeby Abbey, a monastery that prepared men for the priesthood. He had gone because no other option was opened to him.

The evening meal consumed and her household duties completed, Ailish retired to the small cot in the hut behind the house that served as her sleeping quarters. In the darkness she prayed he would not come tonight. An hour later, the door opened. His silhouette appeared and moved towards the cot. She pulled the covers back and lifted her nightgown knowing that any resistance would be futile. It would only delay his departure. He removed his robe and the cross that hung around his neck. His body hovered over her, then pressed down upon her. It was cold and clammy. His breath reeked of beer and the lamb he had consumed at supper. He tried to kiss her, but she turned her head. His hand gripped her jaw and held it firmly while his tongue explored her mouth. To finish the ordeal and be rid of the priest, she spread her legs. He removed his mouth and concentrated on driving his shaft into her. Afterwards, an evil smile spread across his face. The wickedness of that expression, visible from the moonlight that flooded through the open door, sent a chill down her spine.

As the last log on the fire turned to charcoal, Rhone finished his jug of wheat beer. Before he passed out in the chair his thoughts turned to the message he received that morning from the bishop. He had read it over slowly three times to be sure of the true meaning behind the flowery language, written in Latin. Try as he could, there was no different way to interpret the document. All thanes were to be freed on Christmas. And that was only a month away. Anger swelled up in Rhone's chest. The bishop's actions since coming to Marleyfjord were slowly destroying his way of life. No more graft and no more slaves. What advantage lay in continuing to be a priest. And what was to become of his thane, Ailish. He had received her as a gift from a Norwegian chieftain who had acquired her for a gold coin. Only eight at the time, she had been seized from a village on the coast of Wales and blossomed in captivity by the time she reached eleven. It was Rhone's luck that the chieftain had given her to him after he prayed successfully for the man's ailing wife. He remembered his excitement on bringing her home. Such a ripe piece of fruit ready for the plucking, and he had plucked her the first night.

The knar had made port two weeks ago, and Baldar had finished his trading with the merchants. Normally he would hunker down and wait until spring to sail, but only yesterday he heard reports of a plague in the foreign quarter. He knew these reports, if true, could wipe out half the population in a matter of weeks. While he had a healthy respect for the sea in winter time, he had a greater fear of plague. He recalled the numerous members of his clan whose lives had been swept away, and he made a decision to sail despite the weather.

Rhone discovered that a knar from Greenland planned to depart the port. He sensed an opportunity in what he believed was a poor judgment on the part of a young captain. He would offer the man his thane for a reasonable price. After all, he would not own Ailish much longer. But slavery was still allowed in the colonies, so she still had value in those distant lands.

Baldar looked at the female thane who stood before him. The owner said she was sixteen, but he thought she had not reached such an age. She spoke a dialect that was a mixture of Welsh and Norwegian, languages that Baldar had only a limited understanding of from his travels. He did not need her for his personal use, for now he had a wife. But she would bring a good price in the new world where he would voyage. After striking a bargain with the priest, he dropped ten coins into the palm of the man's hand. It was not much for a young, healthy slave. But he had heard the rumors that slavery would soon be abolished here. When the sale was completed, he motioned for her to join the other seven slave girls he had purchased. She stepped aboard bringing nothing with her except the rags that covered her body and a wooden cross that hung from her neck. In the breeze she shivered until Ingri covered her with a coat made from wild animal fur. It would not do to have a valuable asset die from the cold. The next day the knar sailed from port and started the return voyage to Iceland where they would wait in port until the winter season passed before they continued on to Vineland.

It had been weeks since the knar sailed. Rhone looked about the hovel in which he lived. It was dark, and no one had come to care for him. His mind wandered. He screamed out for Ailish, than remembered he had sold her. She was the lucky one, he thought. She sailed just before the small pox spread like wildfire. At first he welcomed the plague. The people gave him things to pray for their sick ones. The corner of his home was covered with these ill-gotten gifts. But soon the people realized that God was not listening to him. Those seeking help turned to others. Some new converts to Christianity even prayed to the Norse gods. But these gods did not hear the cry of the people any more than the Christian one.

The priest hid in his home. He had not been out in public for days because the people were hostile. He sensed in their fear, desperation and danger. Three days ago he had come down with the smallpox and was now near death. For the first time in his life he tried to find God. But his prayers went unanswered. As he drew his last breath, he saw an image of Lucifer, one more evil than himself.

* * *

The storm came suddenly. Giant waves washed across the deck and several times Baldar thought the knar, heavy with trade goods, would sink. But somehow she weathered the storm, which lasted two days. When the cold rain stopped, so did the wind. The knar lay in a calm sea with no movement for many days, a situation Baldar had never experienced. The crowded space created the potential for an explosive situation. It had been weeks since the men had an opportunity to visit whores, and they vied for the attention of the female thanes on board. Fresh water supplies began to dwindle; then catastrophe struck. The plague from Marleyfjord visited a crew member. Small pox was a threat to everyone on the crowded ship. During the night, while Baldar lay with Ingri in the cabin, he heard the infected one cry out for help. He did not stir for he knew the crew in their hysteria was taking the only action they knew to preserve their own lives—throw the infected one overboard. During the next week three more sailors met the same fate; then the plague ended. During the following weeks a strong wind blew across the surface of the ocean and carried the knar upon its surface many miles each day in a direction that Baldar had never sailed. The sun stone he used made of a crystal called *Iceland spar* could detect the sun within a degree on cloudy days. But this compass was useless in his present circumstance. He tried to hide from his crew the fact that he had no idea where they were in this sea that stretched on endlessly. Each morning everyone awoke to stare at the vast ocean. Then one day the temperature went from freezing to as warm as the climate was in Greenland during the summer season. While the weather improved, the food supply continued to dwindle. The remaining fresh water in the wooden barrels was stale and stank from the algae that began to flourish in them. The men used every device available to capture the water from the scattered rain that fell upon the ship to replenish their supplies. Baldar imposed strict rations in an attempt to survive until land was sighted. The crew and thanes shrank until they were so gaunt their bones showed through the skin that contained them. And yet there was no land on the horizon. Four thanes perished, and their bodies were carved up and eaten. And still there was no sign of land. Despair set in, and the morale on board sank until finally the men and passengers became listless and unable to perform the simplest task. They lay upon the deck awaiting death that was only days away. In the cabin Baldar lay on the bed and stared up at the ceiling. Ingri lay beside him. A constant stream of prayers to the Norse gods flowed from her lips.

Beawolf looked out across the horizon. Standing beside him on deck was Ailish, the small-framed, red-haired thane that Baldar had purchased from the priest. He had watched her throw the small wooden cross that hung around her neck into the sea immediately after the priest had released her. This visible show of rejection of that Christian faith guided him to take her under his protection. With the approval of Baldar, he began to train her in the rituals as a step toward making her a priestess of the Norse gods. She was a quick learner, and in a short time she absorbed every piece of knowledge it had taken Beowolf a lifetime to learn. He trusted her to the point that he gave her possession of the two stone statutes of Freya and Frey.

Nor observed the pair from the passageway that ran between the cargo stacked on deck, his body still weak from a fever that had only broken last night. The emotion he felt toward the young thane was foreign to his person. He never liked women. In fact, he despised them. He had hated them as far back as he could remember. At least as far back as when his mother had sold him into slavery at ten. But with Ailish it was different. She had nursed him through his sickness. When the crew wanted to toss him overboard because they were afraid he had the pox, she had prevailed against them, even threatened to bring down the wrath of the gods. During the confrontation, the captain had remained aloof just as he had with the other crew members who were cast into the sea.

The third day after Nor regained his health, Ailish sighted a flock of winged creatures in the distance flying in the same direction that the wind was carrying the knar. Those on board were excited their salvation might lie just over the waves. Baldar knew from experience that land was probably somewhere within a day's journey. He nervously paced the deck trying to keep his concern from his crew. If the birds were from a small island, they might pass near it without sighting the land, especially if it were during the night. He posted two men in rotating shifts to watch, and when night came, he lowered the sail, hoping they would not drift past it during the night.

One morning Ingri and Baldar were awakened by voices outside. They quickly dressed and threw open the door to see what the loud commotion on deck was about. Everyone on the ship was staring out to sea when they exited the cabin. They soon saw the reason for all the excitement. In the water a few yards off the starboard side was the trunk of a tree bobbing in the waves. Perched upon it was a large bird that no one could identify A few minutes later, after making a loud screeching sound, the bird flapped its wings and flew off in a westerly direction.

"Nor," Baldar said, "Raise the sail and point the ship in the direction that the bird flew."

Although they lost sight of the creature, they continued to sail westerly all morning. Around noon the clouds turned dark, and the winds picked up. But Baldar decided against lowering the sail. He must find land soon. Everyone was on the point of perishing. The rain came down in sheets. As the knar was tossed about by the waves, the wind proved too much for the mast. The pressure on the sail caused the mast to snap. When it came thundering down on the deck, it crushed the priest. Ailish struggled from the other side of the ship where she had tied herself to keep from being washed overboard. Beawolf was barely alive when she reached him.

"Father," she called out, using the term as one of affection, because he was the only one who had shown kindness to her.

"Daughter," he answered, for he had come to love her, as if she were born of his loins.

"It is finished. I go to the other side."

"I will pray to our gods that your journey will be swift."

"Do not waste your prayers on me. The gods have already spoken. Pray for the others. Pray that they will survive this storm."

After he whispered those words, the last breath of life flew from his body. He laid still, eyes opened toward the heavens. At that instant, a great wave rolled over the deck of the ship. Ailish was almost washed overboard. However, Nor reached out from his space between the cargo and grabbed her. He held her tight as a second wave washed across the ship. After it rolled away, she looked for Beawolf. He was no longer on the deck. She looked out across the sea and saw his body floating near the knar until a wave washed over it, and then she saw it no more.

The next morning, despite a good sea breeze, the knar was moving slowly with its makeshift sail through the waves, and Nor was pacing about the ship with a worried look on his face.

"Captain, something is wrong. Our speed is slow despite the strong wind that is blowing in a westerly direction. And look how low she sits in the water."

Baldar looked over the starboard side. It was clear to him that the ship was taking in water.

"We must rip up some planks from the floor of the deck," he said.

Nor called out the names of two members of the crew, and they immediately began to pry loose several planks from the center. This allowed Nor, secured by a rope under his armpits, to slip down into the bowels of the ship. Although it was already clear to everyone on deck that water was coming in, Nor needed to swim beneath to find out the source of the leak.

"There's a crack in the bottom, the length of a man's arm," Nor said when they pulled him up.

"How fast is the water flowing in?" Baldar asked Nor.

"She won't be afloat much longer."

Just as the bad news left Nor's lips, Ailish heard a bird in the distance. She turned and looked toward the west from whence the sound came.

"Land," she screamed.

People turned their attention from Nor and looked in the direction that Ailish was pointing. Far away they could see a land mass that ran along the length of the ocean as far as the eyes could see. As they stared, Baldar realized that the knar had almost stopped moving forward in the water.

"We must act quickly," he said at the top of his lungs to get everyone's attention. "We must throw some of the cargo over the side, or we will sink before we reach shore."

Everyone was organized in two groups, one on each side of the ship. Under Baldar's direction they began to fill the sea with cargo that Baldar had hoped to trade. Soon the ship began to move again with the wind. An hour later Baldar spotted what looked like a bay ahead on a coast line that appeared to have a forest in the background. He directed Nor to steer in that direction.

With lumber from the trees we will be able to repair the ship, he thought. Just as that thought crossed his mind, one of the crewmen shouted toward him.

"Captain, the water level is getting higher. He climbed down from the cabin onto the deck and peered into the hole in the deck of the ship.

"The crack must have widened," Baldar said. "We must lighten this ship even more, or we will never reach land."

More cargo was empted into the sea. Then he directed them to uncork some of the barrels and pour the remaining water from them. After they were corked again he directed them to throw them into the sea, if the ship sank they would serve as life rafts.

Standing on the platform built on top of the cabin, Baldar could now see clearly the mouth of a bay. It was high tide. Even with the knar floating low in the water, he hoped the channel was deep enough for the ship to clear the sand that always hugged the entrance of every bay.

The knar scraped the bottom at the entrance, but a few minutes later it slipped over that obstacle. On board, Baldar and Ingri stood beside one another and watched in amazement the beaches that lay on each side. After they passed the white sand, the landscape consisted of heavy marsh and tall cypress trees. On the high elevation in the distance, pine and oak trees reached toward the sky. The waterway around the knar teemed with life. Shrimp jumped in the creeks, which were surrounded by the marshlands, and fish sailed through the air beside the ship. The bay was large, but the channel was deep only in the center. The crew kept the knar in the deepest part to avoid getting grounded. As the ship sank even deeper into the water, Baldar had the men strap some of the empty barrels on each side of the ship to keep it afloat. With only a light breeze blowing, the boat sailed at a very slow pace up the channel.

Baldar was anxious to find a place to land, but the vast areas of marsh denied them easy access. Soon they passed a small river on their left that flowed past a peninsula. On this day from the center of the bay, it had the appearance of a creek to the Vikings. It was small and muddy even at high tide, so Baldar directed Nor to continue on. Only in coming years would later settlers realize that in its upper reaches this small body of water had a depth of thirty feet.

Soon the knar came to several rivers that flowed into the bay. Baldar sailed up the largest one. He could see high ground just beyond where it emptied into the bay.

"That is where we will anchor and go ashore," he said to Ingri, who stood at his side.

As they neared the spot he had in mind, a terrible cracking sound filled the air as a timber in the bottom of the ship gave way. No one had time to prepare before the ship went down. Holding onto the debris floating in the water, the passengers and crew swam toward the shoreline only a few yards away. Baldar and Ingri held onto a floating barrel, while to their right Nor and Ailish gripped a large plank. Once they dragged themselves onto shore, the four climbed up the bank onto a small bluff that overlooked the river. A few minutes later they were joined by the others.

"We must make preparations before nightfall," Baldar said to the survivors that gathered around him. "Nor, pick two men that are your strongest swimmers and recover what you can from the water. Check out the knar also. I don't believe the water was that deep where she sank. If you can't reach her now, then perhaps you will be able to recover some of the cargo at low tide. I will take the rest of the men and find a suitable place to prepare a camp."

"Ingri, you organize the women. Go see if you can recover items that floated to shore. Don't stray too far. We don't know what dangers may lurk in this land."

Once the women were gone, Baldar led the other eight men through the forest along the edge of the river. Soon he reached the spot where he had earlier planned to anchor the ship. It had a small beach with a sloping bluff above it that presented no barrier to the forest beyond. After climbing the elevation, Baldar watched Nor and his men bring barrels and other floating objects from the water to the shore. He noticed the thanes under Ingri's direction were scavenging the shore line.

"Let's explore the surrounding area," he said to the men.

He smiled as he saw them picking up limbs that lay on the ground. His Vikings were brave as long as they held a weapon of some kind in their hand. Baldar spied a four foot limb. If they ran into trouble, he would not go down without a fight. In the forest he made a wide swing that would eventually bring them back to the bluff.

The heavily shaded land they entered was full of game that did not flee at the sight of man. They saw deer at a distance, squirrels playing in the trees above, and the tracks of many small animals. But without weapons they were helpless to use this wildlife as a source of food.

"What we need are bows and arrows and perhaps some spears," he said to the men. "Hopefully, Nor will be able to retrieve some tools from the ship to create weapons for hunting and for our defense."

After curiosity got the best of them, Ingri and the women explored the area around the bluff. They came across a trail made by the feet of men. Afraid the group might alert hostiles, Ingri sent the other women back, except for Ailish. Leading the way Ingri quietly stepped along the path until it ended at the river bank some distance from where the ship had sunk. Three canoes were tied to an overhanging bush, but there wasn't a human in sight.

"Come, we must go back and tell Baldar what we have discovered," she said to Ailish.

Back at the bluff, Ingri told Baldar about the small boats. He looked around at the gauntness of his men, then he turned to Nor.

"You stay here with your party. When the tide is low, get whatever you can from the knar. I will take the other men and find these boats of which Ingri had spoken. I don't know the owners of these crafts, but we must have them. Everyone is hungry, and we shall use them to obtain food from the bay. If we don't do something soon, we shall perish."

"Baldar, be careful," Ingri said, and then put her arms around him.

He held her for a moment, feeling her frail, thin body pressed against him. Then he turned and started with his men down the path that Ingri had spoken about. They carried with them sticks sharpened in such a way that they would hold a fish once it was stabbed, or puncture a man's lungs. The trail that led to the canoes was easily located.

"Let's take these three boats and head toward the mouth of the bay," Baldar said. "With the tide low we shall spear fish where there are pools of water trapped in the marsh."

* * *

To the local inhabitants the weather may have seemed cool, but to the Viking it was warmer than summertime in Greenland. With the bright rays beating down upon their faces, the men in the boats made good time paddling in the direction where the river poured into the bay. In this vast expanse of water, they saw that items cast overboard from the knar had washed up on the mud banks along the marsh.

"The boats are too small for us to collect it now," Baldar said. "We will come back later and recover them when we construct a raft. A few minutes later he said, "It's too difficult right now to return to our people because the power of the current is still running toward the ocean. So, let's continue to where the sea enters the bay. We will stop and stab some fish on the way back."

The speed of the current took them at a fast pace until soon they were approaching the location where they had entered the bay that morning. On their left was a parcel of land with a flat sandy beach, whose terrain was broken only by sand dunes on which grew sea oats that prevented the wind from blowing the soil into the sea.

Upon reaching the beach, Baldar and his men dragged the boats onto the sand to keep them from being carried away by the current. A warm breeze was blowing, but the men did not have time to enjoy the pleasant day or the beautiful scenery, for they were at the point of starvation. Seeing a flock of birds down the beach, they went to investigate what had attracted the feathered creatures to the spot. Even before they reached the birds they could see the outlines of a baby whale which had beached itself upon the land during the storm. Driven by hunger, they whipped out their knives from the sheaths attached to their belts made of rope and carved chunks of meat from it. The whale was still alive and let out a wail that reminded one of a child crying for its mother. While some were sinking their teeth into the raw flesh, one man, who always carried a couple of flints on his person, started a fire from a large mass of dry driftwood that lay near the base of the sand dunes. Soon the smell of roasted meat filled the air as the men held pieces of whale meat over the fire with sticks they gathered from behind the dunes near a pool of brackish water. After they finished gorging themselves, they trekked along the beach and at some distance from the inlet they came across several chests thrown overboard while the knar was still at sea. They had washed ashore during the storm. Inside were a variety of trade goods, including colored beads, cooking pots, blankets, and several single-edged axes. By the time they returned to the boats the sun was going down. In the distraction caused by the events of the day Baldar had lost track of the time.

"We have delayed too long," he said too his men. "We must wait until morning when the tide turns inward to return to our people. Let us make camp here for the night."

While some of the crew gathered enough materials for a fire to last until morning, others scoured the area beyond the dunes for food to supplement the whale meat. They were amazed by the large amount of sea life available to them. When they returned to the beach they carried large quantities of crabs and some flat fish which they had speared in a creek. These were thrown into a cooking pot recovered from one of the chests. The men, who had gone foraging, told the others around the campfire a tale of a large four-legged reptile with razor sharp-teeth in the marsh water. They had avoided it since no one had a weapon large enough to slay the creature.

* * *

That afternoon, after the tide flowed out toward the ocean, Nor led his men back into the river to the spot where the ship deck was now visible beneath the surface of the water. In several trips they were able to salvage from the ship materials that would help them survive. Included in their recovery were axes, swords, cooking pots, and other useful items, such as lead. Although he knew of the chest in the cabin, Nor left it there. It was wiser for Baldar and him to recover the valuables hidden in it when camp had been set up and the group better organized, for thievery was always a problem with a Viking crew.

Yatan watched with great interest from a cluster of trees along the river. Though the winter had not yet ended, a warm day brought him and other braves out of their quarters on a hunting expedition. When they first saw the large canoe with wings glide across the surface of their river and then disappear beneath the water, they thought it was magical. Some of the men feared the creatures that emerged from the water were gods. Yatan was not intimidated by what his eyes had seen. As the warriors gathered around him, he reminded them of legends passed down through the tribe for many generations—how creatures like those before them had once lived upon this shore. These creatures had been few in number and defeat in battle had destroyed their world. The survivors were assimilated into their tribe. Yatan could even trace some of his ancestors to the strange ones. He thought perhaps the creatures who now busied themselves upon the riverbank might be members of that ancient tribe, for they had white skin and were taller than the clay-colored inhabitants. Yatan and his braves waited quietly in the shadow of the trees until dark, than made their way down a path that led to their village.

That evening the tribal elders sat around the campfire. Standing before them was the shaman, the one whose duty it was to know everything. He recounted to them the history of the Winyah tribe, reminding them how their tribe were members of the Sioux Confederation along with the Catawba, Pee Dee, Hooks, Santee, Sampas, and, of course, the Waccamaw, who lived to the north along the ocean shores. These tribes were all that remained of the Sioux nation living in this region since the

Great Divide, an event that occurred a long time ago when the Sioux tribes split into two groups over a conflict upon the death the great Chief Winyaw. One of his sons wanted to follow the buffalo, a beast that was fast disappearing from the land, for as the climate changed along the rivers and ocean, the broad grassland was replaced by forest. As the forest grew thick, the grass died, and the buffalo herds began to migrate west. The other son wanted to stay in the land of their ancestors. He argued the tribe was already supplementing its diet from vegetable plots, sea life, and the wild game from the forest. The buffalo were no longer necessary for their survival. Upon the death of Winyaw, those who listened to the eldest son made their choice with their feet by following him westward. The rest remained and elected the other son their new chief. For several generations they remained under one leader. But disputes arose and they were now divided into different tribes under their own chiefs, though they still spoke the same dialect. After the division the tribes formed a confederation and elected a wise man over it. They gave him the title, 'Datha'. He resided in the nearby region called Duhare. When he died, another wise man assumed the same title.

At a time more distant than the Great Divide, the Sioux had battled for this land. With force they took it from a people with white skin. These former inhabitants had traveled to this place from far away lands during a time when the weather was colder, and ice clung along the edge of the great body of water that bordered the bay. Although they had superior weapons, they were few in number. A generation later the ice melted, and no further migration of the creatures was seen again until today, when Yatan and his men reported them on a small bluff on the Big River.

After the shaman recited the history of their people, the tribal elders discussed what action to take. Some wanted to strike immediately and destroy the strange ones, but Chief Motar and his allies on the council cautioned against it. They wanted the tribe to reach out the hand of friendship unless these strangers proved hostile. After an argument that lasted most of the night, the chief and his supporters prevailed. It was decided that Yatan should go to the camp of the white ones and make contact with them. He would take with him food and two slaves as a gift to show that he came in peace. Yatan was chosen because his bloodline had retained a few chosen words of the ancient ones called the Fish Eaters. With these words they hoped he could establish communication with the strangers on the bluff. The use of these ancient words would turn out to be an act in futility. The earlier inhabitants from which the ancient words came were a pre-Clovis group who had disappeared from Europe long before the Vikings existed as a people.

* * *

The lodge, in which the chief of the tribe resided, was a rectangular structure like many others in the camp, except it covered a larger area because he had many wives. Unlike the tepees used by other tribes, the Sioux used solid log construction, a result of their contact with the Fish People.

After the warrior guarding the entrance allowed Yatan inside, the chief motioned him to a bear rug that lay next to a smoldering fire. Giving the traditional greeting, Yatan sat down beside the chief. In the light of the fire embers, he noticed his uncle was beginning to show his age. The battle scar that once graced his cheek now drooped toward his chin. His remaining teeth were dark and ground down to the gums. He had lived beyond the age of those born during the same season and had outlived most of his children. The tribe believed he was wise, and they continued to follow him even though his prowess as a warrior had long since disappeared.

"It has been many moons since the death of the last Fish Eater," the chief said.

"But they live on through our blood," responded Yatan.

"Yes, it can be seen among many of the Sioux. The tall ones like you have a different coloring."

"Why do you think these strangers have come?" Yatan asked.

"That is something you must find out. Perhaps they come to claim this land."

"But they are so few."

"Yes, but many may follow. Remember the reports we have from the tribes of the North. How they traveled by canoe during the summer months upon the great water and traded in the land of ice with white men that look like these who have appeared on our shores today. I am sending you with the young slaves, Uhan and his sister Kee. They have been with us since we took them as children the day we raided the Cherokee settlement near the mountains. The girl is trained to cook. And with her skinning knife she can clean the animals that are killed. She also knows when to plant vegetable plots and how to bring forth a bountiful harvest. These are skills that will be valuable to these strangers. The male child will soon grow into a man. He is physically strong and will make them a good warrior."

"When do I leave on this mission?"

"Before the sun reaches its height in the sky."

* * *

Ingri sat with her back against a large oak tree whose lower branches rested upon the ground. She stared at the river surface that was barely visible from the rays of moonlight. She wondered what had happened to Baldar and his men. Everyone expected them before dark, but there had been no sight of them. Perhaps they would come by morning, if they returned at all. Her stomach ached from lack of food, and she felt very weak as did everyone. Fatigue and hunger had sapped their strength, and she knew they were doomed if provisions did not come by the time the moon rose the next evening. The only things that had eaten since the boat sank were the insects that hovered in a mass around their bodies. The only relief from their bites was to cover themselves, for any exposed skin was immediately attacked.

Under another tree not far from Ingri lay Nor and Ailish, two individuals with whom she had developed a bond. They were pressed together so tightly that at first glance they were indistinguishable from each other.

They clung to each other beneath green pine branches that Nor harvested to cover their bodies like a blanket. Unlike Ingri, they slept soundly.

Nor was used to living on the edge, and Ailish felt safe in his presence. Sometime during the night he awoke and became conscious of her soft, small breasts pressing hard against his chest through the damp shirt that hung from his shoulders. He looked at her face in the moonlight. In its relaxed state it was the face of innocence. Not the innocence of a female who still had her maidenhead intact, for he knew of her abuse by the priest, but the innocence of one still able to trust another person. Nor understood that in her eyes, he was that person. Despite his age of thirty, he had never known a woman, for he was a damaged article–damaged by the knowledge of his mother's conduct selling him when he was young and also sexually damaged by the conduct of men on ships he served with when he was young. Men who were long at sea without the benefit of a woman always turned to the boys to release their sexual frustrations. This emotional baggage that he carried made him hate women and even hate the idea of sex, at least until now. The anger within him had begun to subside since he had come into contact with Ailish. She was gentle and kind. But he might not have even noticed these characteristics except for his fever. She refused to let the others throw him overboard, and when everyone said he was going to die, she nursed him back to health.

Sometime during the night Ingri must have fallen asleep because she sat up with a start when she heard the footsteps of a man coming through the forest toward them. She was not alone in hearing the disquieting sound, for the rest of the camp stirred quickly with the women cringing in terror and the men reaching for the swords and axes they had recovered from the ship yesterday. Nor shouted an order to the men and they formed a defensive line to meet any assault from the thickness of the forest. As their weapons glistened in the morning sun, they did not look like the fierce Viking sailors who had left Greenland months ago. They were gaunt and disheveled. Their tattered clothes drooped on their skeletal frames. Fatigue showed in their eyes, and the weapons they held were no longer sharp. The shields, which should have been attached to their arms with a leather strap, still lay at the bottom of the river. Nor looked at them and knew a fight against any worthy enemy would end in a massacre. Ingri, sensing his despair, fell down on her knees and cried out to Thor for deliverance. The other women, including Ailish, followed her example. The sound of their cries was picked up by the wind and reached the ears of Yatan when he was still some distance away. It was so mournful that it sent chills down his spine. He turned and gave the two slaves a warning to keep their feet from fleeing in the opposite direction.

Through the foliage stepped Yatan adorned with a headdress made from bird feathers. No garment clothed his torso, except his loins, which were covered by an animal skin wrapped around his waist and held there by a vine rope. Behind him stood two plump and naked Indian children whose hair fell to their waists. The female's flat chest was just beginning to show signs that puberty was near. The male child standing beside her appeared about twelve. He was the color of a clay pot, and the bear grease upon his skin glistened in the morning sun. There was no mark upon his body for he had not undergone a ritual ceremony to separate him from his childhood.

Nor stepped forward from his men.

"I see that you come in peace," he said.

Though he knew the man would not understand the language, he depended on the tone of his voice and the expression on his face to convey the meaning of his words. Yatan, who stood ten yards away, turned and spoke to the boy and girl who then crept forward. They placed on the ground the two baskets they carried before retreating to where the savage stood. Though Nor could not see the contents from that distance, he smelled food. Having dealt with men of many cultures in his travels, he understood what this gesture meant. He stepped forward and inspected the peace offering but did not recognize the foodstuff, for the cooked cornbread was not made of a substance grown in Europe. There were also nuts and strange shells that looked similar to the ones along the marsh bank where the knar entered the bay. He sat down beside the baskets and motioned for Yatan to come forward and join him.

Yatan observed the creature sitting across from him. While strange, he was still just a man and not someone sent from the gods. The other white creatures standing nearby were near starvation. He made hand gestures to encourage them to come forward and take the food. The first one moved forward with hesitation, but once he had taken a corn cake and placed it in his mouth, there was a rush by the others to the baskets. Soon these refugees were spread out under the surrounding trees, consuming the food which Yatan brought. It was so quickly eaten that he knew his village would have to deliver many more baskets of food if these people were to survive.

Nor looked at the collection of numerous shells at the bottom of the baskets and wondered why the man had brought them. Seeing the look on Nor's face, Yatan took the baskets and dumped the shells into a pot of boiling water that the women had placed on a fire built to wash their clothes. Everyone gathered to see the purpose of the savage's action. Soon the shells began to pop open. Yatan motioned to Nor, pointing at the knife secured in a sheath on his waist by a rope belt. Nor, feeling no danger from the man, removed the knife and handed it to him. Yatan pried open a shell with the knife and then cut the meat within from the shell and placed it in his mouth. Returning the knife to Nor, he motioned for him to do the same. The meat in the shell easily slipped down his throat and had a salty taste. Nor gave Yatan a grunt of approval. Their hunger not satisfied by the cornbread and nuts, the others scrambled to retrieve the remaining shells from the pot. Soon the meat was gone, and the empty shells were thrown into a pile.

When Nor sensed the warrior was ready to depart, he placed in Yatan's hand a double- edged ax, a token of friendship he hoped would arouse the curiosity of others and cause them to come with food for his people. He kept pointing to the empty baskets and rubbing his hands over his stomach until he felt the Yatan understood his desire for more food.

Yatan, his mission successfully completed, stood up and gestured he was leaving. A moment later he disappeared into the forest, leaving the young ones behind. Nor realized these two were left as gifts. No doubt existed in his mind that they were slaves. Strange, thought Nor, how everywhere in the world the institution of slavery existed, even here in this untamed land on the edge of the world.

Ingri saw the terror in the eyes of the young girl and felt compassion for her. She walked over and held out her hand. The girl cringed in fear until Ingri removed a silver pendant on a chain that hung around her neck. She placed it on the slave girl. This act of kindness eased the child's fear. Afterwards she followed Ingri to where other women were busy boiling the mud out of their clothing in a large iron pot that Nor retrieved from the ship.

The slave boy Uhan sulked under a tree. He had looked forward to the spring when he hoped the chief would free him. Then he could go through the tribal ritual which would allow him into the ranks of the warriors; now his dream had dissolved. He was to become the slave of a white stranger. He did not know for sure which one was chief, for none had yet indicated ownership of him. Perhaps the small one was the chief of this tribe. He seemed to be the person everyone looked to for direction. He thought that was strange, for only warriors large in stature were ever considered for the position of chief among the Sioux. Perhaps the small one was a fierce warrior despite his size and had been so honored.

* * *

Ingri was the first to see the returning boats, for after the savage left, she climbed into an oak and positioned herself on a large limb that cast a shadow over the river. From this branch she could see almost to the bay. At first the boats appeared as only small dots on the horizon, but soon she was confident enough that she announced to the others that Baldar and his men were coming up the river.

The return trip was not difficult. The men had full stomachs, and the incoming tide made the paddling easy. The need to stop and spear some fish on the way back to the encampment was now unnecessary. The boats were already loaded with whale meat and a variety of seafood taken from the creek behind the sand dunes. The day was so pleasant that for a moment Baldar entertained the thought that this would be a good place for a Viking trading post, and then realized that he might never see Viking civilization again. They were in an unknown land, and the odds were against them ever returning to Greenland. The thought was so desolating that he quickly dismissed it and turned his attention to the figure of Ingri and the others who were waving with excitement from the bluff that lay ahead.

Uhan watched the excitement of the strangers as more of their number approached the shore in crafts that he recognized as belonging to the tribe. The first to step forth on land was a tall one who had a dark growth of hair covering his face. He could tell by the way the people gathered around him that this was their chief. The red-headed small one must have been in charge only during the other's absence. He realized the time for sulking had pass. He must adapt himself to the new circumstance and attach himself to this chief, striving to become so invaluable that this white chief would allow him to become a warrior in this new tribe. Although his first impression had been negative, he now realized that once these men recovered from their voyage, they would become powerful. He had already noticed that their weapons were superior to the Winyah.

Baldar and Nor exchanged their stories of what occurred since their separation, while the men and women left behind on the bluff devoured the whale meat and sea food. Baldar was intrigued by the description of the warrior, whom Nor described as tall like a Viking and with light brown hair–characteristics that Nor pointed out were far different from the two slaves left behind who were more copper colored with jet black hair. Afterwards, Baldar organized a hunting party. An inventory showed the men were now well armed with axes and swords. Most of the men also carried knives in their belts. Leaving Nor in charge, Baldar and four of the Vikings set forth through the surrounding forest. They soon came upon what Balder was seeking, saplings of hardwood trees from which they could make bows and arrows. The arrows they would dip in hot molten-lead which would make a point hard enough to pierce the skin of animals and men. The string for the bows would come from the ropes recovered from the knar. Ingri and the other women could unravel the ropes until they were reduced to the necessary strands.

* * *

Yatan was invited that evening to sit with the tribal elders at the campfire and tell the story of his meeting with the strangers. The shaman was not invited to sit in the circle, but he stood under an oak tree nearby and listened with great interest to Yatan's description of the white ones.

"They are different from the tribes we know. I could not communicate with them in our language or the language of the ancient ones. They carry fearsome weapons that will cut through a man's limb with one blow and have pots not made of clay. But they aren't gods. They are only men. They are of a tribe from across the great water. The giant canoe that sailed upon the surface must have been damaged in the storm that blew down trees in the forest and swept water upon our shores. When it sank in the large river, they were spit upon our shores not by design of the gods but by the storm. Now they are weak, but soon they will gain their strength. We must make them our friends by supplying them with food in exchange for weapons. An alliance with them will help us defend our lands from the Cherokee, who always attacked us in the fall, killing our men and stealing our women."

He then removed the ax which he had hidden within his blanket. The tribal elders looked in awe at this strange instrument attached to a wooden shaft. It glistened in the dark when the light from the fire fell upon it. Yatan walked over to a young sapling that grew out of the ground near where the council sat and with one blow severed it. The men were amazed and each in his heart wanted to obtain this magical weapon. Yatan handed it to the chief who examined it and then passed it around to the others. In the end it was returned to the chief and with him it would remain.

The next morning the Viking posted on the edge of the woods signaled by a blast from a cow horn that someone was approaching the camp. The men rose from their beds of green pine needles and with weapons in hand formed a defensive line in front of the goods they had retrieved yesterday. The women huddled near the edge of the river. The level of fear dissolved when from the edge of the woods stepped the same warrior they had met yesterday. Following him were three other warriors who differed in appearance. They were shorter in stature and more copper toned. Each carried a basket from which the smell of food flowed into the Viking's nostrils. Nor recognized the odor coming from these baskets was corn-bread, though he did not yet know its ingredients.

Nor stepped forward and Baldar followed. When they stood in front of the natives, Nor introduced the captain to Yatan using gestures to indicate the man was his leader. The size of the Viking and the manner in which he carried himself showed clearly he was the chief of these strangers. After Yatan offered the three baskets of food to the Viking, Baldar invited the men to sit by the fire and join them for a meal of fried whale meat. While the meat was tasteless without spices, when eaten with the salted corn cakes, it made for a delicious meal. Yatan noticed the bows the Vikings had made in an outside woodshop they had created under the trees. He walked over and examined them. The workmanship was of poor quality, and the wood chosen was not from the best type of tree. But when his finger touched the point of the arrows, he knew they were superior to the arrowheads used by his tribe. Baldar saw his expression and indicated to him that he would exchange three arrows for three of Yatan's bows. To seal the agreement hands were shaken, a custom foreign to the Winyahs. When the braves were ready to leave, Baldar gave each a handful of beads. When Yatan indicated he wanted an ax, Baldar answered in the negative by shaking his head. The number of axes was in short supply, and the Vikings could not afford to continue to trade them in exchange for food.

"Do you think they will continue to bring us food?" Nor asked, after the warriors had departed. "They were unhappy that we did not give them another ax."

"I have traded in many ports, and I can tell you when the wives see the colored beads, those warriors will have no peace until they return for more."

Baldar was right. The women of the tribe pressured their men to return many times to the camp of the Vikings for more trinkets. On each visit they brought food. Soon the warriors were taking Baldar and his men into the forest and teaching them the skills of hunting wild game.

Eventually, Yatan brought a message from the chief inviting them to visit the village. At last, Baldar thought, we will see their village and how great are their numbers. A Viking was always wary of friendship from foreigners and was prepared to take advantage of any group that showed weakness.

As the Vikings were led by Yatan down a forest trail, Baldar warned his men to be on their guard. Though relationships were on friendly terms, one never knew what was in a warrior's mind. Perhaps they planned an ambush with the aim of killing the men and taking the women as slaves. Such conduct could be expected in the world from which the Norseman came.

It was late afternoon when the party arrived. Word of their coming reached the village from a slave boy who had seen the Norsemen approach when he went to the river to get some fresh water. Excitement raced through the tribe. The members of the tribal council gathered in front of the chief's lodge to await the coming of the strangers.

Baldar was surprised by the size of the village which contained many dwellings. The people appeared well nourished. At the end of a long avenue that ran down the center of the village stood their chief surrounded by his nobles. Baldar sized up the chief, as Yatan led the party to his leader. The chief was very old. In the land of the Norsemen he would be called ancient. He was not almost naked like the other men who stood around him. Instead, he was clothed in animal skins. A black bear wrap was thrown over his shoulders and on his head were perched bird feathers of many colors. The skin on his face hung loose, as it did on the other visible portions of his body. But the smile radiated a genuine happiness at their arrival. Yatan spoke words of introduction. When he finished,

Balder and his men bowed before the old man as a way of acknowledging that they were visitors in the land of the Winyah.

The day was one that revolved around the men feasting around a large fire built some distance from the village in an area that had been cleared of all undergrowth. The chief and his council sat across from the Vikings. They were joined by Yatan who acted as interpreter. He had learned a limited number of words in the language of the Norseman.

The shaman once again watched from the edge of the woods, but he could not decipher the words of the strangers. He understood they represented a new force in the land. They were a people he did not understand, and ones over which he had no control. He must acquire their language and learn their secrets, or he would eventually lose his power over the Winyah. His mind churned on how to accomplish this feat. When he closed his eyes and focused his prayers to his gods, the image of his slave girl Myi appeared in his mind. That was the answer from the heavens. He went back to the village to seek her out.

While the men feasted with the leaders of the tribe, the Viking women were taken by the Winyah women to the other side of the village. The chief's first wife, a woman with little hair and no teeth, mumbled words that could barely be understood by even her own people, led the way. Soon Ingri and the others were invited to sit on animal skins laid near a large tree in a small clearing. In the center were several clay pots and other vessels. The smell of food rose from them and filled the surrounding air. Once they were seated in a circle, Ingri spoke to Kee.

"I need you to interpret what they are saying."

Following Baldar's instructions, Ingri had worked daily to learn the tribal language and to teach Kee the Norse language. The effort had been intense because Kee seemed just as determined as Ingri to bridge the gap of understanding each other's spoken words.

"The old one, Medi, is the chief's first wife. She extends the hand of welcome and invites you to eat of the bountiful harvest the gods have provided," Kee said.

Ingri could only understand a few of the words that fell from Kee's mouth, but they were enough to grasp the meaning. The Winyah women offered to their guest large shells gathered from the ocean and invited them to use these to scoop food from the pots. Ingri and the others soon found themselves enjoying a variety of food that included venison, fish, and the cornbread for which they had already developed a taste.

Ailish watched with keen interest the actions of the native women. Despite the fact they seemed to stand in awe of their guests, she did not trust them. She listened to their conversation and could understand some of the words spoken. She too had focused on learning the language of the Winyah. The old one, while she smiled at her guests, kept muttering about how the white women stank, and that no warrior would ever want to sleep with such sacks of bones. The other women laughed with her and joined in making derisive remarks. She noticed Kee did not try to interpret these negative words to Ingri. She was not surprised, for she did not trust the young slave. She had watched with alarm the growing attachment between her lover Nor and the one called Kee. Each day the jealous demon grew within her soul.

* * *

In the weeks following the visit to the village, the atmosphere between the Vikings and Winyah relaxed to the point that visits became frequent between the two settlements. When spring weather appeared, Kee showed Ingri and the other women how to prepare plots of cleared land for vegetable gardens. Then with seeds received from the tribe, the first crops were planted. During this same time the men with tribal warriors at their side hunted, fished, and explored the areas around the bay.

As spring gave way to summer, the shaman suppressed his fears and superstitions enough to enter the camp of the strangers. He took with him Myi, a child of thirteen who had been his slave since she was a baby. She had been taken during a raid on an enemy village. During the raid her parents were hacked to death in front of their tepee. The shaman seized the opportunity to take possession of the child. No warrior contested his claim because their preferences were for women to perform domestic chores or boys to be initiated into the ranks of warriors.

By the time the strangers arrived, Myi had grown into a beautiful young woman, and according to tribal custom the time had come for her to take a man. But the shaman intervened every time a warrior showed interest. It was not because he had an interest in her for himself. She had become like a daughter to him. But it was more than that relationship. As his bones grew old, he needed someone to replace him as shaman on his death. Myi he observed had a special connection with the gods. She was a good student of his magic and quickly grasped everything he taught her about the spirit world. For this reason he felt she must never take a man just as he had never known a woman. She must forgo those pleasures to become a spokesman to the gods. He believed only those who had never tapped their sexual energy could effectively communicate with the heavens.

The shaman needed Myi to learn the language and ways of the strangers. This was the first time in their relationship that he would be the student and she the teacher. As she acquired knowledge, she would pass it on to him. At first he thought of giving her as a slave to the white chief's wife, but he could not find it in his heart to part with her. So instead he decided to build a lodge in the woods near the stranger's camp for the two of them. That way he could keep Myi and at the same time observe the activity of the strangers.

Ingri knew the shaman and his slave were constructing a dwelling nearby. When it was completed, the young woman called Myi came into camp and attached herself to Ingri. When the sun went down in the evening, she always returned to the shaman. A competition soon developed between Myi and Kee. This proved fruitful because their knowledge of the Norse language developed rapidly. Ingri was then able to learn a great deal from them about the planting of indigenous crops and the gathering of herbs. The women weren't the only ones to exchange information. While the warriors taught the Vikings how to hunt the wild animals and gather the produce of the waters, these Norsemen returned the favor by helping the warriors construct additional lodges by using their axes. Soon thereafter, the warriors came to the camp and assisted the Vikings in building lodges so they too would be protected from the weather when the coming winter fell upon the region. By the time summer ended and the cold wind of winter approached, each civilization had been enhanced by their contact with the other. But all was not happy in this paradise, for Nor was restless when Kee was about him and Myi stood in awe of the Norse chief, Baldar.

* * *

The Cherokee warriors followed the well-worn path from their mountains to the land that lay along the ocean. It was their custom to raid when the frost was on the ground, a season when the mosquitoes no longer attacked the human flesh with their blood sucking stings. The travel to their destination took many moons. By the time the warriors reached the vicinity of the coast they had exhausted the fried cornbread and dried jerky carried in their leather pouches. As they neared the Big River, the appearance of smoke rising above the trees was a welcome sight. A village now lay within an hour's march. But they waited, for the sun was still high in the heavens. The leader ordered the men to a place beside the trail. Here they would hide in the underbrush until the sun set. Then the men would travel nearer to the site of the village and position themselves to attack as the sun rose the next morning. At that time the Winyah warriors would be asleep in their strangely constructed homes, and they would present an easy slaughter. After killing the warriors, they would take the young women captive and smash the heads of the old ones. The boys near puberty would also be taken back to the mountains to become Cherokee warriors.

The Winyah Chief, Motar, awoke from a troubling dream. He turned over beneath the warm animal skins and looked into the face of the young woman he had recently taken as his wife. She was the youngest daughter of a warrior he had fought beside in battle. She had been conceived the year before the warrior's spirit was taken. Knowing his own days were numbered, Motar tried to impregnate this young one, but his manhood had escaped from him. He was unable to penetrate the band of her womanhood which blocked the channel that led to her soul. He knew there would be no more children from his seed. Though he still hoped to see another spring, he was doubtful he would survive through the next winter. Thoughts of his youth passed through his mind–the many battles fought, the young flesh taken. He dozed back to sleep. Later something woke him. He did not know why, but he had an unsettled feeling. Unable to sleep, he arose, wrapped the bear skin around him, and then stepped outside. A Cherokee tomahawk struck him from behind with such force that it split his skull open like a ripe melon. The brain tissue filled with the memory of a lifetime poured forth and fell upon the ground.

Yatan had also awakened in the early morning hours with an uneasy feeling. As a warrior he learned to listen to that inner sense of danger. He stretched out his arm until his hand felt the cold steel of an ax he had finally convinced Baldar to give him, when a Viking died of an unknown disease five moons ago. He rose to his feet and looked out the opening of the lodge the Vikings helped him complete. In the mist of dawn he saw figures in the shadows moving about the village. Quickly he woke his ten-year-old son, Cherco.

"Go to the camp of Baldar and tell him that we are under attack. Ask him in the name of friendship to come to our aid."

The boy scampered off into the darkness. The only others in the lodge were his wife, Winoa, who was asleep with their infant girl in her arms. He whispered into her ear.

"The enemy is upon us. Take the child and flee into the forest."

Dressed only in a light pullover made of deerskin and holding the infant close to her breasts, she ran toward the trees. A Cherokee saw her through the mist that was quickly evaporating. Days without a woman diverted his attention from the objective of the attack. He crept through the forest in the direction she fled.

Under the needles of a cluster of long-leaf pine saplings, Winoa watched as the shadow of a man came ever closer to her hiding place.

He almost passed by, but the baby, hungry for her mother's breast milk, cried out to be fed. Winoa knew at that moment that she and her child were doomed.

After Winoa disappeared into the woods, Yatan let out the cry of alarm. The braves of his tribe dashed forth from their lodgings, but before they could prepare a defense the Cherokees were upon them. The fight was short and bloody. Trying to avoid being cut off and eliminated as individuals, a group of braves managed to join Yatan to form a last line of defense. With tomahawks they beat back several assaults. Yatan slew several of the attackers with his ax. Cherokees warriors were fascinated by the instrument of death in his hands. Some of them lost their lives trying to take the ax from the Winyah warrior. When all seemed lost, a loud cry came from the forest. Out onto the cleared area that bordered the village charged Vikings wielding swords and axes. Behind them a man followed who was constantly blowing on a cow horn and creating an awful racket. The Cherokees were stunned by the appearance of these strange creatures. Though the strange ones were few in number, their sudden appearance caused panic. Thinking they were demons, the courage of the Cherokees deserted them and they fled.

The battle over, Yatan looked around for his wife and infant child. She was not in the village, and no survivor had seen her.

"I am missing my wife and child," he said to Baldar.

Nor, standing nearby, offered to go with the warrior and help find them. As Baldar watched them walk toward the wooded area where Yatan last saw them, he was touched by the anguish in Yatan's face. Compassion swept his emotions. He suppressed this strange feeling that he was unaccustomed to, and then he turned his attention to more pressing matters at hand.

The infant body lay on the grass next to the tree where her head had been bashed against its trunk. Nearby, Winoa's nude body, beat to a bloody pulp with a tomahawk, was sprawled over a tree stump, a sight so gruesome, even Nor, a veteran killer of men, was sickened. Yatan reached down and picked up his wife and holding her against his chest, he returned to the village; Nor followed him carrying the dead infant.

Although only fifty Winyah braves survived the attack, few of the women and children were harmed. The survivors looked to Yatan as their new leader. He felt the heavy burden of responsibility that now rested on his shoulders. The very survival of his tribe was at risk. The limited number of warriors meant that many maidens would be without mates unless the existing braves were willing to assume the responsibility of taking on more wives than the traditional two. The thought occurred to him that these strangers could be a source of strength, for though they were few in numbers, their aggressive nature would greatly increase the ability of the Winyah to defend their traditional territory along the river and bay from encroachment by other tribes.

"Baldar," Yatan said, "Your people could easily be wiped by a hostile tribe. You should consider moving to our village. Together we are much stronger. With the cold time coming, wildlife will be scarce, and the gardens will die. Our tribe has stored corn and other produce for the winter. With the death of so many of our people we now have sufficient stores to provide your Norsemen with enough food to survive the winter."

"I will hold a council and talk to my men," Baldar said.

But he had made a quick calculation and already knew the answer. Without help from the Winyah, he believed his people would starve when winter came. Not knowing the climate in this land, he expected a winter as cold as Greenland, where families retreated to their longhouses and did not come out until spring. He would soon find out that the winters along the bay were warmer than the summers at home.

* * *

The Winyah rarely hunted in the winter because the weather was too cold on their naked bodies. But the Norseman, surprised by the mildness of the winter, had no difficulty in organizing hunting excursions. They were successful in killing wild game in sufficient amounts to feed not only their people but also the Winyah. Yatan, who had adopted the Viking's custom of wearing clothes, joined his new friends in the hunt. Other warriors soon followed the actions of their leader and by the end of winter the wearing of clothes made of skins by all members of the Winyah tribe became common place.

Baldar's residence in the village that winter included Ingri, who was heavy with child and the thane, Ailish with her lover, Nor. The slave, Kee, also lodged with them. The quarters were crowded, but not to the extent as the other longhouses where the rest of the Vikings were housed. In due time the long houses were built larger and divided so that men and women were separated. The discomfort of close quarters in the lodges this first winter in the new world was only relieved by days when the sun shone bright and warmed the crust of the earth.

With spring around the corner, the sap began to rise in the trees and in the humans. Myi wasted no opportunity to be in close contact with Baldar when he was out of Ingri's presence. He thought it was funny at first the way her big eyes danced with excitement in his presence. As time progressed and with Ingri so pregnant that a sexual relationship with her was no longer possible, he felt a growing desire in his loins for the young slave girl. Morality was not a problem for him because he never accepted the Christian god and instead had remained faithful to Thor and the other Norse gods. Age was also not a factor because females frequently lost their maidenhead in Greenland when they entered puberty. So Baldar's problem was not one of religion or custom, but one of fear–fear of Ingri's reaction. He had never known love before, but he now had those feelings toward his wife. They had grown close during their time together, sharing joy, life-threatening crisis, and a new land. Now their life was blessed with the excitement of a child, who with Thor's blessings would soon enter this world.

Spring would be the fifteenth such season since her birth, and Myi was battling the hormones that unmarried females dealt with at her age. The fact she was attracted to the Norsemen did not help matters. She was held back from expressing her feelings by the watchful eye of her master, the shaman, and a fear of Ingri. Although she liked the woman, she knew the Norse woman was not one to trifle with. For despite the considerate way she treated her, Myi knew beneath the surface of kindness lay the fierceness of a puma. Despite this and even knowing a loss of virginity would bar her from becoming a shaman, she felt her resolve weaken every time she was in Baldar's presence.

The shaman was wise. He had over the years observed the nature of animals and the movement of the stars. He also was an observer of human behavior and, therefore, was not surprised at Myi's temptation, which he sensed from her body language when he saw her in the presence of the Norseman. Each night after she taught him all she had learned that day at the lodge of the strangers, he took the precaution of feeding her a meal into which he had mixed a concoction of herbs, which he hoped would limit her restlessness. Since no other was available to replace him, he must try to protect her purity. Already she knew secrets he had spent a life time learning, and she was ready to assume the mantle of shaman upon his death.

* * *

Nor saw Kee in a clearing near the river some distance from the village. She was gathering the tender leaves of wild greens that had sprouted from an old garden plot under the warm rays of the spring sun. With the coming of warm weather she had discarded the clothes of the Norse women that she wore during the cold winter time. Now only an animal skin was tied around her waist. It hung just far enough to cover her womanhood. Her firm naked young breast bounced in the afternoon breeze as she moved about placing plant leaves in a basket she carried upon her hip. Nor paused on his way back to the lodge and watched her for a moment from the shadows of a tree near the edge of the forest. His thoughts of the first person he ever loved, Ailish, dissolved from his mind, and were replaced by lust for this slave girl. The hunger in his loins drove away all reason as he stepped from the shadows and walked in her direction.

Kee felt his presence, and she knew his eyes were watching her every movement. It was not by accident that he had come upon her that day. For during the past she had watched carefully his routine walks in the woods every afternoon, and she had positioned herself to be observed. Though she was just a slave girl and her age was fourteen winters, she had a typical woman's instinct when it came to men. During the long winter months in the lodge, she felt his eyes were upon her at night even while Ailish lay in his arms. She had encouraged him by exposing parts of her body while pretending to be asleep. She had never known a man but she intended to. She had chosen Nor, for he had the courage of a warrior. Though this was important to her young heart, it was not the most important thing that attracted her to him. She recognized gentleness about him. It lay just beneath that hard exterior. Now as he crossed the open area toward her, she knew that the time had arrived. She turned around and faced him while he was still several yards away. Her hands undid the skin garment around her waist and let it drop to the ground. In another moment he would take her, and she was ready to submit to his passion.

She knew. How Ailish knew defied logic. And her heart was broken. She could not accept his relationship with the slave girl, even though to have done so would not have violated the customs of her society. Viking men frequently bedded numerous women. She sulked about the lodge for days. Then one morning she packed her few belongings and moved to the edge of the forest where she built a makeshift hut near the shaman's lodge. Nor came and tried to persuade her to return, but she would consent to do so only if Kee was expelled from their quarters. This Nor could not agree to. In her pitiful hut she remained until Myi and the shaman with compassion in their hearts invited Ailish to come and live in their lodge, which was large enough to accommodate three adults. There she embraced them like a family and soon they became as one.

* * *

The birth was not an easy one for the channel was narrow and the child large. But the old women of the village had delivered many children in the past and when logic dictated that they should give up the mother's life and save the child, they did not. The child Kendar was born and Ingri lived.

"It is a healthy child who will grow up to be a leader among the Vikings," Baldar said to his wife who lay on a new bed he had constructed for her.

She looked up and smiled.

"No, he will be the leader of all the Sioux tribes in this new land. We are Vikings no more but the fountainhead of a new civilization. He will take a Winyah woman as his wife and she will bear him many children. Around the camp fires in the future, the tribes will speak of the white ones who came from across the sea and taught them how to wear clothes, forge lead arrow heads, and defeat their enemies. This is how we will be remembered when our bones have turned to dust."

Though Ingri survived the birth, her health never recovered. Something had torn within her and never healed properly. The following spring she became dependant upon Myi to help her in planting the plots of land with sweet potatoes, tubers that came from trade with tribes that lived far to the south in a world far removed from the more primitive indigenous tribe that lived on the east coast. Other seeds planted that spring were also received from trade conducted along the numerous trails that ran for hundreds of miles down the coast and into the interior of this land. The most important to the Winyahs were squash and corn, a staple upon which the people of a distant southern tribe based an entire civilization— a civilization so advanced that it rivaled that of ancient Egypt. Of this civilization Ingri, and the tribes about her had little knowledge. They received these items from tribes much closer to their world after they had passed through many hands along the trade routes.

Now that Nor and Kee had constructed their own lodge, Ailish began to come with Myi each day and help Ingri with chores. And in the evening Ingri and Ailish would instruct Myi on the hierarchy of the Norse Gods. Though there were many, Myi was more taken to the gods represented by the stone statues. Like the human race from the beginning of time, she found it easier to believe in something she could see with the visible eye. Soon the statues no longer represented the gods but became the gods. Each day she offered prayers and requests to them. The shaman found this disconcerting. As her belief in these two gods grew stronger, he knew that to resist them would be futile, so he incorporated them into to the spiritual world which existed in his mind before the coming of the strangers. They were added to the gods of the water, animals, trees, and sky. Every day prayers were made to all of these forces that the humans did not understand but whom they believed decided their fate.

By the end of summer season Ingri sensed death was upon her. At night her dreams were filled with scenes of the life she had known before the voyage on the knar brought them to this strange place. When the fever came during the midst of the summer season, the earlier pleasant dreams turned into nightmares about her son being left alone in the forest with no one to care for him. One day in a moment of clarity she watched as Myi sat at the foot of the bed holding Kendar. She realized that the answer lay with the shaman's slave —she recognized the young woman was bonded to the child. In order to assure her plan, Ingri felt she must give up her man to another. And to bring peace of mind, it must be before her death. That was the only way to be sure such a union would take place. It was a heart-wrenching decision, but it must be done and soon.

"I will not do this," Baldar said to his wife one night after she made the stunning request. It would not please the gods."

"Since when have our gods objected to a man having more then one woman?" she asked.

"I do not desire another woman."

The words were spoken because he truly did love the woman that lay beside him, but they were not totally true. For the desire for Myi had grown in intensity during Ingri's pregnancy, and since then thoughts of her clouded his mind. This situation was aggravated by the fact that Ingri was not physically capable of lovemaking since the birth. On the days when he was in Myi's presence, beyond the view of the lodge where Ingri lay dying, he sensed she felt the same attraction, and it took restraint not to act upon his desire.

In his sleep, Baldar turned over during the early morning hours and reached out for his wife's hand. When he touched it, the cold lifeless feeling of the flesh woke him. In the flickering light of the burning embers that remained from last night's logs, he saw her eyes were wide open, and there was no light emanating from them. The color of her lips was a dark bluish color, and her chest did not move from the exhaling of breath. He dressed and went to alert his clan that Ingri was dead.

The Viking men and women gathered around the grave dug in a patch of land on a spot were a village once stood. Many Winyah people came to mourn with the strangers from the sea. In the short time the Norse had lived among them, they had come to admire the wife of Baldar. The shaman danced around the grave and called upon the spirits to guide her along the journey to the afterlife. For the first time Myi participated in the spiritual ritual. At the end the two of them offered a prayer to the stone idols that Baldar had brought to the grave site. Baldar intended to place the idols in the grave with Ingri, but he was prevented from doing so by the restraining arms of the shaman and Myi. He finally understood they wanted these Norse gods to live on by incorporating them into a place of honor in front of the shaman's lodge.

* * *

In the middle of the night Myi slipped from her bed of straw. Her feet followed the trail through the woods to Baldar's lodge. The moon was high in the sky, and its reflection cast off light so that a burning torch was not necessary to guide Myi on her journey. A chill hung in the night air, and it caused the nipples on her small breasts to stand rigid. They were dark purple in contrast to the copper-colored flesh on the mounds from which they protruded. From a distance she saw Baldar's lodge. As she approached, she looked through an opening at the glimmer of light given off by the hot coals from the remains of burning logs. Later, she stood in the doorway for a moment and observed the sleeping form of the Norseman. He was alone, for Nor and Kee had moved many moons ago to their own dwelling. She approached quietly and stood over him. The muscles in his chest, which was covered by thick black hair, moved as his lips sucked in the cool fall air. The exhaling breath looked like smoke coming from his lips. After placing over him the cover that had fallen on the dirt floor, she slipped beneath it. She felt him stir, then reached out for her.

Aroused from a deep sleep, at first Baldar clouded mind thought it was Ingri who lay beside him. The cold nipples that pressed against his chest caused a dream of Greenland to flee from his mind, and he opened his eyes. Myi's soft voice spoke to him in the darkness. He pulled her close, and his hands began to explore her body. As he caressed her, he could feel the urgency of her flesh beneath his touch, and it matched his own. As he took her, she screamed out a short cry of pain, and then their bodies joined in a mating rhythm used by humans since the beginning of time.

Words did not have to be spoken. The shaman knew when he looked into the face of Myi that her purity was gone, and that she would no longer have access to the gods. It broke his heart, for now his link to the heavens that protected the Winyahs would die with him. Who would then come forth from his tribe and speak to the spirit world, he wondered. A week later he fell ill with fever after a storm caught him a great distance from his lodge. After several days of sickness he drew his last breath and was buried near the spot where Ingri had been placed beneath the sod.

* * *

The source of the pestilence was of an unknown origin. But in its path scores were left dead. Not only members of the tribe were swept away but also all who had crossed the sea, except for Baldar, Nor, and Ailish. They somehow survived the onslaught without any sign of the symptoms that made the others sick. The sickness seemed limited to the Winyahs and the strangers that had come to live among them. Those who lived in the adjoining regions were untouched. During this crisis the Winyahs were without a holy man. But Ailish with the knowledge gained from the shaman fought back against the reaper with herbs and prayers to the heavens.

Myi served as her right hand during the crisis, and though many died, others were saved by their efforts. Something unusual happened when the unknown passed. The new chief Yatan and the tribal council allowed Ailish to become the new shaman, ignoring the fact that she was not a virgin. They put their faith in her and in the two new gods brought from across the sea.

"We have been reduced to thirty braves," Yatan said.

"And the number of women and children number no more than one hundred," Baldar replied.

"It is too few to resist our enemies."

"We must move to a place easily defended until our numbers have been replenished."

"You have uttered wise words. Let us take our peoples to the land across the marsh."

And so it was that the Winyah moved to the area in the land between the waters and dwelt there. In order to strengthen the tribe, each warrior was required to take as wives any widows or unattached women over the age of twelve and adopt their offspring. Soon there was an explosion in the tribe's birthrate.

The passage of time allowed the Winyah to expand the size of their tribe. Because they were hidden in the mosquito-infested area of the coast, the other tribes did not for a long time contest their right to reside there. Yatan gave Baldar command of his warriors. The Norseman taught the warriors tactics that were different from those used in the region. Over the next few years, Baldar led raiding parties into lands far to the south where boys were taken captive and brought back to the Winyah village where they were prime candidates for initiation as warriors.

The isolation the tribe created for their group could not last forever. In the tenth fall after the great death, a band of Winyah men on a hunt near the mouth of the Big River spotted a band of Cherokee warriors with canoes coming downstream. The gods were with them for darkness soon fell upon the land, and the Cherokee stopped to make camp for the evening. The Winyahs were then able to cross the water and reach their village without drawing attention.

"We must strike tonight while they are asleep around their campfires," Baldar said.

"We have never attacked at night," Yatan replied. "It will disturb the spirits who wander the woods in the darkness, and they will bring their wrath upon us."

Knowing that arguing with Yatan would be futile, he decided to try another tactic.

"Let us consult the shaman for she knows the ways of the spirit world."

They found Ailish in her lodge. She listened carefully to Yatan's story about the Cherokees and the tactics Baldar proposed to defend the village. She went outside and knelt before the two idols and began to speak in a language that no one understood. They assumed it was in the language of the spirits, but actually it was Welsh, the language of her people. When she finished, she looked up at the two men.

"The spirits invite you to enter their world this night and strike the intruders."

Yatan had his answer.

"We will take the experienced braves and go," Yatan said.

"No, you should remain behind. For if we fail, you must lead the remnants of the tribe into the marsh islands for safety until the enemy has departed."

"I want to lead my warriors, but you speak wisely. I will stay and prepare our people. May the gods grant you victory this night."

They paddled to a bluff downstream from the Cherokees' encampment. From there the men followed a trail through the forest that passed a short distance from where the enemy slept by their campfires. Having no obstacle in their way, Baldar and his warriors found the camp without alerting them.

The sentry felt no sense of danger, for after the exhausting journey that day his eyelids grew heavy, and he fell asleep an hour before the Winyahs arrived. This young buck would never need to worry about rest again. The double-edged ax split his skull open from one blow delivered by Cherco, son of Yatan. It was his first time in battle, and the sight of his enemy's blood had an exhilarating effect upon him. The fight was over in a matter of minutes. Twenty enemy bodies lay upon the ground. An equal number had fled into the woods. Baldar did not pursue them. He wanted the survivors to spread the message about the fierceness of his adopted tribe. This would act as a deterrent to others who previously may have thought the Winyahs incapable of defending their own territory.

The Cherokee continued to raid the coastal area in the fall of each year, but they avoided the bay area. Their defeat at the hands of the Winyah taught them that any invasion into that tribe's territory would not come without a great cost in lives.

In the twentieth fall after the great death, the Winyah tribe split into two groups. Yatan led most of the tribe back to their ancestral home near the mouth of the Big River. Baldar remained on the land near the beach with the remainder of the tribe. The separation was a friendly split with Baldar still recognizing Yatan as his chief. The cultural divide continued between the two groups as Baldar's people built separate lodges for the men and women. Some of them were large enough to house fifty individuals. Yatan's group continued the practice of family lodges in the tradition handed down many years ago from the Fish People. Ailish chose to join Yatan on his trek. She took with her the two stone Norse gods. Nor and Kee did not want to leave Baldar, so they remained behind with their five children.

THE
WELSH

It was the worst of times. The ancient land of the Welsh suffered from a violent and devastating civil war that engulfed the land. Hope was at last brought to the region of Gwynedd by Prince Madoc and his brother Rhirid. These bastard sons of King Owain of North Wales had been caught in a storm while exploring the western ocean. Lost at sea for many weeks, their ships, the *Gorn* and the *Sant*, were carried by the winds to a strange new place. Now a year after their disappearance, they returned to their home and spoke of the riches of this new country. They described it as a paradise where land was available for everyone, and food was plentiful in the rivers and great forests. Excitement was at fever pitch among the inhabitants when word spread that the brothers planned to return in ten ships, eight of which had recently been seized by their father from his enemies. Passage was free to those willing to undertake this dangerous voyage to the edge of the earth.

Among those who dreamed of a new life was Ava, an educated Welsh woman, twenty years of age, who had lost her husband in a great battle between the forces of the king and an English noble. After her husband's death, the king took her into his castle at Dolwyddelan, for her husband had been one of his finest warriors and a close confidant. During the following two years, she served as governess to the young children of his new mistress, Rendar. The woman was jealous of Ava, who soon realized there was no future for her in the kingdom. When Ava heard of the expedition, she persuaded the king to allow her to depart with the fleet as a passenger. He granted her request in order to end the domestic friction which was making his life a living hell within the very confines of his own living quarters.

* * *

The captain noticed Ava immediately for she stood out among the throngs of downtrodden peasants that the king had allowed his sons to take from his kingdom. Standon was not surprised by the king's action, nor was his friend Prince Madoc or the prince's brother, Rhirid. These illegitimate sons of the king did not expect their father to release valuable assets from his land, not even for the two sons he had recognized before the law. The only men of quality allowed to leave were the twenty soldiers personally loyal to Madoc. At least the illiterate peasants from the bottom rung of society were healthy, for the brothers had focused on picking ones who could survive the journey. These peasants were willing passengers—willing to face any danger to leave a place where hope was extinguished. They numbered three men for every female. The two brothers knew a ready supply of women was available from the primitive people they lived among during their journey in paradise, women who could be easily taken by force of arms if necessary.

It was late spring when the ships sailed from the Afon Ganol at Rhos on the sea. The fleet was adequately stocked with food for the journey. Many of the old and weak who were left behind would starve in the coming months because the quantity of food stored on the fleet meant there would be less surplus in the land. The women were restricted to three of the ships. The brothers thought it easier to maintain order this way. In their experience at sea the presence of females on board always became a source of problems once men were at sea more than two weeks. They anticipated it would take much longer to reach their destination.

Ava was one of seven women on board the *Pedr*. The others were the wives of crew members. She soon learned from the gossip of these women that her suitable quarters and fair treatment were because of the captain, a man who it was whispered was a close friend of Prince Madoc. She was immediately suspicious of the captain's motives. In her world such men usually expected something of value in return for favors. Ava was keenly aware her body was the only thing of value she possessed that would interest him.

* * *

In his forty years of life Captain Standon had experienced many adventures. Born the son of a landowner he was trained to be a warrior. But for some unknown reason he was drawn to the sea. He had rejected her until a plague took his wife and three children. Then the sea's call to him became irresistible. Now for years it had become his only solace.

Giving up the life of a land warrior, he learned to be an expert sailor by working on merchant ships carrying goods to Iceland. It was during one of these trips that he met Prince Madoc. He learned the prince also had a love of the sea, and the two soon became close friends. The next few years he served as first mate on the prince's ship. In their fifth year together they were on their way to Iceland along with Prince Rhirid when a summer storm blew their ship off course. Weeks later, suffering from starvation, they sailed into a body of water that later Europeans would call Mobile Bay. Dropping anchor they set about exploring what to them was a tropical paradise. One day while on a hunting expedition, Prince Madoc and his brother were surrounded by savages whose action indicated they thought the Welsh were gods. The Welsh leaders were quick to take advantage of this misconception. Now furnished with food on a daily basis, the men quickly regained their health. Using the savages as their guides, they mapped the area and discussed establishing a Welsh settlement. When they sailed away, they carried with them two savages to display when they reached home to add credibility to their story of a new land. Unfortunately, the savages became ill on the way back to Wales and had to be buried at sea.

* * *

Standon watched Ava come out of her quarters the first morning of the voyage and go to the starboard side where she emptied the night bucket into the sea. She was a thin woman whose long red hair fell to her waist. On this particular day she wore a black skirt that brushed against a set of beautiful ankles. He had first noticed her down at the docks. Attracted to her kind face, he had inquired who she was from a servant on the dock. When he later discovered that she was going to sail with the expedition, he had Madoc assign her to the *Pedr*, a ship he was to command for the voyage. He wondered what had driven him to take this action as he watched her boarding the morning of departure. The justification in his mind was that he did not want a lady of breeding to suffer sailing among the mass of illiterate peasant women. Deep inside he knew that was not the real reason. He was lonely, and she was a woman of good breeding whose smile radiated light into the darkness that surrounded his soul—a darkness that was previously only relieved by the sea.

It was the second day at sea, and Ava was leaning on the rail, looking out in the direction of the other ships, when a voice behind her interrupted her thoughts.

"I knew your husband."

She turned and looked directly into the face of the captain for the first time.

"We fought together in the battle at Gandar," he said. "That was before you were wed to him."

She was startled by this bit of information and for a moment did not reply.

"If I can be of any service, please call upon me."

Such a use of good language, she thought. He must be of noble birth.

"Thank you, Captain. I am a widow, and I am used to taking care of myself, but your offer is appreciated."

As he walked away, she noticed what a commanding presence he had. It reminded her of the husband she had lost after only six months of marriage, a marriage that she thought might never happen. She had turned down many suitors, and by the time she met him she was over eighteen years of age; in her society that was considered old not to have wed. However, when they first met he was as smitten with her as she with him. Wasn't it strange, she thought, how she could handle the loneliness before marriage better than after she became a widow. Perhaps it was preferable never to have loved than to have lost the one you had given your heart to. And then there was the sexual frustration that never existed before. This situation was aggravated by the fact that over the last two years the king had been always trying to get her alone, and his mistress was constantly watching her with suspicion. It was all too much to deal with. She sucked in a breath of the fresh salt air. No matter what happened, she was glad to be free of Wales.

Ava did not try to avoid him. Even if she had, it would have been an act in futility. The deck of the ship was not that large, and she could not remain in the stifling heat of her cabin during the day.

"I lost my wife and children during the plague," he said to her one morning.

She was touched by this information.

"I am sorry," she said.

"It nearly drove me mad."

"I have lost my parents and my spouse, but not children. So I cannot feel that pain, but it must be a terrible ordeal."

"Worse than death."

She saw from the look on his face that it was as he had spoken.

After their conversation, Ava felt compassion for the captain, and thereafter each day they spent time on the deck together. Despite her efforts to avoid it, her heart opened up to him. Soon she no longer worried about him forcing his way into her cabin, but instead she waited up at night wondering how long before he would come to her bed.

* * *

It was the end of the third week when one evening a knock came on Ava's cabin door. She did not rise for her instincts told her who it was that had knocked.

"Come in," she said, after having sat up in the bed.

When he entered, she observed a strained look on his face.

"We have the pox on board. It is one of the women."

"But how is that possible? We have been away from port a long time."

"I don't know, but I'm afraid it will spread."

"Bring the woman to my cabin, and I will take care of her."

"It's too late for that."

"Has she died?"

"I had the men throw her overboard. It was necessary to protect the rest of us on this ship."

He saw a look of revulsion on her face, and it was directed toward him. Suddenly, he was filled with the horrible thought that she despised him. As he turned to leave, he expected her to say something, but her lips remained silent.

In the following days the pox spread. Those who contracted it tried to hide the sores for they knew what fate awaited them. Standon had a policy of checking everyone, and over the next few days three more women and two crew members were thrown into the sea. That was the end of the pox problem. The crew breathed a sigh of relief, and Ava who had remained in her cabin, finally came out onto the deck.

Ava saw him instantly. He had changed since the night he visited her cabin. It was more than the loss of weight. His face was drawn, and when he looked up and saw her face, she felt pity on him. She knew the decisions this man had made were necessary, or they all might have perished.

She walked over to where he stood and slipped her hand under his arm. He did not acknowledge her presence but instead continued to gaze out at the ocean. After a moment she leaned over and whispered in his ear.

"Come to my cabin tonight. For I have waited too long, and our lives are filled with so much uncertainty."

A surprised look came across his face. Though he did not reply, she knew he would come when darkness fell upon the ship.

On the fourth night that he lay in bed beside her, they were both awakened by the roll of the ship before it righted itself between the angry waves of the sea.

"I must get on deck. A storm has come upon us while we slept."

After he left the cabin, she got up and looked out the shutter at the angry water. She could tell from the sound of the wind outside, and from the way the ship was rocking back and forth, this was no ordinary storm.

Standon and the crew battled to keep her afloat. By the break of day, he felt they might be fighting a losing battle, for they were in the midst of something none of them had ever experienced. A hurricane was sweeping across the eastern coast of what later in history would become the Carolinas. In the distance Standon thought he saw land, but he could not be sure because of the heavy sheets of falling rain. When all seemed lost, the winds suddenly died down, and the rain slackened. An eerie calm settled upon the water. Standon saw the relief on his men's faces. But he did not share their new-found optimism. Instead, he sensed this calm was unnatural and that the storm would return in all its fury.

"Is it over?" she asked, when he entered the cabin.

"No, I don't believe so. I'm sure the storm is going to return. When the rain slackened, I spotted land, but it was a great distance away. I have ordered the sails hoisted. We are going to make a run for it. Hopefully, we will find a bay where we can seek shelter."

"What about the other ships?"

"Lost sight of them in the storm. I'm sure they are scattered across the ocean."

"Will they be able to find us when this is over?"

"I don't know how much distance lies between us. But if we follow the coast line after this storm, we will locate the place where Madoc and Rhirid plan to start their settlement."

He paused for a moment as they both heard the wind begin to whistle through the sails.

"Dress in something you can swim in," he said, "In case this ship doesn't make it to safe harbor."

He looked into her eyes one more time. She saw his lips form the words, *I love you* and then he was gone. She dressed as he suggested, than emptied a small chest containing clothing onto the floor. While she listened to the cries of the crew outside trying to lower the sails, she focused on securing the lock on the chest. She then took a rope that lay in the corner of the cabin and ran it through the steel handles that were on each side and tied the two ends into a knot. When she finished, she sat down and waited for Standon to return.

He had ordered the sails lowered when the storm returned with more ferocity than before. In the short time the sails had fluttered in the wind, the ship had made great progress in closing the distance between itself and the land that lay on the horizon. Just when Standon began to think they would make it to safe harbor, disaster struck. He heard a loud crack in the center of the deck. The ship was breaking in two. He rushed toward the cabin, but he was swept away before his hand could reach for the door.

When the ship broke apart, Ava grabbed the ropes that she had securely tied to the handle of the chest. Seconds later she was in the water. It was daylight, but the high waves blocked her view from seeing the others struggling in the water. She held on tight as the water constantly broke over her. In between the constant coughing up of water, she cried out for Standon. Instinctively, she knew no one except her had survived when the ship went down. In the distance she saw land, and she kicked her feet to push her body in that direction.

* * *

Members of the Winyah tribe were walking the beach that morning after the storm. They had come when young boys from the village brought news of strange items washed up on the sand. Kendar, son of Baldar, was one of the first adults to arrive at the scene. Several bodies lay upon the beach. They were dressed in strange clothing. He was shocked when he turned one of them over and saw in the man's face a reflection of his own characteristic. His mind raced back to the stories his father had told him many times of the land from whence the Vikings had come. Surely these must be of the same tribe. As he explored farther down the beach, he saw what appeared in the distance to be the body of a female. When he walked up to get a closer look, he saw that her hands clutched a strange type of vine that was attached to a round container made of wood. He saw her chest move and realized she was breathing.

For hours Ava had struggled to reach shore, and when all seemed lost, the current changed and pulled the wooden chest in the direction of land. At the time it was still a long ways away, and sometime during the ordeal she sank into a semiconscious state. Even then her hands still gripped the rope. The current brought her into shallow water, and when the water receded, it left her body upon the surf. The following weeks would only confirm what she already knew in her heart. Standon and the others on board the *Pedr* perished. She thought that perhaps those on board the other nine vessels had also perished.

Unknown to Ava, the *Gorn* and the *Sant* survived and would arrive badly damaged at their original destination. There the Welshmen would forcibly take the women of the local inhabitants and breed with them. The Welsh's advance organization and knowledge would serve them well in this new world. Later settlers would find the remains of their forts in regions of Alabama, Georgia, and Tennessee. Ultimately, because they were outnumbered in the new country, they would be conquered by the Cherokees and assimilated. English settlers would frequently remark upon the unusual facial features of that tribe when they came into contact with them.

* * *

When word reached Ailish after the storm that a stranger had washed up on the beach, she immediately convinced some warriors to take her there by canoe. The strange one was asleep in a makeshift tepee at the foot of sand dunes at a place English settlers in a later era would call Pawleys Island. When she gazed upon the figure that lay on mats woven from sea grass, her emotions were stirred. The woman before her was a reflection of Ailish's people. She had lived in this new land so long and become so embedded into the Winyah tribe that she had almost forgotten her home, the land of Wales where as a child she had been kidnapped by Vikings and sold into slavery in Norway before being purchased by the Norseman, Baldar. Now as the memory of her earlier life flooded her mind, she felt grief, and her heart ached to be among her own kind.

Was it all a dream? Ava had a flashback memory of opening her eyes and seeing that she lay on a sandy beach. A man with brown eyes, dressed in strange clothing, hovered over her. He spoke a strange language she did not understand. Then others, who looked different from the first stranger, appeared. Their skin was the color of clay and their hair jet black. They had pressed to her lips a gourd, and from it water flowed into her mouth. Then her eyes shut and darkness overcame her. When she woke a second time, she was in a strange dwelling constructed of animal skins. A female was placing in her mouth a soft, warm, mushy substance which had a salty, gritty taste to it. Then sleep had overtaken her again. Now in the deep recess of her mind, she felt as she lay there in a semiconscious state, that she was standing on a line between life and death, and she was not sure on which side of the chasm her spirit would fall.

* * *

The Winyah's gathered all the materials washed ashore and carried it to the village. They were placed outside the old chief's hut. Inside on the soft skin of a black bear rug sat Baldar. An old man who suffered from poor health, he knew his days upon the earth were numbered. He looked forward to the afterlife where he hoped to see Ingri and Myi again, though he did hate that his departure from this world would separate him from his favorite child, Kendar. He was the warrior in line to succeed him as chief. Memories of a prior life flooded Baldar's thoughts. For a moment a sense of regret settled upon him. It did not last long, for this land had been good to him. And the Winyahs, who lived on the land between the waters, had flourished under his leadership since the death of Yatan. It was true that some of the customs and traditions of the land had changed since his arrival. The Winyahs no longer were almost naked, but instead they wore garments made from animal skins, a change in their culture that allowed them to roam the forest even during the time when cold weather visited the earth. The changes to the Vikings were even more pronounced. Baldar and the descendants of the others had adopted the language of the tribe. Except for the difference in skin, hair color, and stature, they were now indistinguishable from the native inhabitants.

* * *

When the first words dropped from the stranger's lips, Ailish recognized the language of her people. A long time had elapsed since she last heard such sounds from others, for even the statements that Baldar used on occasion in his native tongue were of Norwegian origin. The only way she kept the Welsh alive, even in her own mind, was by using it in her communications with the gods. The Winyahs always stood in awe when she did this in their presence. They believed she was speaking to the gods in the language of the spirits.

A year later as Ava set around the campfire in the village, her mind wandered over what had transpired. The adjustment was not as hard as one would image. One reason was that Ailish was in constant contact with her. Since they both spoke Welsh, it was easy to learn about the world into which she had been cast. The language barrier was broken during the first few months when Ailish helped her learn Sioux. The days had their lonely moments when she thought of Standon and her deceased husband. They were the only portion of her prior life that still held an emotional attachment for her. While the mores of the tribe were different from her own, there were many similarities. They both were warrior cultures, and in the arena of life, even outside of war, the men were dominant and women were frequently treated as serfs. She knew from Ailish that soon she would have to choose a man. At her age it was not acceptable in this tribal culture to have it otherwise. As men found every reason to flock about her, the women, who were jealous of her, turned a cold shoulder. Deprived of female companionship, except the days that Ailish came from the mainland, she began to consider who to choose as a mate. One that attracted her was a warrior named Kendar, the son of Baldar. Though the mother, Ingri, was dead long before her arrival, Ava had spent many hours around the campfire with the father, Baldar. He spoke frequently of his deceased wives, and he hungered for news about the European world. In their conversations the father encouraged her toward Kendar because he wanted to keep his bloodlines pure, at least for another generation.

Baldar gave counsel to his son on marriage, as he did on other aspects of his son's life. In the past he had encouraged him to marry the daughter of Nor. She turned out to be barren, and after five years she died from an unknown cause. He had waited through two springs after her death and now it was time to take another wife.

"Take the stranger," Baldar said to Kendar one evening. "And once a male child is born we should arrange for you to marry a maiden from each tribe of the Sioux."

"That is not the custom."

"In Europe that was the way a man became a chief and his descendants became king. It is no different here. One day your line from the stranger will produce a chief of all the Sioux. Then one of his descendants will become king.

Though he could not understand Europe or what a king was, Kendar understood what chief of all the Sioux meant. He had been taught the legend of the Great Divide, and the fact that before this event the tribes of the Sioux were all united under a great chief.

In the spring of the year a new lodge was built, and after a proper tribal marriage ceremony, Ava moved her belongings into the structure. When she first entered, she was surprised that the trunk Baldar had frequently mentioned was there with its lid opened. She was taken aback by the amount of silver it contained. This trunk had been recovered by Baldar's trusted friend, Nor, when their ship sank in the river. She knew what the delivery of this meant. Baldar had a premonition that death would soon arrive on his doorstep, and he was passing this treasure on to the next generation.

The night she moved into their dwelling, Kendar came to her. She was not submissive like his first wife. Her hands moved with skill over his body. Though it increased his desire to explode within her sacred cavity, she prolonged it until at last her hand guided his firm shaft. The long delay, he soon realized, made the final act so much more pleasing, as he was carried to the pinnacle and then released.

It was different, she thought, perhaps because he was a younger man. The only thing she knew was that he touched something within her not touched by her first two lovers. On future nights, as they lay in bed together, she worked with feverish effort to please him, and he allowed her to do so. When the male child was born nine months later, Kendar was free to begin the task of collecting a wife from each tribe, one per year in the spring of each year. Eventually, Kendar would become chief of all the Sioux and would be called the Datha. Thus a confederation was established that would continue until the coming of the Spanish to their shore.

THE
SPANISH

Spring at last, Ana de Becerra thought as she looked out at the landscape below. The fragrance of flowers flowed through the stone window of the small castle that clung to a hillside in Toledo. Though she was delighted cold weather had disappeared, it was more than the change in weather that had her emotions flowing. An exciting day lay ahead. Lucas Vazquez de Ayllon was coming to meet with her father. She knew he was contemplating offering her hand in marriage to this man whom she had never met. In the short time since Ana learned of the stranger's coming, she had worked feverishly through her contacts in the city to find out more about this adventurer from the island of Hispaniola. Although he was from her city, he had left Spain many years ago to seek his fortune in the new world. Yesterday, she had received notes from her friends that spoke glowingly of the man's accomplishments on the island. If he is so successful, she thought, might he not seek a wife who would be more advantageous for his future than what I offer.

Rising from the hot tub of water which her servant had poured, Ana looked into the full length mirror attached to the wall in her bedroom. Physically she had a lot to offer. She was sixteen and her body has never known a man. Then she frowned at the tanned complexion of her skin, a pigment resulting from a corruption of her bloodlines during the five hundred years the Moors ruled Spain. She wondered about his complexion. Did his bloodline flow from the north of Spain or did it flow from the south like hers. It was something that mattered to a man, especially if a girl's dowry was small. Her father, though a man of influence at the king's court, did not have a large sum to offer, for much of his wealth had been spent arranging marriages for her older sisters. But if this stranger did not offer a proposal, what would become of her. Ana's father was old, and his estate was laden with heavy debt. She cringed at the thought of slipping from the thin layer of the ruling class to what lay below. The last thought filled her with such horror that she became determined to convince this stranger that she was a prize worth having.

The father sat in his study behind a beautiful desk having his morning sherry.

He had known Lucas' father, a prominent lawyer in Toledo known for his intellect and honesty. He hoped the son would exhibit the same attributes. These factors were very important in arriving at a decision on whether the son was a suitable groom for his daughter. But it was not the only consideration. Of equal importance were Lucas' prospects. The father looked down at the correspondence that he recently received from a relative.

My good friend,

I am sorry you have not been to court of late. It distressed me to learn your health will not permit a return in the near future. I know you are concerned with Ana. I share this concern, for she is like a daughter to me. I would like to recommend to you Lucas Vazquez de Ayllon. He is a man of intellect, education, and integrity. Since he arrived in our colony of Hispaniola in 1502, he has accumulated a great deal of wealth. This man's success in managing his sugar plantation has attracted the attention of the king. He recently was rewarded an appointment to the Royal Council of the Indies and also appointed as a judge for His Majesty's government on the island.

I have spoken to him with such glowing terms of the beauty of your daughter while he was visiting in Seville that he inquired if I would write a letter recommending him to you and secure an invitation to visit. He will be returning home to Toledo soon to visit his father's grave before he departs Spain again for the island.

* * *

The land of his birth seemed foreign to Lucas. He longed for the gentle climate of the Caribbean where he had lived since his youth. But there was one thing that was missing on the island. The population contained few women of noble birth. The shortage caused many men to become desperate, and some had even been reduced to marrying Indian women. He felt the same desire but resisted it. Although many reasons existed for this trip to his homeland, on the top of his list was finding a suitable wife. His opportunity to find a spouse had greatly expanded when word of his success preceded his arrival in Seville. Many fathers were now anxious to push their daughters in his direction. But he found these women at the king's court frivolous in their thoughts and demanding of his attention. None he met seemed suitable for life in the new world. So, he had returned to the city of his birth in hopes that he might find a woman who would share his love of the island. One prospect stood out above the others, a young woman recommended by a counselor of the king. He had spoken so highly of her that Lucas requested an introduction to the young lady's father.

Ana was nervous. The two men had spent the last two hours conversing in the study. What could they talk about in such great length, certainly not her for such a long period. Her young servant girl tried to listen at the door for her, but the father's housekeeper had discovered the girl and sent her scampering away. Finally, she heard the dinner bell ring. At last the waiting was over. She took one more look into the mirror. This was it. If he found her acceptable, perhaps the lack of a large dowry would not be a barrier.

The dining room's cold, damp, stone walls were heated by a blazing fireplace. Although spring had arrived, the evenings were still cold within the castle walls. The father sat at the head of the long table, and Lucas was seated at his right. The table was filled with dishes that contained mutton and a variety of local vegetables.

Earlier, each party at the table had a delightful conversation about the politics at the king's court before discussing more personal matters. Lucas knew his host was influential. A marriage to his daughter would mean an advocate for his dream, an ambition far more expansive than just being a wealthy and influential person on Hispaniola. He wanted a charter from the king to plant the flag of Spain on new territory to the west of the island. There he would establish a colony of his own, one his future sons could inherit.

When Ana entered the room, he felt his heart begin to pound. The reflection of light from the fireplace upon her face caused its beauty to be illuminated. As she gracefully walked toward the table, he rose along with the father to greet her.

"Ana, this is Lucas Vazquez de Ayllon. He has agreed to join us for dinner."

"Everyone knows who you are," she said. "All of Spain is filled with your stories of Hispaniola."

"Your beauty is greater than I was led to believe," he said.

"Then those who described me must have been fathers who desired you for their own daughters."

He was taken aback by her boldness. But the comment was not made with a malicious tone. And she smiled in such a way that he could not measure the intent of her statement. After she was seated across from him, he felt a little embarrassed when she caught him staring down the cleavage of her blouse. She didn't seem to take offense and continued to pepper him with questions about life in the new world.

Ana had struggled with the old servant who resisted her efforts to wear a revealing top that showed cleavage, but in the end she prevailed. Although it was more than she had ever revealed before, she knew this was her only opportunity to get his attention. Now, sitting across from him and watching the direction of his eyes confirmed she had done the right thing.

When it was time to depart, Lucas regretted the evening had passed so quickly. The daughter of his host was not like the other women he met in Spain. Ana had depth and purpose. He was amazed by her knowledge and interest in the island. Unlike many of her gender, she was literate. This made her more attractive to him as a wife than even her beauty. Although, he was aware many men in Spain did not want a wife who was educated and independent-minded, he liked those attributes in a woman.

* * *

"Father, have you made an arrangement?"

"Nothing is sealed."

"When will you know?"

"Lucas is coming tomorrow."

"For what purpose?"

"I am to go with him to the cemetery to visit his father's grave. A good man he was and trustworthy. The son's reputation is like the father's. You could do worse."

"Lucas is handsome don't you think?"

"You are wiser and have more depth than that."

"Yes, you have taught me well. I shall go with him tomorrow to the cemetery. And you shall be too ill to accompany us."

"You have all the intelligence and cunning of your mother. Bless her soul."

"Afterwards, I will invite him to dinner."

"Will I be well enough to attend?"

"Yes, father. And do not let him leave this house without getting him to commit."

"Are you sure this is what you want?"

"A woman doesn't have much choice in our world. As you said, it could be worse. The thing I hate most is leaving you."

Both knew they would never see one another again if she went to Hispaniola. When she saw tears form in his eyes, she walked over to him and the two embraced.

Lucas lay awake turning over in his mind what decision to make. Rationally, he knew a more desirable advantage from marriage could be had. Although the father had many important contacts at court, his health was poor. If the old man died, those contacts would be of no use to him in getting favors that he needed to pursue his dreams. The dowry offered was small, and there would be no inheritance for Ana. The old man was deeply in debt. On the other hand, she was of noble birth, literate, and intelligent. Not many women in Spain had all those attributes. Soon his thoughts turned from the more practical to the emotional. An image of her long black hair that fell to her waist, the olive skin that enhanced her beauty, and a set of eyes that seemed to penetrate his soul flashed through his mind. Then there were her lovely firm breasts that caused such a stir in his loins. He tried to sleep, but it was futile. After tossing and turning he went down to the tavern below. The young peasant girl he had seen earlier was still sitting in the corner. She was a professional in her trade and knew the look of male frustration. She joined him for a drink. Later that night, when she slipped from his bed and returned downstairs, she had a smile on her face. Such passions she had never felt from a man. She almost felt guilty keeping the gold coins he placed in her hand.

* * *

Ana watched Lucas from the window as he approached the castle. He seems to walk with a bounce in his step today and looked so much more relaxed. Perhaps, he had a good night's sleep.

She did not let the servant answer the knock but instead went to the door herself.

"I'm sorry, but my father is not feeling well. I told him not to worry, I will accompany you."

He seemed at a loss for words for a moment.

"I am sorry about your father's health, but I will be delighted to have your company."

"I had the servants pack a lunch. I know of a spot where we can be alone from prying eyes," she said, as a servant stepped out the door with a basket and a blanket in her hands.

The walk was almost a mile. The trail was well worn and the day pleasant. Ana engaged him in conversation, and soon she heard him laugh over something she said. Moments later it seemed they both found reasons to laugh, but when they reached the grave a more solemn atmosphere ensued.

"He died while I was away."

"I'm sorry."

"What about your mother?"

"She died many years ago and was buried on her father's estate near the coast."

"My mother is buried on the other side of that hill," Ana said.

"Would you like to visit her?"

"If you don't mind."

After spending a respectable time at his father's grave, they walked along a path that ended in another part of the cemetery. The tombstone there was weathered. Already the inscription had begun to fade.

"She died in childbirth," Ana said. "It was my birth. I never knew her. Older people say my father's heart was so broken, he never wanted to remarry."

"Sounds like the same story they told me about my father," Lucas said.

"Come let us go to the far side. There is a small stream where we can spread out the blanket and have lunch."

It was a beautiful place, a spot hidden from the outside world where a small stream flowed through its lush surroundings. The servant followed Ana's earlier instruction not to follow them to the secluded spot. When the servant handed the basket to Lucas, her expression clearly showed her disapproval of the action of her mistress. But she let them go on alone, while she rested under a large tree and awaited their return.

It was late morning when Ana watched him spread out the blanket beneath the trees. When that was done, she reached into the basket and brought forth some cheese, fresh- baked bread, slices of roasted beef, and a bottle of red wine. Afterwards, she sat across from him, and the loose-fitting dress she wore inched its way up to her knees. She didn't seem to notice, as she flooded him with questions of his life on the island. The wine was consumed along with the food and still they were engaged in conversation. Suddenly she stopped him in the middle of a sentence.

"I have never been kissed by a man, except family."

Ana leaned over toward him and her lips moved in such a way that he knew she wanted to be kissed. He held back at first. To do so would compromise her in society. She was so close that he could smell her body, and when she pressed upon him, she became irresistible. The kiss was like nothing he experienced before. When she withdrew her lips, he was hungry for more. Without saying a word, Ana got up and started back in the direction of where the servant sat under a tree. He grabbed the blanket along with the empty basket, and ran behind her. Thinking he had offended her, Lucas apologized profusely, but she never turned around as her feet kept moving away from him.

Ana was glad he could not see her face at the moment, for then he would have been able to discern her true feelings. She wanted him now. This whole day was planned to make him desire her enough to ask her father for her hand in marriage. What she hadn't planned on was to find out that she felt a strong physical attraction to him. On the way home she didn't speak to him. Not knowing the true measure of her feelings, he remained silent. When they were in sight of the castle, she directed the servant to go ahead; and when the woman was out of earshot, Ana stopped and turned to him.

"I have behaved badly today. My father would be ashamed. But you should know this. I would make you a good wife, a life partner sharing with you the dreams you have in your heart. I know I am young. You are much older and experienced in the ways of the world. But I am a quick learner. And I will listen when you speak wisely. I will always be faithful and when you are away you need not worry that someone else will share my bed."

She then turned and walked toward the castle, leaving him standing there dumbfounded, wondering what had just happened.

* * *

The father was watching from the window and saw the servant return alone. Shortly thereafter, his daughter came running across the field. He went downstairs to meet her.

"Where is Lucas?

"I don't know."

"Is he coming for dinner?"

"I did not ask him."

"What?"

"I changed my mind. And I don't want you to offer him a dowry to marry me," she said just before going down the hallway to her bedroom.

He shook his head.

"Women. Who can understand them," he muttered. "She is like her mother. A wonderful person, but I never knew what was going on in that head of hers."

* * *

After Lucas had left Ana, rain set in before he could reached his lodging above the tavern. Downstairs he passed the girl from the night before, and she whispered an invitation to him, but he shook his head and continued up the steps. He had no need of her tonight for his thoughts were full of another. The next morning he awoke with a fever. A doctor was summoned and bled him. It did no good. Each day he grew weaker until Lucas sensed he was on the point of death. In his dreams Ana was there. At times he saw her face clearly and then he would descend into darkness.

The father received word that Lucas was ill. When he went to the tavern, he immediately dismissed the old hack that the locals used as a doctor and sent for one who had treated him many years earlier. The man arrived that afternoon, and his prognosis was that the patient was lingering between life and death. When he returned to the castle, Ana was in the big hall sitting beside the window looking out at the surrounding countryside.

"Father, where have you been?"

"At the tavern where Lucas is rooming."

"I don't want you to offer anything to him to take me as his wife."

"Silly child," he said impatiently. "He is gravely ill. My doctor says he may die before the morning."

She sat there stunned for a moment.

"Take me to him."

"I cannot do that. It would not be proper."

"I love him," she cried out.

Ana did not leave his bedside for three days. She prayed to her God and to all the saints that she could remember. Promises were made that no human being could ever expect to keep. On the morning of the fourth day, the fever finally broke and Lucas opened his eyes.

"I have been praying for you," she said in a calm voice.

"I know. I heard you in my dreams during the time I was in the gulf between life and death. And I was praying that I might live so that we could be together.

He tried to get up, but she restrained him.

"You must stay down a little longer."

"I am going to ask for your hand in marriage."

"You must not make such statements. You are not well yet."

"It is the will of God."

She would have rather heard the words, *I love you*, but she felt in time those words would be spoken.

* * *

The wedding ceremony over, the newlyweds departed from the cathedral in a carriage pulled by four white horses, a fitting end to Ana's life in Spain. When they arrived at the port in Seville, she was filled with excitement at the caravel which awaited them—a ship that would transport them to Hispaniola.

The ship was fully loaded, and all passengers and crew were already on board.

"The only thing delaying our departure," the captain said to some impatient passengers, "is the arrival of a most important personage. The Honorable Lucas Vazques de Ayllon is sailing on this voyage with his new wife, Ana de Becerra."

On board watching the couple's carriage approach the dock were two sailors who would later play an important role in Lucas's adventures. Francisco Gordillo was the first mate and a rising star of the crew, and the pilot, Alonso Sotil. Both had experience crossing the Atlantic, and love of adventure flowed in their veins.

"It is our pleasure to welcome you aboard," Captain Gomez said. "My first mate, Gordillo, will show you to your quarters." After acknowledging them, Gordillo turned and ordered two crewmembers to gather up the baggage. He then led the couple to their accommodations. While it was the best on the ship, the room was small and sparsely furnished. It did have the advantage of a shuttered opening that allowed its occupants to look out at the sea. The benefit of having a breeze circulate through the cabin would not be noticed until they reached the warmer climate of the Caribbean.

The first night at sea, Lucas walked the deck impatiently. How much longer should he wait. It was dark now. Surely it was appropriate for him to return to the cabin. But he didn't immediately leave the deck. It would be her first time, and he wanted her to have good memories of their first night together. This evening would be a first for him also. He had known other women, but they were prostitutes or women of ill repute. Of course, there were the virgins from among the young Indian slave girls on his plantation. But those matters had only been about satisfying his hot Spanish blood. This time it was different.

A chill in the air caused Ana to pull the heavy quilt up over her body. She didn't know whether the shaking of her body was from the temperature or from the nervousness of waiting for Lucas to return. Why was her husband taking so long? She had stripped her gown off and slipped under the covers after he left the confines of the cabin, expecting him to return quickly. Now it was dark in the room, except for the beams of moonlight that seeped through the cracks of the shuttered window. She was just beginning to get a little irritated at him when at last the door of the cabin opened, and she saw him standing in the entrance.

She heard him remove his clothes, and then his body slipped beneath the covers. She jumped when his naked body first touched her, for it was cold from being outside. But her body heat soon warmed them. After their lips met in the darkness, his hands began to explore. He was very patient and moved slowly not wanting to frighten her. Finally she urged him on for he had delayed too long in quenching the fire that burned within her.

* * *

The first day of the voyage Ana had seen the small-framed man walking the deck of the caravel. His priestly garb was made of the same type cloth used by the peasants on her father's estate. She ignored him the first week. Since he was obviously on the lower end of the church hierarchy, he must have done something that offended the authorities. Otherwise, why would a man of his age still hold such a lowly position with the church.

Dominican Father Antonio Montesinos slept at night in the cargo between two large crates. He didn't mind. He was just happy to be allowed to return. At least he was not in chains on this return voyage to Hispaniola. Before his exile, he had made powerful enemies by speaking against the enslavement of the local Indian population on the island. When the arrest came in the middle of the night, he was surprised by the action of the council. He always believed the church would protect him from their vengeance. He was mistaken. No one raised a voice when he was deported in chains on a merchant ship returning to Spain. It was only the blessed action of a fellow

Christian, who had the ear of the queen that gave him his freedom back. Now with the protection of a royal writ in hand, he intended to preach against the sin he believed would lead to the damnation of his country if the hearts of the authorities in the new world were not changed.

Ana was with her husband enjoying a change in the weather when the captain approached them.

"I feel it proper to disclose information about the priest who travels with us."

"Please do so. For my wife and I have not had confession since we left port. She believes him guilty of some heinous crime because of his low status in the church at his age and is, therefore, reluctant to call upon him."

"In that case, I'm afraid my information might appear rather boring. He was reduced to his present status because he has preached against the enslavement of the Indians. I don't need to tell such an important personage as you the reaction from the planters on the island. Now since he has a writ of protection from the queen, I expect he will stir up more trouble when we reach port."

"You are right. Slavery is ordained by God, and the economy could not function without their labor."

Ana sent word to the priest to come to her quarters to take her confession. She no longer felt uncomfortable once she learned his problems were of a political nature and not as a result of a moral deficiency in his character.

When the cabin boy brought him a perfumed note written in a feminine hand, he knew even before he read the contents the identity of the person who sent it. He had wondered since the voyage commenced how long it would take before this woman of such high breeding would request confession, even if it had to be before such a lowly priest as himself. It took longer than he expected. What terrible sins could one so young have committed to feel the need to confess?

The priest listened as Ana poured out her heart to him. It had weighed heavily on her soul that she enticed Lucas to marry her using her flesh as a magnet for his attention. The priest restrained his smile. Only the innocence of youth would believe using such methods to obtain a proposal of marriage was sin. She must indeed have lived a sheltered life in her father's castle.

"Will you come every week to hear my confessions until we reach land?" she asked, when he was getting ready to leave.

"Certainly, but as I said moments ago, you should not worry yourself over imperfections in thoughts and deed. Even the saints of the church were human. Of course, prayer and confession are always good for the soul."

Ana felt better about the state of her soul after the priest's visit. He did not feel she had done anything awful in the way she obtained Lucas's attention. She put the idea of her prior actions being sinful out of her mind and never thought of it again.

* * *

The weeks after Lucas and Ana arrived in Puerto de la Plata were busy. The couple moved into a small dwelling on the plantation. Nearby, Lucas had a hundred Indian slaves busy constructing a grand home where he hoped many children would be born.

First, the curse of Eve was not on time. After she missed it a second time, she suspected that Lucas's seed might be growing within her. This was confirmed when she developed morning sickness. Lucas was excited at the news that she might be pregnant. The next day a doctor came from town and examined her. His conclusion was the same as Ana's and all the adult female slaves who worked in the household. She was indeed with child.

Montesinos lived in a small hut near Ana's new home, which had been recently completed. Lucas, at his wife's urging, had allowed him to move there when others on the island refused him shelter. Lucas received veiled threats from fellow planters over the situation but chose to ignore them. Since their time on the caravel, Ana and the priest had established a close bond; and when the child was born, he waited with Lucas on the veranda until the doctor announced the news that the mother had delivered a boy. All had appeared well at first. Then two weeks after the birth, the child developed trouble breathing and at one time even appeared to have turned blue.

Lucas and Ana watched with deep concern as the priest prayed over the child that carried the name of his father. As Father Montesinos' large hands moved over the young body, the blue coloring receded and the child commenced normal breathing again. From that day forward, the doors of the home were always opened to the priest, and Lucas even built him a small chapel nearby where he could minister to the Indian slaves.

* * *

In the two years since Lucas returned to the island, death from disease had wiped out a large number of the Indian slaves. Ships were now constantly scouring the surrounding islands within a five-day journey seeking a fresh supply of labor. The shortage of Indians caused many enterprises to fail, and even Lucas had trouble harvesting his crops. So he was greatly relieved when the council gave him four hundred recently captured slaves in payment for his services as judge during the last two years. While this reduced the pressure on his growing enterprises, it brought him into disfavor with his priest.

The time had come to confront his patron on the slavery question. Montesinos conscience would not allow him to remain quiet any longer. It was not an easy decision to make, for his benefactor had been generous to him. Lucas had paid the costs of enlarging the chapel building to meet the needs of a growing congregation whose members now included Spanish families from the lower classes. The Bishop at Santo Domingo had recently assigned two new priests, Father Antonio and Brother Pedro de Estrada, to help with the services and pastoral duties. But Father Montesinos felt God's hand upon him, so he was prepared to face the consequences of confronting Lucas on this moral issue. Tonight when he dined with the family, he would bring up the matter and be prepared to vacate his chapel if he could not sway Lucas on the issue. He was not without hope of convincing his benefactor, for he had constantly guided Ana toward the realization that salvation for their family lay in ridding themselves of this scourge. He felt she would now be an ally with him on this issue. Ana's influence on Lucas was great for he was deeply in love with her.

There was a deafening silence in the room. Lucas looked over at his wife and saw in her eyes that she agreed with the priest. In his soul he knew the priest was right, but he was not yet ready to yield on the subject.

"The colony cannot survive without the forced labor of our Indian slaves," Lucas said.

"It is immoral," Father Montesinos replied. "It is also against the king's law. Under his edict and the orders of the Pope, they have been found to be among the branches of the human tree. They have souls. Many are of the opinion they may be the lost twelve tribes of Israel. We are under a duty from both our sovereigns to bring the word of God to them, not enslave them."

Lucas' thoughts of the moral issue were briefly pushed aside by the economic one. They were dying in the field by the thousands. Each day ships had to go farther out into the western sea in search of a fresh supply. They were not a sustainable force of labor.

"And what of the Africans?" Lucas asked. "As you are aware two-hundred were brought to the island last month as slaves?"

"Blacks are the sons of Ham," Father Montesinos said. "Their position in life was approved by God when his servant Noah placed a curse upon Ham and proclaimed that his descendents would be the servants of his brothers' seed. Thus it is in accordance with God's will that their status in life has been forever set. Man is only following a holy edict when he holds them in slavery, and no sin arises from such action."

Thus it was settled that night. No further Indian slaves would be purchased by Lucas, and when sufficient black slaves were obtained for the plantation, the remaining Indians would be granted their freedom. A moral crisis was averted and an economic one as well. Now both Lucas and Ana felt their souls were safe, and a priest believed he had successfully acted as the instrument of God.

* * *

The three were sitting in the corner of the tavern drinking rum. One of the men, Gordillo, had recently earned his rank of captain. He was celebrating the occasion by buying the other two men a drink. His companions Sotil and Quexos were unemployed pilots. The two, who were cousins, had never sailed together, but they had served at various times under Gordillo when he was a first mate.

"There are no boats to be had right now," Gordillo said.

"It is a tough time for men of the sea," Sotil responded.

"I have a prospect," Quexos said.

"From whom?" Gordillo asked.

"The word is that Juan Ortiz de Matienzo is sending out ships to catch some wild Indians," Quexos said.

"That's against the edict just issued by the Royal Council of the Indies," Gordillo said.

"I would rather risk the dungeon than starvation," Quexos responded. "Besides Matienzo is himself a member of the council. Surely he would protect those in his service."

"Perhaps he might or then he might not," Sotil said.

"I will wait for an honest job," Gordillo said.

Every ship that sailed had a full crew, but the docks were still filled with unemployed sailors. In the previous years, Spanish seamen converged on the island when word spread that slots were available on ships sailing to the Spanish settlements in the west. The shortage had ended, and the port was now filled with sailors who were becoming a menace to the local inhabitants.

Now the time was ripe for Lucas to pursue his dream. He looked over at Ana, who sat in a chair beside the fireplace. Curled up in her arms was their infant daughter. The child was in a state of perfect contentment, as her lips sucked on the nipple that set upon an enlarged breast filled with milk. His family was well settled. His new gold mine was producing, and the sugar plantation continued to show a profit. He could not wait any longer. Others would claim all the land and glory. Already Cortez and Pizarro had created empires for themselves. Every day other explorers set sail to the West. The pressure had become unbearable. That very night he sat down at his desk and plotted a plan of action. First, he must find a good captain, then send him to explore the lands an old Indian slave had spun stories about. This man had been Lucas' house slave until he was granted his freedom last year. The man had been captured and taken from his tribe who lived on an island he called Yamos. He often spoke about his island. Sometimes he would speak of another land, one that lay to the west of his home. It was a place covered with trees and wildlife, a land where pearls and gold were plentiful. The people who lived there were over six feet tall and were fierce warriors. Most of these statements Lucas discarded as fiction. But the part about the existence of land he believed. He knew that at the heart of every fanciful tale there always lay a grain of truth. If it existed, he would get a king's charter.

A caravel that lay in the harbor was for sale. According to rumor the ship was cursed. The owner was ill, and the ship had lost its captain and several crewmen during a voyage that proved financially unsuccessful. It was the perfect opportunity for Lucas, and he did not intend to let it slip through his fingers. When he had heard about it, he kissed Ana and the children goodbye, and then he sped to the port of Santo Domingo. After an evening of haggling over the price beside the bed of the owner, the purchase was agreed to and the necessary documents executed. His mission accomplished, he went to the tavern where he normally rented a room upstairs when he was in town. No sooner had he sat down at a table in the corner of the bar than a man with a bushy beard approached him. When he looked into his eyes, he recognized him as the first mate on the ship that brought Ana and him from Spain.

"Your Honor, I have heard that you are in need of a captain and crew."

"Gordillo, the last time I saw you, your face was smooth shaven."

"And I was much younger too, Sir."

"Well, we both were. Have a seat and I will order us a drink."

"My pleasure, Judge."

"How did you know I was looking for a captain and crew?"

"The docks are full of rumors and half-truths. I remembered some of our conversation when we last sailed together. And when your name was attached to the rumors, I knew you had decided to strike at last. I'm a captain now, and if you will put me in command of your ship, I will sail anywhere in the world you want her to go."

"Are you willing to sail west where no others have been?"

"You mean a place where I will not have the guidance of charts?"

"Yes."

"If you provide me with a sea-worthy ship and let me choose my own crew, I will sail to the very ends of the earth."

"Its late and has been an exhausting day. I am staying in a room above this tavern. Let me think it over tonight. I will meet you here tomorrow morning, and we can continue our conversation."

"I will be here. Remember, you will not find one of greater skill. I have sailed the sea since I was a boy, and I have worked my way up through every position. No one knows the sea better than me. Hope you come to that same conclusion."

After Gordillo left, Lucas had one more drink and then started toward the steps that led upstairs. He was stopped by an attractive young woman who spoke proper Spanish.

"Senor, would you like to spend the night with a widow woman of high birth who has fallen on hard times?"

He respectfully declined her invitation for he had remained faithful to Ana since their marriage. But feeling compassion for her condition, he placed gold coins in her hand, then turned around and walked upstairs where he slept soundly throughout the night alone in his bed.

* * *

Although Ana did miss Puerto de la Plata, she enjoyed the hustle and bustle of Santo Domingo. She particularly loved the new home Lucas had recently purchased for his family in the best part of the city. Its two-storied structure had a double veranda. On the lower one, she could be close to the street and neighbors. On the second floor, the sea was visible and the air fresher. She was drawn into a vibrant social life because her husband was recognized as a man whose star was on the rise. If there were a fly in the ointment, it was Lucas' preoccupation with planning an expedition to the new world. Though she supported him in this endeavor, sometimes she wished he could be happy to just be a member of the ruling class in Hispaniola.

During June in the year 1520, the first steps of founding a colony were about to begin. The departure of his recently purchased caravel named the *Choruca* had been delayed. There had been unexpected repairs and also a problem finding sufficient supplies. Now at last everything was ready for the long voyage. Lucas had given the captain orders to explore the lands north of Florida and find a suitable place for a settlement.

As the *Choruca* lay in the harbor at Santo Domingo, Lucas looked upon her with an admiring eye. She had a high rounded stern with a large forecastle and bowsprit at the stern. It had a square-rigged on the foremast and mainmast. This design made her large enough to be stable in heavy seas and roomy enough to carry provisions for a long voyage. As he walked toward the ship, he could see Captain Gordillo and the pilot Sotil engaged in a conversation on the deck as men scurried around making last minute preparations for the voyage.

"Judge, all the supplies have been loaded," Gordillo said to Lucas.

"When will you sail?" Lucas asked.

"At high tide, tomorrow morning."

"Remember, do not take any slaves from the lands you visit. We must not create hostilities among the Indians who reside there. Trade and settlement are our objective, not plunder and enslavement.

"I understand, though you know the mindset of my crew. It will not be easy to change their behavior, especially those who have in the past sailed with other expeditions."

After Lucas left, Sotil approached Gordillo.

"I'm glad the judge decided not to sail with us," Sotil said.

"He wanted to, but he just couldn't leave his businesses in the hands of others."

"I would never leave this land if I had a wife so beautiful," Sotil said, as a lustful expression spread across his face. "But I know he has dreams that have blinded him."

"By the way, I'm sorry we weren't able to enlist your cousin, Quexo, with this crew."

"He couldn't turn down the opportunity to be the captain of his own vessel."

"You are right. That was a good offer from the merchant Juan Ortiz de Matienzo. But I don't think the Indian-catching expedition has the sanction of the council."

"I agree. Especially since that priest, Montesinos, is stirring up trouble with his outspoken statements on slavery."

"He has the judge on his side now. And there is the problem of the constant flow of correspondence to the queen on the Indian slavery issue. Soon I expect it will be banned from the island."

"Captain, another ship of Africans arrived yesterday. I suspect the planters intend to rely on this new source of labor in the future."

* * *

Gordillo had wanted to sail in the early spring. He hoped that, by leaving port at that time, he would avoid the storm season that frequented the sea from late summer until early fall. But various delays had prevented a departure until June. Nevertheless, he followed the maps in his possession and arrived without incident off the Florida peninsula. He avoided contact with his fellow Spaniards by turning north. He traveled up the coast keeping his ship a great distance out at sea. A cautious captain, he was afraid of running aground in uncharted waters. But when his supplies began to run low, he had no choice but to hug the coastline in search of a harbor in which to anchor his ship and gather fresh supplies.

Early one morning out of the mist, a bay appeared surrounded by marshlands. He sailed into the bay on August 18th, Santa Elena day in the year 1520. He wrote on the chart the name Punta de Santa Elena, an area later called Hilton Head by the English. Once the ship lay at anchor, he loaded two row boats with sailors and landed near a village that a crew member had spotted from the starboard of the ship.

The tribe that Gordillo made contact with was the Guale, whose leader was called Huspa. Although skilled in the ways of war, his tribe was not one of the most aggressive ones in the region. They restricted themselves to an area that would later be called Port Royal. Their lives revolved around hunting and harvesting the sea life that lay in abundance at their fingertips. They often traded shells and pearls with the Indians in the interior in exchange for gold brought down from the mountains. This they used to fashion ornaments, which they either hung around their necks or wore as bracelets on their wrists.

The appearance of the Europeans did not have the effect it would have had on tribes in the interior. The Guale were aware of the Spanish from their trade contacts with the tribes in Florida. Neither was the sight of white skin a novelty to them. When trading with the Sioux that lived to the north along the coast, their warriors had noticed that among the chiefs were men with a white complexion. One disturbing thing the tribe knew, from their contacts in the south, was that although the Spanish had exciting trade goods, they were violent men. Without provocation, they would slaughter warriors and take their women. So Huspa chose to lead a delegation of his strongest fighters to meet these strangers, while the others left the village and sought refuge at a hidden location farther inland.

Near the village, Gordillo came across a large cleared patch of land. As they entered, several Indians emerged from a thicket nearby. They were naked, except for animal skins strapped around their waist. Their leader was dressed the same as his warriors, except he had a gold band around each wrist, and he wore a headdress made from bird feathers.

He approached without showing fear and uttered a few words that the Spanish could not understand. There followed an exchange of words between the two groups; and when this failed, hand gestures were employed. Afterwards, Huspa and his men led them to the village. Gordillo was surprised to see it was deserted, except for a few old women. He surmised that the others had intentionally abandoned it as a strategy until they could ascertain the intentions of his expedition. After the men were seated in a circle, the old women brought them wooden bowls filled with food from large pots nearby. The bowls contained a mixture of shrimp, corn, and scallops. After they had eaten to their heart's content, Gordillo had one of his men open a small chest that was brought from the boat. It contained the type of trinkets the Spanish learned from prior experience fascinated the primitive inhabitants in the new world. Afterwards, jewelry, mirrors, and a music box emerged. Before he left, Gordillo indicated with hand gestures that he would like food for his men left behind on the ship in exchange for the trinkets. Huspa, who was able to understand what the stranger wanted, agreed to the conditions of the bargain.

It was late afternoon when several canoes approached the caravel. They brought with them a variety of food in hand-woven baskets. After some encouragement the warriors were convinced to come on board the vessel. When they left an hour later, they were given Spanish clothing and some iron pots to carry back with them to the village. The women, upon seeing the trade goods left by the strangers, insisted that they be allowed to return to the village so they too could participate in trade with these strangers.

The second meeting two days later was without the fear of hostility. Gordillo and several of his men went directly to the village where they entered into negotiation with Huspa for the delivery of more food to the ship. The scene was changed from the first visit. The women and children had returned. The Spanish noticed that many of the women had gold bracelets and around their necks hung strands of pearls. When pressed about the gold, Huspa again indicated it was purchased in trade from Indians who lived in the mountains.

Gordillo decided to stay in the village and use it as their base of operation for exploring the surrounding countryside. In just a matter of days the harmonious relationship began to break down. Many Indian women were attracted to the Spanish men. The ire of the warriors was soon aroused. But having been long at sea, the sailors could not resist taking advantage of the situation. Knowing that trouble was brewing, Gordillo ordered his men back to their ship. The next day they sailed out of the harbor and headed north along the coast. Left behind in the village were women who in the coming months would give birth to babies with a different complexion than the other children of the tribe.

* * *

The decision to leave the Guale territory was an easy one. Gordillo had decided the area was not ideal for settlement. While it had a deep waterway, the area lay close to Florida and the claims of other Spanish explorers. Huspa had described to him another bay that lay further north, a place he said was rich in pearls, gold, and silver. The area was ruled by a powerful chief who had skin colored like the Spanish. And the soil was so rich that the tribes living there were able to grow an abundance of vegetables.

The first day after they sailed, the weather turned stormy. The captain lost sight of shore as he struggled to keep the boat afloat in the high waves. After two days the foul weather relented during the night. With the rising of the sun the following morning, he tried to find the coastline. Farther out at sea then he realized, it took another day before land was sighted. The body of water that appeared on the horizon was not the one Huspa had mentioned. The storm had carried him to the north of his destination. He sailed into the harbor, which he named the River Jordan. Soon Indians appeared along its bank. They gathered in clusters and appeared fascinated by his ship and the crew. He decided to take advantage of their presence before dark by boarding a row boat with several of his men. When they approached the shore, the Indians disappeared into the woods.

But Gordillo had learned from prior experience that they would not have gone far. They were still somewhere nearby watching him. He had his men unload a trunk from the boat and he removed several items. He placed them on a sandy area near the water. Then he and his crew departed. Before they reached the ship, he observed the Indians come out of the forest and struggle over the possession of items left behind.

Chief Neus sent a runner to the Datha to advise him of the strangers who had arrived on the river near his village. Though Neus was the chief of the Waccamaws, he paid homage to the Datha who lived in the land of Duhare. This leader was a man of gigantic height, and he was recognized as the spiritual leader of all the Sioux who had remained behind after the Great Divide. He knew the Datha was already aware of these strangers from contact with another Sioux tribe that lived in the south of Chicora, a name given the territory controlled by the Sioux from modern-day Cape Fear to McClellanville.

The next morning Indians gathered around Gordillo after he had disembarked from his ship and sat on the river bank for an hour. They were more anxious than afraid. For like all the indigenous tribes, the trade goods of the Europeans attracted them. The chief and several warriors were among the group. Gordillo spotted him right away from the respect shown him by the other Indians.

In a matter of days a friendship arose between Gordillo and Neus. As a result of this bond, many Spanish left the *Choruca* and become embedded with the tribe at their village. But the curse that seemed to follow the Spanish everywhere in the new world soon came to visit them at this new outpost. Trouble developed between the Indian warriors and the crew over the young maidens of the village. Despite efforts by Gordillo and Neus to quell the sporadic violence, it became obvious that the Spanish would have to retire to their ship. For several weeks after this event, the tribe continued to trade, and Gordillo used this opportunity to acquire supplies for the long voyage back to Hispaniola.

* * *

Loaded with supplies of corn, venison, and dried fish, the *Choruca* sailed out from the Jordan into the sea. Its captain set a course for Hispaniola. The voyage had not been financially rewarding for the crew. Despite being informed of the purpose of the expedition from the start, they still had dreamed of gold and silver that could be plundered, a dream not realized. Now when they returned to their home port, all they would have to show for their months at sea would be the meager wages promised them. The grumbling reached the ears of the captain who did not lightly dismiss them. Mutiny was always a danger on the high sea, especially when men journeyed for an extended period of time. The fact that his own purse would be meager did not cause him the same discontent. He knew when the settlement expedition was launched, he would be in command of the fleet. The judge had also promised him a grant of land when the colony was established. That would fulfill his dream of a landed estate on which he could build a home, marry, and have children. An estate would be the rock upon which he could base his place in society, and it would provide security when he no longer was able to command a ship.

Other than the discontent, Gordillo expected the journey to go well. The ship was in good shape, and the hold was packed with provisions of food. He wanted to explore farther north, but after sailing in that direction for several days, the crew rebelled and demanded an end to further exploration. Disappointed, Gordillo turned his ship toward home.

On a pleasant day, only a short journey from home, a sailor on lookout spotted a caravel just as the *Choruca* neared the island of Lucayoneque, a large island that was later called Bahamas.

Sotil was filled with emotion. He recognized the Nantos and knew that the captain of this vessel was his cousin Quexos. With his captain's permission, he took command of a rowboat that was being launched to go to his cousin's ship.

"Sotil," Quexos cried out, as his relative came aboard.

They hugged without hesitation in front of the crew, for their long separation made each lonely for the companionship of the other. After a brief conversation on deck, the two went to Quexos' cabin where they indulged in strong drink.

"I have been weeks searching these islands for Indians," Quexos said. "But there are none to be found. If I return without slaves, Matienzo will make sure this is the last ship I command."

"He is indeed a hard and unforgiving man. His hardness is well known among those who have had dealing with him."

"What should I do?"

"Where we have explored there were many Indians. If we can convince Gordillo to return with you, we could all show a profit for this voyage. The crew members are dissatisfied, and I don't look forward to returning from a voyage where all I can claim are a first mate's wages—wages that will not tide me over for more than a few months. If I cannot find a slot on an outgoing vessel, it will mean poverty for me."

"Will he agree? I have heard the judge forbade him from taking slaves."

"That is true, but there was an exception in his orders. We may take slaves captured in war. So any incident with the Indians would justify it, and a justification is something that can easily be created."

When Sotil returned the next morning with his cousin to the *Choruca*, word swiftly spread among the men of the proposal. Gordillo did not like the position he was placed in by Sotil. To not accept would mean mutiny, and he did not have the means to prevent it except by agreeing to the proposal. So he yielded to the circumstances that confronted him. The understanding reached between the two captains was reduced to writing. The document provided that they would equally share the number of slaves taken. The next morning, the ships sailed with Gordillo following a course to the land he had recently visited. But as often happened in those days, the ships ran into a storm and were blown off course in a southerly direction. Gordillo soon realized he was in the vicinity of the land he had been searching for when another storm had propelled his ship to a more northerly harbor. He steered along the coast hoping to catch a glimpse of the bay described by Huspa.

On the third day just before noon the lookout shouted that there were Indians on a beach. It was an exciting moment for the crew. Riches from the sale of human flesh were standing in full view before a cluster of sand dunes that stood over twenty feet high. A small channel ran at an angle from the ocean to an area behind the dunes. The channel was much too small to even consider trying to take a caravel through, so Gordillo launched two row boats commanded by Sotil.

As the row boats approached the beach, the Indians fled across the dunes, but the quick action of four sailors allowed them to capture a man and woman. The two were clearly frightened. Sotil gave each a piece of molasses candy, and they calmed down. Then by hand gestures he indicated there was more on the ship. They willingly climbed into the row boat. On board the ship, Gordillo presented to each of them some bright clothing and a package of hard candy. Then he had them returned to the beach, where they ran out of sight as soon as their feet hit the wet sand. Sotil stood with a puzzled look on his face until they reappeared a short time later. They brought with them twenty Indians of various gender and age. There was one among them whom they deferred to. The Spanish were surprised by the man's appearance. He was whiter than the other Indians who were of clay-colored complexion. His hair was brown whereas the others were black. The man had a height that towered above even Sotil, who was the tallest among his crew.

Sotil had brought a trunk on the rowboat filled with colorful trinkets. After distributing these trinkets, he decided it best to make camp on the beach and spend the night with the natives. He sent one of the rowboats back to inform the captain about his plans.

The Indians were a friendly lot, and after a time of appraising one another, he inquired about food by using hand gestures. A few Indians disappeared and soon returned with sea food they had obtained from the surrounding creeks and marshes. After building a fire, they proceeded to cook these items for the Spanish. Once their hunger was satisfied, Sotil inquired about the location of a large body of water by drawing a picture of it in the sand. Once they understood his question, they all eagerly pointed to the south.

The next morning, Gordillo arrived on the beach with several of his sailors.

"They say that a large body of water lies a short distance to the south," Sotil said.

"Are they willing to guide you there?"

Sotil turned to the tall one and posed the question. After explaining what information was desired by making drawings in the sand and getting a response, he turned back to the captain.

"They are willing to take me to where a big river flows into a great body of water. Apparently there is a trail on the other side of the marsh that lies behind these dunes. The tall one has indicated that it leads to a village near the mouth of a big river."

"Our provisions are getting low. You need to explore the countryside and obtain food for our voyage home.'

"We should go there and establish friendship with this village chief."

"Quexos and I will take the caravels and follow the coastline until we find the bay. Then we will sail up it until we come to this big river. That is where we will meet. And if we don't make contact in the next forty-eight hours, we will both plan to return to this place."

"When will you sail?"

"Tomorrow."

"Then we will start for the trail immediately, since it may take us longer to reach our destination."

At low tide the group waded across a creek behind the dunes and quickly located high ground where there was a trail. It hugged the elevated land on the interior side of the marsh. The path was well worn so that it was easily traveled. Before the sun set that afternoon, there appeared before them a small village. It was built on a bluff overlooking an expansive river. From this elevation one could see the point where the river emptied into a bay. Sotil calculated that the ocean could not be too far away.

Word of the arrival of these strangers preceded them. When they entered the village, people were gathered to meet them. The chief, like the tall one, had a coloring not far removed from that of the Spanish. He wore clothes made of deer skin and carried a long staff. The women of the tribe immediately brought food. Fish and a type of cornbread comprised most of the meal. Afterwards, the tall one and Sotil sat alone upon the bank of the river and engaged in conversation. Although hand gestures were still important to their communications, the two were able to speak a few words of each other's language. Sotil was in an advanced position in understanding the native language because of the time spent on the Jordan where the tribes spoke the same dialect. And the tall one seemed focused from his first contact on the beach with learning Spanish. As a result of their conversation, the tall one convinced his father, who was the chief, to send runners to other villages in the vicinity to request provisions for the big boats that would be coming up the river the next day.

* * *

Gordillo located the bay easily. The entrance was surrounded by estuaries. He called the bay Saint John the Baptist, a name that would not survive. The channel on the north side appeared the deepest. Now he sat at some distance from its entrance with anchors securing the ships because the channel was too shallow at low tide to gain admittance. He waited in frustration for the tide to change. When it did, he delayed until the tide was at its high point. When the two ships entered from the north side, it was deep enough that they did not scrape the bottom. The Spanish saw a waterway with marshes on both sides. Throughout this area were small creeks teeming with sea life. Oysters were embedded in mud banks nearby, while shrimp and fish were constantly jumping in the water, as flocks of birds passed overhead. He kept the ships in the center of the channel to avoid going aground. They sailed by a small river on their left that had a peninsula of land jutting out into a river. Farther upstream, he saw several other bodies of water that emptied into this bay. The one to his right was definitely the largest, so he gave orders to steer toward its mouth. He named this river Gualdape. A few minutes afterwards, he saw several of his men waving from a bluff up the river.

During the three weeks the ships were anchored in the river near the village, Gordillo learned much about the land and its people. The tribe who lived on the bluff called themselves Winyah. They were in a confederation with other tribes that spoke the same dialect. The Winyahs were somewhat different than their brethren. They had a separate oral tradition that involved a bloodline that came from across the sea in boats. The tall one described these boats as similar to the Spanish but with only one mast.

Gordillo and the crew established trust during their time with the Indians, and many items were traded between the two parties. Soon the ships were full of tanned animal skins. several bushel baskets of pearls, two pounds of gold, and some silver. The silver obtained was sparse and held to be of great value by the tribe. The tall one said the amount was once greater. It had been brought from across the sea. Over the years, it had been used extensively in trade, so very little remained in the tribe's possession.

* * *

"It is time," Quexos said. "The men are anxious. They have been away from home too long."

"Yes, we must sail back to our island," Gordillo responded.

"How many shall we seize?"

"Not too many or we shall not be able to control them."

"How do you plan to do it?"

"Announce that we are leaving. Then we'll invite some on board to spend the last night with us. While they are asleep we shall sail in the darkness."

"They will panic."

"Those who are sleeping off a drunk will not. We will convince the others that we are only going back to the spot where we first met members of their tribe."

"You mean the land with the high sand dunes."

"Precisely."

"I believe that plan will work, but I hate to waste the last of our rum on these savages. The men will be upset not to be able to have rum on the way home."

"It is best if they are sober. We'll have less chance of problems. Particularly with any Indian women we may have on board."

"I shall have the men get the chains and ropes ready."

The tall warrior awoke with a blinding headache. He felt the movement of the ship upon the seas. When he tried to rise, he found that his movement was restricted by chains that were bolted to the deck of the ship. As others awoke, the air was filled with loud wailing of men and women who realized they had been stripped of their freedom and separated forever from their people. The tall one tried to console the others, but even he saw only darkness in their future. He looked around to see how many others were prisoners and counted forty heads. He was grateful that only five were women. The rest were men of various ages. He saw some of his tribesmen on the other ship but, because of the distance, he could not count their numbers.

By the fourth day three men who refused to eat were dead. The others were seasick. Most of the food they consumed was thrown up on the deck of the ship within minutes after it was ingested. As a result each day that passed, they grew weaker.

The women were visited by the crew at night while the captain was asleep in his cabin. They cried out as the sailors took them in a manner that showed no compassion for the pain inflicted as every cavity was explored. By the tenth day at sea, all the women were dead.

The storm came suddenly. One moment the sun was bright, and the next moment the sun had disappeared behind clouds in a sky that was pitch black. Gigantic waves washed over the deck of the *Choruca.* In the distance, Gordillo saw that his fellow captain was losing his battle with the sea. But he could do nothing to help him. Then just before the winds died down and the sun returned, he saw Quexos' ship, the *Nantos*, capsize. Crew members were in the water holding on desperately to floating objects. An hour later the winds subsided, and Gordillo was able to pick up the survivors, which included Quexos. The Indians on board the *Nantos* had been tied or chained to the deck, and they were all lost to a watery grave.

* * *

Lucas was furious. Word reached him in Puerto de la Plata that Gordillo had sailed into the harbor at Santo Domingo with Indian slaves on board the *Choruca*.

"Get my horse ready," he said to his newly acquired African slave who took care of his stables. "Saddle one for yourself. I shall need you to accompany me on a journey. And make haste."

He then gave orders to the African slaves in the kitchen to pack food for the journey.

Ana tried to calm him down.

"You must control your anger. Perhaps there was a good reason to disobey your orders."

He ignored her statement.

"Go see Father Montesino and tell him what we have heard. Have him meet me in Santo Domingo. His tongue may be useful there."

"I will have my carriage made ready."

If there was a way to be angrier than Lucas, Father Montesinos found it in his self-righteous soul. Words bordering on the profane flowed from his lips when Ana delivered the news. He was still issuing threats of taking the matter directly before the queen, as he rode away from the chapel in the direction of Santo Domingo.

Out of the eighty slaves taken onto the two ships, only twenty-eight had survived the journey and the tall one was among them. Recognizing immediately that this man had the respect of the others, Gordillo had released him from the chains. He hoped this Indian would be useful in helping the Spaniards deal with the other captives.

The tall one had used his liberty to ensure his fellow captives were properly fed and received their water rations.

"We must do as we are told," he said to them. "Do not give up hope. Surely our gods will rescue us and send us back to our people."

He did not believe the words he spoke but knew, if these men had no hope, they would perish.

The Indians had already been removed from the boat when Lucas arrived. They were in a barracon, and their arms were chained to the inside wall. He was disturbed at his captain's actions. Unfortunately for Gordillo, he walked in just as one of the slaves was being beaten for an infraction. The full weight of Lucas's anger fell upon the captain. When Lucas left the barracon, Gordillo had not only been stripped of his command, but his employment was terminated. There would be no command of a fleet, nor an estate in the new world. His inability to control his crew was fatal to his career. His claims that circumstances justified his actions were given no weight. The captain's last days would be spent working at a brothel as the doorman and living off the meager wages he received.

* * *

The order from the court was served on Lucas before he had time to leave Santo Domingo. It was signed by one who was a friend of Matienzo, and it was *ex-parte*. No notice had been given and no right to be heard granted. The order made a finding as a matter of law that Matienzo was entitled to half of the slaves brought to Hispaniola on board the *Choruca*.

"This is outrageous," Lucas said to Father Montesinos, who had just arrived. "I shall bring this matter immediately to the attention of the Royal Council of the Indies."

"I shall go with you."

"It is best that you don't. They are all slave holders, and they still hold it against you for pressuring them to free their Indian slaves. But you can go to the Bishop and enlist his help in speaking to the council on behalf of the church. Surely men will listen if they believe their very souls are at risk."

"I will do as you ask."

"The council is meeting next week, and by that time I will have a writ in their hands asking for relief from this order."

The council met at the palace in Santo Domingo where the Governor-General of the Indies was to preside over the hearing. His given name was Diego, and he was the son of Christopher Columbus.

When Lucas arrived, he caused a stir for he had brought with him one of the Indians. The man was tall in stature. He had brown hair, which he wore in a braided knot at the back of his head. His skin color resembled the pigmentation of many Spanish inhabitants in the south of Spain.

"Why have you brought this slave before the council?" Diego asked.

"According to the case I presented in my petition on which you signed a writ, he is not a slave, but a free man who is entitled to be returned to his own country."

"What was your purpose in bringing him here?"

"He was chosen by members of his tribe to speak for them."

"Speak for them. How can that be possible? We do not know his language."

"But he knows ours, Governor. At least he knows some of it. I myself was surprised that in his short time among us, he has conquered our words. He is a most amazing Indian, and I would like to call him to testify."

"That is not possible. He cannot take an oath for he is not a Christian."

"He has converted to our faith and has been christened Francisco Chicora. The reason for the first name is obvious. The last part of the name assigned to him is Chicora. He has told us that the land from whence he came to us was called Chicora."

"Who is the priest that can vouch for this Indian's conversion?"

Into the room stepped the bishop.

"I can Your Excellency. He was converted by Father Montesinos, but I have questioned him and was truly amazed by his knowledge of our Lord. You may give him the oath for he is a member of the true faith."

"So let it be done," the governor said.

A portion of Francisco Chicora's testimony taken before the Royal Council read:

"I come from Chicora. It is the land of the Sioux. There are many tribes, and each has its own chief. But we live in peace with one another. We are organized into a confederation to protect us against other tribes who seek to take our lands. The spiritual head of our confederation is the Datha. He resides in the land of Duhare. He is taller than all men. And his wife Ingris is as tall as he. He is whiter than the Spanish. I am the son of his brother, who is the chief of the Winyah. Our tribe lives on the bay and along the rivers that feed into it.

We were captured by Spanish sailors who came up the Big River. Many of my tribe died along the way of sickness and abuse. We were free men and ask to have our freedom restored so that we can be returned to our own country."

After the full testimony of the Indian, Lucas and Matienzo argued the law before the council. At the end of the argument, the council took the matter under advisement and asked that the two litigants return in three days for the verdict.

* * *

"Francisco, the council has placed you in my custody pending the outcome of this case," Lucas said. "You will return with me to my home here in Santa Domingo. My wife and children have just arrived here today from Puerto de la Plato, and they are excited to meet you."

Francisco understood enough of the spoken word to know he must go with his benefactor. Outside the great hall Father Montesinos was waiting. The three of them departed the governor's palace together and entered a carriage that was waiting for them outside the building.

At home Ana and the children waited with anticipation to see the savage that everyone in the city was talking about. They did not have long to wait. Through the front glass windows they saw the carriage arrive. Out stepped the savage they had been waiting for all afternoon.

Not comfortable with having Francisco sit at the dining room table in his own home, Lucas had the priest take him to his small house that was located next to the chapel. There he would have the evening meal with the three priests. The food was provided from the kitchen at Lucas's home. Afterwards, the priest would return with the Indian who would sit on the floor before the fireplace and tell the family about life in Chicora.

"The ruler of the Sioux is the Datha. He lives in a house built upon a mound so that it overlooks the homes of his tribesmen. In front of this house are two stone statutes that were given to his ancestors by the gods who sailed from across the sea and taught us many things.

"The Datha and many of his extended family are descendants of these gods. But even before the gods came, there were others who were called the Fish Eaters. They were different from other man in that they had tails and could not sit down unless a hole was first dug in the ground for their tails or they sat in a specially built chair that was high in the air. They lived along the ocean and rivers until the fish gave out; then they perished from hunger.

"Near my home is a Sioux tribe called the Tihe. They are the priests of all our tribes. They are the descendants of the god, Nor, and his wife, Kee. They know all the healing herbs and can communicate with the gods in the language of the spirits. They have stone gods similar to the one that graces the home of the Datha. In time of battle they care for the wounded and bury the dead.

"In my land we keep doe deer penned up and milk them every morning. During the day we let them out, and in the evening they return of their own accord. We make cheese out of the milk and use the milk in cooking many of our dishes."

That night and the next, Francisco spun many tales to the judge's family, and they were greatly entertained by the stories of his land and people. After everyone had gone to bed, Ana prayed to her god that the council would render a just verdict. In the church a short distance away, three priests joined in that prayer.

* * *

In the great hall the council sat. The two vacant seats would normally have been occupied by those who stood before them. Rising from his seat, the governor announced the judgment.

"It is the finding of this council that Lucas Vazquez de Ayllon gave specific orders to his captain not to take possession of Indians as slaves. It is the further finding of this body that the captain violated his orders when he seized these Indians that he brought to Hispaniola. Now Juan Ortiz de Matienzo claims an interest in these Indians as slaves because of the agreement between Captain Gordillo and Captain Quexos, to share the Indians captured equally. This agreement has no weight of law for the reason that Juan Ortiz de Matienzo sent his ship out for the sole purpose of capturing Indians as slaves. This action was in direct violation of a decree of this council issued at the direction of our king. Therefore, it is the judgment of this council that the Indians are declared to be free. But in light of the danger this freedom may present to the island, they are to remain in the joint custody of Lucas Vazquez de Ayllon and Juan Ortiz de Matienzo until they can be transferred back to their homeland. If an appeal is filed with the king, then the order today will be stayed until such time as the king issues his verdict. In the meantime the parties before this court will be responsible for the maintenance of these Indians."

The decision having been made, the council adjourned.

"I will appeal to the king," Matienzo said to Lucas. "My brother-in law is a lawyer at the court, and he will present my petition."

"I am aware of your connections in Seville. But until the appeal is heard we should agree on the division of custody."

"Since you are so concerned with their liberty, I suggest that you have possession and bear the expense until we hear from the king."

"I accept your offer provided you will reimburse me the cost of maintenance and the cost of transporting them back to Chicora if I prevail."

"Agreed."

A handshake sealed the bargain. Lucas made arrangements that very day to have the Indians transported to his plantation at Puerto de la Plato. There, under the supervision of Father Montesinos, they would work in the fields until a final decision on their legal status was determined.

* * *

"Lucas, what did the council decide?" Ana ask.

"They ruled with me on every point, but Matienzo intends to appeal to the king."

"Will you defend the verdict?"

"I must go to Seville and argue the case personally. Otherwise, I fear the appeal will go against me."

"That's a lot of trouble and expense just to protect these Indians."

"There's a more pressing reason for my returning to Spain. While there, I will petition the king for a charter to the lands that Captain Gordillo explored. If he grants my petition, I shall plant a settlement in the new world that will rival those that have already been established for Spain."

"Will we be coming with you to Spain?"

"My dear, I fear the dangers of such a voyage for you and the children. Also, I need you to stay at Puerto de la Plata and oversee the operation of the plantation and gold mine. There is no one else that I can trust.

"When do you expect to take your leave?"

"A ship sails next Thursday. I have already made arrangements with the captain for passage. It is rumored that the captain is carrying appeal documents which he will deliver to Matienzo's brother-in-law at the king's court."

"I do not like Matienzo. He makes me uncomfortable whenever I am in his presence."

"You should be careful of him. He is not a trustworthy character. Always have Father Montesinos with you when he is in your presence."

"Is there anything else I should know about your trip?"

"I am taking Francisco Chicora with me. He is a very smart one. I think his presence at the court will attract favorable attention."

"You are right. The nobility will be fascinated by this savage. I certainly was taken by him."

"Of course, I shall see your father while I am in Spain, and I will deliver the correspondence I am sure you will want me to place in his hand."

* * *

Francisco woke early that morning. He rose from his bed and went on the veranda of the home where he resided with the three priests. His tribesmen were not as blessed. They lived in a large rectangular hut in the compounds that also housed African slaves. Those slaves were a strange group. They were black as pitch and spoke neither Sioux nor Spanish.

When Francisco visited his people, he was amazed by the change in them. Despite the fact that they were required to work long days in the field, they had recovered physically. The gaunt look had disappeared as they adjusted to the food served on this island. Only four had died since their arrival at port, and none had expired since coming to the plantation. The priests were strict with them, trying to control every aspect of their lives. At the same time they were more kind than other men.

What is this place called Spain? Francisco wondered, as a priest packed his belongings for the journey. The judge had told him tales of this strange land and the priests had as well. But his mind could not picture the things they described. What a strange place it seemed to him. And yet, could it be any stranger than what he had already seen since his capture on the Gualdape. His thoughts briefly strayed to where his people lived a more simple life than the world where he presently was being held against his will. He quickly pushed thoughts of his tribe from his mind and focused on adjusting to his present situation. Otherwise, I will go mad, he thought. As mad as my four kinsmen went when the ship sailed into the port of this strange place. They died of heartbreak. He silently prayed to the gods of his tribe and to the new Christian god the priest had taught him about. He didn't really understand this new god, but he was good at regurgitating the words taught him by the priests. This seemed to please all the Spaniards with whom he came into contact.

* * *

Lucas had sailed three weeks before Matienzo made his first appearance. It happened when the priests were in town buying supplies. Probably the man knew this, and his appearance when Ana was alone was by design. When he knocked on the door of her home at Puerto de la Plata, she had to invite him in. To do otherwise would show a lack of civility. She made a pot of tea, for the servants were away on another part of the plantation. Even the children were at school in town.

"Lucas will be gone a long time."

He let the statement hang in the air for a moment.

"If you should need help on any matter please send word, and I will come immediately to your aid."

She did not respond immediately. Instead she looked at him seated across the table and wondered if all the rumors of him rutting with anything that was female were true. Probably, she thought. He was handsome in a rugged sought of way.

"Thank you. I will sleep better at night knowing you are nearby."

Even while the words fell from her lips, Ana knew she would secure her bedroom door at night. When he finally left, she felt relieved. In the future she would attempt to make sure someone was always with her. The days and nights would be lonely before Lucas returned, but she intended to keep the promise made to Lucas long ago before they were married. No one else will share my bed, she had said to him. And those words rang as true today as when they were first spoken.

On the way back to town Matienzo kept the image of Ana in his mind. Her husband would be away a long time. Her resistance to his charm would grow weaker in the weeks ahead. Lucas was a fool to leave her alone. He filed the appeal only because he knew Lucas would go to Spain to defend the judgment of the council. Lucas' departure had given him the opportunity he had been waiting for since Ana arrived on the island. What a tasty morsel she would be when he finally bedded her.

* * *

It was the first time Lucas remembered a voyage where there had not been a serious storm for the entire trip, though the weather was a constant cold. Francisco shared a cabin with him. He spent a few hours every day teaching him about the western world. Though the man was bright, he knew that sometimes he only pretended to understand the information given.

Francisco spent time each day explaining to him the world of the Sioux. There were many gaps in the history of the tribe. Apparently in the past there had been several contacts with other worlds, but the details of these were lost in time. Only scant information was retained by oral tradition. Too bad the tribes did not have a written language. Apparently the earliest inhabitants were referred to as the Fish People and were present when the Sioux arrived. They were killed or assimilated. Later there was another contact with a more advanced civilization that was also assimilated. Although from this last group, the Datha and all the other Sioux chiefs were chosen. In their veins ran the blood of a personage they called Baldar whom they considered a god. These special individuals had different characteristics than the other members of the tribe. And Francisco was one of those special individuals. To try and make sense of the stories Lucas decided to write down in his journal information on the land of Chicora as related to him by Francisco.

Tribes

The Sioux tribes live in a land call Chicora.

One of the Sioux tribes called the Winyahs live around the bay and on the banks of a big river. Francisco is a member of this tribe.

Other Sioux tribes include the Waccamaw, who live around a bay a great distance to the north. The Hooks, the Pee Dee, the Sampas, and the Santee live on various rivers that empty into the bay.

The Catawba is the largest Sioux tribe. They live near mountains and trade with tribes that dig for gold and other precious metals

Francisco Chicora's ancestors

The Fish People taught the Winyah the planting of crops and the building of log homes.

The bearded ones with brown hair and tall in stature brought the stone gods and silver.

Francisco Chicora's ancestors are considered gods. Francisco's pronunciation of their names sounds European to the ear.

Baldar, Nor, Ailish, Ingri

SPAIN

The last week in March a vessel carrying Lucas and Francisco dropped anchor in the river Guadalquivir in full view of the inland port of Seville. Lucas explained to his Indian friend that this was the capital of his country, and that the king lived in a palace in this thriving city of 500,000. Inside its commercial and residential districts dwelt not only Spaniards from every part of the land, but also thousands of foreigners. This glorious city had a monopoly on trade goods coming from the new world. In order to obtain these items it was necessary for merchants from other parts of Europe to gather at this port.

When their feet hit the dock, they did not have long to wait before a carriage pulled up in front of the wharf. Lucas had sent a correspondence by ship several weeks before he left Hispaniola. It was addressed to his friend Stephen, whose father was the Count of Parmel. Stephen was an influential person he knew on a social basis from the time he visited Spain on his last trip. He expected an invitation to stay with him at the Castle Galicia would be forthcoming, but no such reply had arrived by the time they left Hispaniola. It was apparent now that the reply had been written though not received.

Inside the coach were Stephen and his sister Isabel, a girl of sixteen who was one of the most frivolous women Lucas had met at court. Her father had pursued a possible marriage, but Lucas had managed to escape to Toledo in time to avoid that entanglement.

Stephen stepped from the carriage.

"My servants brought me word this morning that your ship was seen entering the mouth of the river. So I had a lookout posted to alert me on your arrival at Seville."

"I did not expect you since I never received a reply."

"That is strange. I personally delivered it to the captain of a caravel sailing to Santo Domingo."

"Unfortunately, it may be a case of another ship lost at sea."

"I am afraid you might be right. One fourth of our vessels that leave for the new world are never heard from again."

"Excuse me for my bad manners. This is Francisco from the land of Chicora."

"Welcome to Spain. Lucas has written me about you and the predicament that your people in Hispaniola are in with the authorities. I am sure the king will do the right thing. I have already made a plea with his councilors for a quick hearing on the appeal. That request was well received when I explained your story. Coming here personally will certainly help your cause."

"Thank you, Excellency," Francisco replied in Spanish.

The weeks at sea with the judge prodding him on had greatly improved his use of that language.

Their conversation was interrupted by an intentional coughing from the lady in the carriage who was tired of being ignored.

Isabel had been watching the savage who was dressed in breeches made of deerskin and naked from the waist up. He was a fine specimen of manhood. His skin was no darker than some of her cousins who lived on the Mediterranean coast. But the odor of the men who had spent weeks at sea without proper bathing reached her nose. Strangely, she did not find it offensive. In fact, the smell of this savage excited something within her. She blushed at the thoughts that began to run through her mind.

She was literate and had read the lengthy letter sent by Lucas to her brother, and had even discussed the contents with her friends. They were as excited as she to meet the savage, but she wanted to be the first one to do so. It had taken little effort to convince her brother to bring her along when he came down to meet the ship.

"Isabel, you remember Lucas."

"Certainly. He is the one who fled when my father tried to wed us. But do not concern yourself over that lost opportunity."

Lucas turned red in the face, and Stephen was taken aback by his sister's bold statement. He quickly covered from his embarrassment by introducing Francisco.

"The ladies at court are looking forward to seeing you there," she said to Francisco, a devilish smile creeping across her face as she delivered those words.

Francisco was embarrassed standing beside the open door of the carriage, not because of the words spoken but because of his clothes and his partial nakedness. Lucas had reminded him many times on the voyage of the need to appear in his native dress for the impression it would have upon the people. To dress like a European will weaken our cause he had said. The population expected a savage from the new world and he must not disappoint them. Francisco would not be the first one they had seen. Every explorer since Columbus had brought natives back to exhibit to the populace. Lucas had decided the way to impress was to present a savage with the manners of a noble and the speech of a Spaniard. In case that was not enough, he had taught him the basics of reading and writing.

* * *

The Castle Galicia was near the center of town. But the busy traffic did not press upon it, for the structure was surrounded by gardens. The area was completely encircled by a wrought iron fence eight feet high to discourage intruders. When they arrived, a line of servants greeted them and took their baggage and deposited it in bedrooms next door to each other.

"I am sure you will want time to bathe before dinner," Stephen said. "The servants will bring pails of hot water to your rooms where they have already placed copper tubs. They will remove all clothing from your bags and see that they are washed."

"We will retain clothing for dinner, of course," Lucas said. "It will not be offensive for we were careful to air them the last day of our journey."

"I am sorry to inform you that our father will not dine with us tonight. Indeed, he will not be in the city for some time," Stephen said. "He has been ill of late and is visiting his country estate on the Mediterranean."

"I hope his health improves and he returns before we depart Spain."

"I am sure he feels the same."

* * *

Isabel left the company of their guests when the carriage arrived at their castle. Upon reaching her room, she sat down at her desk and composed notes for her best friends. She knew the description of her meeting with the savage would make them turn green with envy. After she placed them in the hand of a servant boy for delivery, she had fresh water poured for a bath. While it was cooling, she studied her wardrobe trying to decide which dress to wear for dinner. She could wear something bold this evening because her father was not home, but it could not be so revealing that her brother would scold her later. When she finally made a decision on the dress, she stripped her clothing off, took one look in the full-length mirror and satisfied with what she saw, stepped into the tub. As she enjoyed the warm water, thoughts about her wedding in the coming weeks flashed through her mind. Her groom to be was old—at least sixty, maybe older. But he was rich. As her father had pointed out, his royal blood was not restricted to Spain. If the right people died or met some unfortunate end, perhaps a male child born of this union might become king somewhere in Europe. While that prospect excited her, the thought of having her body taken by such a wrinkled old man made her skin crawl just a bit.

The long dining table seemed empty with just four people seated there. The lamb kidney with sherry sauce served with a side dish of potatoes from Peru was tasty, especially after the fare eaten on board the ship during the long journey. The coffee from the African colony went well with the fried slices of bread covered with honey.

Every time Lucas heard Isabel speak, he knew the right decision had been made in fleeing the capital and going to Toledo to find his wife. The fit of that dress she wore was outrageous, he thought. Most of her bosoms were revealed. She must be trying to show him what he missed by marrying Ana. But her conduct only made him certain that he made the right decision. Beneath these righteous thoughts lurked others of a sinful nature. He had been at sea a long period, and Ana was a long ways from Spain. His body yearned for the feel of a young woman beneath the sheets next to his own. He suddenly realized he was staring at her in a lascivious way, so he turned his head to engage Stephen and Francisco in a deep conversation about the settlement he wanted to plant in the new world.

* * *

The palace would make a great impression on even the most sophisticated traveler, but Francisco did not fit in that category. He was overwhelmed by the beauty of it all. It was so overpowering that for a time he suffered from a form of mental confusion. There were comments muttered by those in his presence, from the lowest servants to those who held the rank of nobility, about the strange expression that dominated his demeanor as his mouth hung wide open at the things he was viewing around him. This did not mean they were not drawn to this curiosity that stood in their presence and gazed at everything. The visit to the palace was only for the purpose of an appearance among the ruling class. Nothing was scheduled for the day at this center of power. That would come later.

Even before his appearance at the palace that day, Francisco had become a celebrity. In fact, Stephen was flooded with requests from the nobility of the city who desired an opportunity to introduce this curiosity from the new world to their inner social circle.

At the Castle Galicia the tailors were busy cutting and stitching clothes for Francisco, all of which were supposed to reflect the native apparel that the man wore among his kinsmen in the land of Chicora, but, of course, it did not. They only represented what the people of Seville in their wildest imagination thought such savages would wear. Lucas smiled with amusement at the outfits that were in Francisco's room. He was amazed how quickly and brilliantly the man had understood it was all an act. Francisco was willing to play along, in order to free his tribesmen to return to their home.

* * *

The stage was set. Isabel had arranged to have her friends to an afternoon tea where the guest of honor would be the savage whom they had heard so much about. It would be her last private party before she married the Duke of Ortiz. She was delighted to be the envy of all her friends, as well as those who suddenly wanted to claim a social connection with her. She spent the whole morning getting ready, changing many times what clothes she might wear. Even her own servants became frustrated with her. Marie, her keeper since birth, finally put her foot down and made the decision. Isabel was not happy with the choice. Too conservative, she thought. She would have protested but knew her friends would be dressed even more conservatively because they had to pass the scrutiny of their mothers. So, she relented and accepted Marie's choice.

The weather was perfect for there was not a cloud in the sky, and the temperature was neither hot nor cold making it a most pleasant April day. The ladies were full of questions, and a nervous giggle followed every comment that Francisco uttered. It took a little time for Isabel to overcome an initial resentment that she was not the center of attention. But once she noticed how infatuated her friends were with Francisco, there was no room for such feelings because jealousy filled her emotions. Her friends all enjoyed the gathering, but she was glad when it was over. Strangely, she had not realized when she organized this event that she did not want to share his attention with other women, not even her own friends. It was at this time that she realized she wanted this savage. From that very point she turned her back on the great cultural divide that existed and focused on seducing him.

* * *

The three left by carriage from the castle and traveled down the cobblestone streets of Seville to the oldest section of the city. When the driver stopped, Isabel tried to get Marie to remain behind, but she gave her a stubborn look and joined them for the excursion. The first place visited was the city cathedral, the most beautiful church in Spain. When the Muslims were driven out, no expense was spared in creating this tribute to Christendom. The building was huge, and the impressive outside was matched by the exquisite beauty of the sanctuary. Isabel did not know much about its history for such things had never been of much interest to her. Uncharacteristically for a servant, Marie, a devout catholic, filled the gap by telling stories to Francisco of the infidels who once inhabited the place and the part played by the church in driving them back to North Africa. Later they visited other historic buildings, all of which reflected the influence of Muslim architecture. Around noon the three went back to the carriage. There waiting for them was a basket of food and wine the servants in the kitchen had packed. Isabel had planned a meal in a city garden area near the river after their tour of the historic buildings. Nothing went as she had planned in her mind. Marie would not leave their presence, and Isabel's attempt at flirtation in the manner of Spanish women did not seem to strike a cord with the savage who sat across from her on the blanket that had been spread out under the shade of the trees. By the time they returned to the castle she was angry at Francisco, her servant, and even more at herself. Consumed by thoughts of this savage, she had given no thought to her upcoming marriage. That was about to change, for when the carriage finally reached the castle, a letter from her father was waiting for her. He was coming home next week.

* * *

Francisco was not a virgin. At the age of sixteen he had married his cousin. This practice was followed by those whose bloodline could be traced to the strangers who came from across the sea. Marrying a relative had been the custom for generations to keep the characteristics of their forefathers. Unfortunately, his wife had died in childbirth a year before Lucas' people appeared on the banks of the Big River. At the time of this occurrence he had made overtures to Cofita, Chief of the Pee Dee tribe for his youngest daughter, a maiden of thirteen seasons. But the matter had not been consummated before he was taken aboard the *Choruca*. Now his thoughts had returned to her, a young woman who carried the scent of the tribe to which she belonged: a mixture of food cooking in the communal pot, the freshness of her hair after a swim in the river, and the smell of wild flowers that she wore in her hair. These were the things that his body yearned for during the night when the hardness of his manhood would not let him sleep. He felt no attraction for the sister of Stephen, although he had begun to understand that she was using the techniques of her culture to indicate an interest in him beyond being a friend. However, he had learned enough about those among whom he now lived that any consummation of her desire would not sit well with his host, or with his benefactor, the judge.

* * *

The queen and her ladies in waiting sat in a semicircle listening to the tales that flowed from the mouth of Francisco. He told them many stories. Some of these were true, but most were created out of thin air. He had come to realize that these people, who felt themselves superior, were willing to believe anything about his world, for their minds were an empty slate, and he wrote upon that slate many falsehoods. He had no way of knowing that for generations into the future these stories would be accepted as factual and totally twist the European recorded history of his people and the land upon which they lived.

From his friend, Lucas heard that Francisco's meeting with the queen had been successful beyond expectations. Stephen thought this would help him get a quick hearing from the king on the appeal from the council. Now perhaps a positive audience with the king would also be forthcoming on a royal charter recognizing the lands he had explored and approving a settlement. He was appreciative of his man, Francisco, doing everything in his power to make this trip to Spain a success. He no longer thought of him as a servant or even as an Indian, but as a friend. Having recognized the change that had occurred in their relationship, from that date forward he would think of Francisco's interest as well as his own.

* * *

The castle on the river had once been the residence of a Moorish King, before he was driven out by other Muslim factions. The castle had changed hands many times before Seville fell to the forces of Christendom. But somehow, throughout the various conflicts, it had somehow remained unspoiled. The present occupier of its grand and expansive rooms was Duke Cuellar, the oldest son of an advisor to the king. The ballroom was more than sufficient to accommodate the hundred people who clustered around the room, all waiting for the musicians to commence playing so they could dance. And they waited for word from the duke, who stood impatiently near a large window where he had a view of a tree-lined avenue. His impatience ended when he caught a glimpse of several carriages. As he turned around and faced his guest, his expression clearly showed that the king had accepted his invitation to attend. An immediate quiet swept the crowd, followed by a rush of private excited chatter when the doorman opened the double doors of the ballroom and announced the king and queen. The room fell silent once again as everyone formed a greeting line for the royal couple to pass through.

The royals wasted little time in moving through the greeting line where Lucas and Francisco stood near the end. They did, however, pause briefly in front of Francisco. The queen stopped and whispered in the king's ear something that caused him to look past her face and into the eyes of the one dressed differently from the others in the room. Afterwards, they finished the procession down the line to the portable throne brought by the king's servants for the occasion and already set up at the far end of the room.

Between every dance the ladies worked their way through the crowd to the corner where Francisco was located so they could engage him in conversation. At the same time the noblemen lined up to speak with Lucas about investments in the new world. This activity did not go unnoticed by the king who had felt the pressure from his queen to favor Lucas with a charter and to grant the savage his freedom. Then there was his mistress who espoused the same cause as the queen. While everyone chatted and danced, the king made a decision, after which he pushed it from his mind and watched his subjects enjoy themselves.

* * *

The word came without warning on that day in the middle of May. The king wanted to see Lucas at the palace. He wanted him to bring Francisco. The word was brought by Stephen, who was as surprised as Lucas at the message he was delivering. He had been at the palace on other business when one of the king's councilors approached him. The king would see Lucas and Francisco at noon. That was less than an hour away. He had rushed to get word to Lucas. Now the time was short to make an appearance. Thank goodness both were at the residence and not on one of those constant tours of the city. The horses remained harnessed to the carriage that waited outside while the three men inside hurriedly dressed in suitable attire.

On the way over to the palace, Stephen instructed Lucas and Francisco in the proper decorum when approaching the king. Lucas was nervous for he had only spoken once to the king, and that was in the receiving line at the ball weeks ago. Francisco reacted to the body language of Lucas so that by the time they arrived everyone was edgy. But the meeting went unexpectedly well. When they were brought in the room, the king sat with his councilors at a long table. The king spoke briefly about the appeal, and then he declared that he would uphold the decision of the Royal Council of the Indies to free the Indians that had been captured on the Gualdape River. After the decision was announced, they were summarily dismissed.

"That was over quickly," Stephen said when they were a great distance down the hallway.

"I am glad the audience is over," Lucas said. "But what about my petition for a charter?" he asked.

"I still haven't heard from my contact in the palace. Perhaps it will be soon."

* * *

Isabel was excited and petrified at the same time when she learned the Duke of Ortiz was coming to the city. He was moving into temporary quarters where he would live until the wedding. She had never met this man who was to become her husband. The marriage set for June 16, 1523, was only weeks away, and there was so much to do in preparation. Not having a mother to help made everything more difficult until the queen intervened. At the queen's request, Isabel agreed to let the queen's lady in waiting take charge. Isabel hardly knew the Countess Dona Corpa, although she was a distant cousin of her mother. She had mixed emotions about the situation. She both resented it and was pleased. With the groom a prominent member of the nobility and with the countess on the inner social circle at the court, she knew this marriage might gain her an entrance into the social life of the court. Of course, if the countess was assisting, then a chance existed that both the king and queen would attend the wedding. The thought of this thrilled her.

* * *

An arrangement for their departure was accomplished when Lucas discovered that anchored in the harbor was the *Breton*. This four-mast ship's destination was Hispaniola. As soon as this word reached him, he went down to the wharf and paid the captain a sum of money for passage. The amount paid was large because Lucas wanted the best accommodations on board, and that happened to be the captain's cabin. The man had reluctantly given it up when he saw the bags of gold coins that Lucas was willing to place in his hand.

After he left the dock, Lucas purchased the services of a coach and driver to transport him to Toledo the next day so he could spend a few days with Ana's father. That would still give him sufficient time to return to Seville before the ship left port. Unfortunately, word reached him that evening by a courier that Ana's father was gravely ill. After leaving Francisco with a few words of instructions and an ounce of wisdom on being careful how he conducted himself, Lucas departed posthaste for Toledo the next morning. Lucas regretted that he had not had an opportunity to leave Seville earlier and visit him, but he had been in contact. The letter from Ana to her father had been sent the first day after Lucas' arrival in Seville. In the weeks that followed, the father-in law and he had exchanged several correspondences.

* * *

The countess moved into the Castle Galicia so she could better coordinate the wedding that was to be at the city cathedral which lay just a short distance away. Her days were busy meeting with the bishop, who was going to perform the wedding, as well as time spent coordinating with the other participants.

Though she was the bride, Isabel was pushed aside and ignored during the preparations. At least tonight she would be the center of attention. The Duke of Ortiz was coming to dinner. What was the man like? He had a reputation as a fierce warrior who had defeated the king's enemies on several occasions and thus secured the king's throne. He had outlived three wives and had no need for a stepmother to his children. They were all of age, married, and had estates of their own.

The evening came at last. Isabel looked out the window to catch a glimpse of the Duke. It was too dark to see clearly, but he seemed to be short in stature and slightly bent over. This was not encouraging. Her previous excitement was now replaced by the dread of seeing him in a lighted room. Summoning up her courage, she stepped out into the hallway and walked slowly down the stone stairway that led to the receiving room for the twelve guests who were joining them for dinner. When she entered, her father was standing in front of the fireplace with the male guests discussing what profits could be made from commerce, while the women were gathered on the opposite end, commenting on the latest fashions. Her father saw her enter the room and motioned for her to come and join him. As she approached, the Duke of Ortiz turned and looked her directly in the face. She had to restrain the revulsion that wanted to rise to her face. He was a wrinkled old man with a long scar that ran from his temple to his chin. He looked at her in a lascivious manner. She felt naked, as the man's eyes filled with lust, stripped her.

"This is Isabel."

"The reports of your beauty have spread even to my humble estate at Murcia," he said.

"And your fame won in the service of our king is known throughout Spain by those loyal to our majesty," she replied.

At this moment a servant arrived at the outer door.

"I believe everything is ready for us to dine," Isabel's father said, as he correctly read the body language of his servant.

"May I escort you to the dining room?" the Duke asked.

"I would be honored," Isabel replied.

She put her arm through his, and together they led the others to the large room where a table was covered with traditional foods from Spain and new dishes from various parts of the Spanish empire.

* * *

The countess knew her place. She maintained a low profile during the dinner and let Isabel bask in the glory of being the center of attention. It was always wise to constantly build alliance. Although Isabel was only sixteen, in the coming years who knew what influence she might wield. She understood that at the end of the day her power and influence rested on being the mistress of the king. The queen did not like her for obvious reasons. Though it might seem strange that she was the queen's lady-in-waiting, it did not to those who understood how the levers of power really worked. The queen owed the countess' husband a favor and it was returned by the queen making her a lady in waiting. Once in the palace, she caught the eye of the king, just as her husband had hoped. He had thus ingratiated himself with both powerful figures. But she knew her usefulness was almost at an end; her womb had produced neither a child for her husband nor a bastard for the king. In this the queen took great pleasure, for she had produced eight children and she constantly reminded the countess of this fact, implying thereby that her lady-in-waiting was deficient as a woman.

The countess had been in the presence of Francisco several times during her stay at the castle. She was attracted by this man. Initially it was because he was a curiosity. Then she found his conversation more interesting than the frivolous bantering that pervaded the court. Finally she found him not just interesting but complex. Thus she was drawn to him until she desired to discover what existed beneath those layers of complexity. She knew the dangers. Although he had given no indication of a mutual attraction, she knew beneath the surface he was a man just like any other, for she was wise in the ways of the world. Once she analyzed all the facts, she made a decision. And once she made the decision, she planned. So it was that one night when the moon was high in the heavens, and Lucas was away in Toledo, her feet crept through the darkness They stepped quietly up the stone stairway and then down the hallway to where the door of Francisco's room stood ajar.

Francisco saw a shadow glide through the door and reflect off the masonry wall. In the moonlight rays that flooded his room, he recognized the countess' silhouette. She slipped beneath the covers and pressed her body against his. Francisco was not surprised. He had felt her attention upon him for several days. Despite their differences, he knew if her civilization were stripped from her, she had the same needs as a Chicora woman. But he found her method different. Unlike Indian maidens, she was aggressive and sought to please, putting her own satisfaction last. This was a new experience for him. But he knew in the end, she also found pleasure. Though they would never have another opportunity for intimacy, the seed he planted that night would take root, and both king and husband would take credit for the deed.

* * *

When Lucas arrived, the three oldest daughters were gathered around their father's bed. He passed by a room where the old man's son-in-laws were engaged in an argument on how the assets should be divided. He did not stop to acknowledge their presence but instead went directly to the dying man's bedside. The daughters stepped aside when he entered the room to allow him access to the gaunt figure that lay upon the bed, gasping for breath.

"We have sent for the priest," one of them said.

"Where is the doctor?"

"We have dismissed him. He can be of no further use, and it would have been a waste of money for him to have remained," the oldest said.

"Daughters, let me have some time alone with Lucas," the father said.

He could tell they did not like their father's request, but they nevertheless stepped away from the bed and departed the room.

"Juan," said the dying man, "Close the door and put the lock on it. I don't want to be disturbed by others while I speak to Lucas."

For the first time, Lucas noticed an old man in the corner whose age was ancient. The old one shuffled across the room and did as he had been told.

"I haven't long to live. Already the vultures outside my door are arguing over my assets. But except for one item, which I will disclose only to you, there will be nothing, for my estate is heavily in debt. When creditors learn of my demise, they will converge upon this place like locusts and strip it of everything. Juan, you must come closer so I can whisper. Who knows what ears may be pressed upon the outside of that door."

The old man shuffled across the room and stood beside Lucas. The dying man spoke so low that both individuals standing beside the bed had to lean over and place their ears near to his lips to catch the words emitting from them.

"Juan, remember the secret chest? The one we hid when we came back from the war?"

"Yes, Master."

The old man paused for a moment and cast a glance toward the door before he continued.

"Take Lucas to it. It shall be my parting gift for Ana, the only daughter who has remained loyal to me and the only one whose husband is a man of honor."

"Lucas."

"Yes."

"This is booty from the battles Juan and I have fought. I must tell you there is blood upon it for which I shall pay when I face the Almighty on judgment day. Take this treasure and use it for the benefit of Ana and the children.

"I shall."

"There is but one other thing that I must have you promise before you leave this room."

"Speak to me of it."

"You must take Juan with you to Hispaniola. He has been with me since my birth. We share the same father, but he was a bastard child. My mother was of noble blood, and his mother was of peasant stock. The man will starve when I am gone if he remains here."

"You have my oath on it."

"You must depart Spain quickly lest family and creditors get wind of this treasure."

"My ship leaves in four days."

"That should be soon enough. Go now and do not return for there is nothing more either of you can do for me."

* * *

The light was beginning to fade when the two men left the carriage and its driver beside the highway and walked up the hill where the remains of an old Moorish fortification clung to the hillside. When they arrived Juan went straight to a large stone. It took the efforts of both men to roll the stone over. Juan began to dig with a shovel he brought with him. Soon it struck the sound of something solid. A few moments later a small chest appeared. Lucas opened it and looked inside. Staring back at him were gold and silver coins. It was heavy, but soon they managed to get it down the slope and inside the carriage. Though darkness was falling, Lucas did not think it wise to return to his father-in-law's residence. So they traveled toward Seville. When it became so dark the driver could not see, Juan took the horse's bridle and walked in front of him. After traveling two hours in the dark, they came across a village where they spent the night at an inn beside the road. The next morning just as dawn was breaking, they once again set out for Seville. When they arrived in the city, Lucas pulled out a purse full of gold coins and convinced the carriage driver to sail with him to Hispaniola. That way Lucas knew there would be no loose lips left behind who could spread word of the treasure.

Back at the Castle Galicia, Stephen greeted him by waving a parchment in his hand.

"The king has signed it," he said, excitement flowing in his words.

"The charter?"

"He executed it without even requiring an audience with you. That is unheard of at the court. You must have had a contact close to the king of which I was not aware—a person who has the ear of his majesty."

Lucas looked bewildered.

"I am at a loss as to who that person could be. Your contacts are my closet connection with the king."

He took the document from the duke's hand and slowly read it, pausing occasionally to absorb the meaning of the words. Later after drinking several rounds of rum to celebrate Lucas's success, the conversation turned to his journey back to Hispaniola.

"I am sorry you must leave tomorrow. The wedding is only three days away. I know Isabel will be disappointed."

"I wish we could stay, but there will not be another ship sailing to Hispaniola for months."

"It was too bad about your father-in-law."

"Yes, he was a good man. I know Ana will take the news of his death very hard. She was very close to him."

"What time are you leaving tomorrow?"

"I have already made arrangements for a carriage to deliver Francisco, Juan, and me to the ship at daybreak. We will say our goodbyes to everyone this evening. We would not want to disturb the household at dawn."

"I will have the kitchen servants pack food for you."

"That would be appreciated. We are not looking forward to eating ship ration for the next few weeks at sea."

* * *

Stephen had the servants prepare an evening feast for his departing guests. Other than family, only the countess was invited to dine. The platters were filled with fried breaded squid, choes, and tender young lamb. Traditional Spanish vegetables from the estate's garden graced the table, along with some vegetables introduced from the new world. For dessert, rum cake and Ethiopian coffee were served. Everyone indulged in emptying several bottles of red wine. The conversation was light and went on for over two hours. Everyone had a good time, except Isabel who kept her feelings well hidden.

Isabel was tense, and there were many reasons for it. On the top of the list was the wedding, now only days away. She was also unhappy that Francisco was leaving. Although she was perturbed with him right now. Lately he had been distracted when in her presence. She did not like it when she was not the center of attention. Then there was the countess. Isabel sensed something between her and Francisco. What it was she did not know. With Francisco leaving, she would probably never find out. Isabel watched the two exchange glances across the table. An intense jealously rose within her. She became so stressed that she asked to be excused citing a headache as the reason.

Francisco was the next guest at the gathering to retire to his room. He knew the judge would expect him up early the next morning for the trip to the docks, and he wanted an opportunity to read the charter. The judge had given him permission to remove it from his room provided it was returned that same evening. When he had arrived upstairs, he had found it on the table beside the judge's bed. His hand shook with nervousness when he picked up the four-page document which had the king's seal on each page, red wax with an imprint of his majesty's ring. Back in his room, he read each word slowly because he was still unsure of his ability to translate and interpret the meaning of many words contained on the written page. The language of the court was a little different than the language he learned from the inhabitants on the street.

"Inasmuch as you the licentiate Lucas Vazques de Ayllon, our judge of the Royal Court of the Indies which is held on the island Hispaniola, told me that a caravel under your control and ownership discovered recently.....I therefore grant you permission to go or send others to prosecute the discovery of said lands,.........Moreover, I order that in such land that the indigenous Indian population not be enslaved....You will agree with the Indians of the said lands that they will be protected...Of such lands you shall be governor and upon your death, a son designated by you will assume the governorship... To you and your heirs are granted land fifteen league square.....as well as fifteen percent of all profits from the colony.....you shall explore the land and find if there is a waterway that leads to the riches of the Orient."

For a long time after he had read the charter, Francisco held it in his hand. To him it was a sacred document. He believed that the force of it would make possible peace between the people of Chicora and the Spanish. He had discovered that there were many good men among theses Europeans. Foremost among them was the judge, a man he had come to respect in the same manner as he respected the Datha in the land of Duhare.

Alone in her bed, Isabel tossed about unable to sleep. With no one around she now tried to collect her thoughts. She had to confront her feelings. She had to admit she was attracted to this savage. Despite the fact he had conducted himself in a civilized manner during his stay, she still considered him nothing but a savage, though a handsome one–one whose attributes stirred a sexual feeling in the place her husband would soon explore.

Only sixteen, Isabel's judgment was no different than others her age might have exercised. She got up, washed her body with water in a basin. After she had bathed in this manner, she rubbed her body down with the peelings from an orange. She looked at the clock. It was after midnight. Everyone would be asleep at this hour. She crept down the passageway to Francisco's room. After opening his door, her feet stepped quietly across the stone floor to the bed where he lay naked, the covers having fallen to one side of the bed. Her eyes examined his body. What she saw made her afraid. How could such a large appendage ever enter her. It must be painful. The thought did not deter her, for along with the initial fear she began to feel excitement. She slipped onto the bed and lay still beside him, not knowing what the next step should be on her part.

Francisco was fast asleep and did not hear Isabel come into the room, nor did she awake his slumber when she lay down beside him. But sometime in the early hours of the morning, he became aware of a woman's presence. He reached out in the darkness thinking the countess had returned for another night. When his hand touched a small firm breast, he knew it was not the countess. The body beside him went rigid, though his fingers could feel the nipple swell. Only when he heard her mutter something indistinguishable did he recognize from her voice the identity of the young woman. His hands moved about caressing her body until finally he felt it relax beneath his touch. Realizing from her initial reaction to his touch that Isabel had never known a man, he exercised skills he knew from experience until he felt her body was ready, then he entered the place where his people said the soul of a woman dwelt. When he did, she let out a short cry as if she was in pain. For a few moments afterwards she lay still while he penetrated her. Then her body seemed to take on a life of its own as it began to move in rhythm with his just before the sacred substance of his body was planted deep within her.

RETURN TO HISPANIOLA

From the deck, Lucas looked out into the mist that surrounded the ship. He could no longer see the buildings of Seville. In the distance he heard the roar of the waves and knew the ship would soon leave the river and enter a vast ocean on which he would sail to his beloved family; an image of them standing on the beach waving goodbye the day he departed briefly flashed through his mind. Suddenly he felt very lonely. His thoughts were interrupted by Francisco who came out of the cabin and spoke words expressing hope that the voyage would not be hindered by the storms of the Atlantic. He turned and looked into his friend's face and wondered how Francisco would ever adapt to his own society again, after he had seen the civilized world. Lucas understood the difficulty because, after having visited Spain, he would never want to live in the old world again. This was the first time Lucas realized, that although he was still a Spaniard, his roots were now firmly planted in the new world.

Many of Lucas's thoughts were also on the mind of Francisco. He still looked forward to returning to Chicora, but he was a changed man. He knew it would be impossible to ever explain the things he had seen to his people. They would think his tales were from an overactive mind. Then there was the question of succession. He carried the blood in his veins that made him a candidate for the possession of the title, Datha, upon the death of that great one who now held the power over all the chiefs of the Sioux. Would his time away and his contact with the Spanish be viewed as an obstacle? The chiefs of the tribes were the ones who choose the Datha. Though he had never held the position of a chief, he had hoped one day to be leader of all the Sioux like his ancestor, Baldar.

* * *

As the ship traveled upon the sea in the direction of Hispaniola with two passengers who had different agendas, an important event had taken place in the Seville city cathedral, the wedding between the Duke of Ortiz and Isabel.

Isabel had retired to the bedroom chamber early. Now she waited to perform her wifely duty. Neither excitement nor dread flowed through her veins. Instead her emotions were numb toward her new husband. She knew he was with his friends drinking. Hours later she heard his footsteps coming up the stairs. Before the Duke reached their room, she turned over and pretended to be asleep. She knew this would not discourage his advancements, something she did not welcome but something she desired. Not physically, but out of neccessity, for she had a premonition that the seed of the savage had taken root in her womb. She understood the need to forever hide the actions of another night when she had given away her virginity. Once her husband penetrated her no one would be the wiser since there had been no witness to her transgression except the savage. And he would never be seen in this part of the world again.

The Duke slipped into bed beside her, cupped one of her breasts with his hand, and kissed her behind an earlobe, then nothing. She did not move for a few moments expecting him to pursue the matter by removing the beautiful white nightgown that the countess had chosen for her wedding night. Then he began to snore and she realized he was sound asleep. She removed his hand and then sat up in the bed. She couldn't believe what she saw in the dim light provided by the candles in the window. The man had not even removed his clothes. She was furious, an emotion she felt sure very few maidens experienced on their wedding night. But she calmed that fury when she realized that if her premonition was right, her sin could be discovered. I have plenty of time, she thought. But then she began to worry about whether he would be able to consummate the marriage. This thought caused her to panic, and the impatience of youth drove her thoughts. Downstairs she went and woke a servant who was asleep on the kitchen floor.

"Boil some water and bring several buckets of it to the door of your master's bedroom. Do not enter the room. Just knock, for I will pour the water in his copper tub myself. He is anxious to bathe before we make love again. And if I hear that you have disclosed what has been said here tonight, I shall accuse you of being a heathen and turn you over to the inquisition. The priest will tear that busy tongue of yours out by the roots. Now be quick about what your new mistress has directed you to do."

The servant was now fully awakened from his deep sleep and thoroughly terrified. Even before she left the room, he was busy adding wood to the fireplace and placing a big black pot on a contraption that allowed him to boil water.

Back in the room she began to undress the Duke by first removing his boots. He awoke as she pulled his breeches down past his knees.

"What is going on?" he asked, as he attempted to sit up.

"I have waited for hours to enjoy the pleasure you can bestow upon your virgin wife," she said.

She was surprised how easily the words came out with such a soft tone. "My body has yearned for you since the first day we met. I can wait no longer."

These words from the lips of his young wife caused the clouds in his mind to clear, and he began to assist her in removing the rest of the clothing.

A knock came at the door.

"Who can that be at this time of night?" he asked.

"The kitchen servant. I had him prepare bath water for you. I shall pour it in the copper tub myself. It shall be my first act as your new wife. You already know what my second act will be, my dear."

Despite his age, her words made the Duke feel young again. After the bath was ready he sat in it as she poured water over him. When he had finished soaking, she dried his body while he stood on the floor beside the tub. Without hesitation her hand touched his manhood and for a moment he thought it might once again rise to the occasion. In bed again, he waited in anticipation for her to join him. Before she did, his new wife went over to a canister filled with rum and poured herself a glass. He had never seen a lady of breeding drink rum before this night. As she curled up beside him, she explained her actions and he understood.

"I am afraid of the pain. Women have told me it is that way the first time. Please be gentle with me."

The next morning she slipped out of bed, dressed and went downstairs. She had been careful not to wake him. Sitting out on the terrace drinking a hot cup of tea, she cringed when thoughts of the prior evening entered her mind. She had used every method she knew to get him to the point where he was able to enter her. Finally he had and the explosion that followed from his manhood would leave no doubt in his mind that he had sired the child, if she was indeed pregnant. But it would be the last time she would allow him intimacy. She would always use a litany of reasons. Finally, just to keep his young wife happy, he would quit asking.

* * *

The messenger brought word from the port. Lucas had returned. Ana issued a list of orders to the African slaves on what needed to be done before the master arrived. Then while her personal slave girl dressed the children, she prepared herself to meet him. When all was ready, she had one of the Indian servants, Touppa, drive her and the children from the plantation to

Santo Domingo. Even from a distance she easily picked out the vessel on which she knew Lucas had arrived. As she stepped down from the carriage, he appeared out of nowhere from a building and called out her name. The children hearing his voice scampered out of the carriage and reached him before Ana. When the children finally released their father from the grip of their small hands, Ana was standing there.

"Lucas, I have missed you so much."

He reached out his arms and she literally fell into them. Such a public display of affection was generally frowned upon in their society but for a moment they forgot convention.

Watching this unusual show of affection was Juan. Lucas had promised him a position in his household. Observing Ana, he knew that the rest of his stay on earth would be a pleasant one.

* * *

The charter had a time-restraint built into its terms. A provision contained within the document required Lucas to establish a settlement within three years or lose all rights granted him by the king. While it may have seemed a reasonable time to the king and his councilors at court, in fact this condition would require Lucas to act quickly, strain his resources and test his ability in order to act within the time-frame. Though he would have liked to have spent the first few weeks after his return to Hispaniola with his family, he could not. Time was of the essence. Everything depended on him and there was no one to whom he could delegate authority. Once again, he must depend on Ana to have a heavy hand in overseeing the operation of the plantation and gold mine. In addition, he had purchased a sugar processing plant mill at Puerto de la Plata with the treasure given him by her father. It was an investment that he thought would further guarantee the financial security of his family; an enterprise that would produce an annual flow of cash income. And this could be important if something happened to him on the voyage that he would eventually have to make to the land of Chicora.

Francisco's first action upon returning to the island was to meet with his tribesmen. He found though they respected Ana, she was only involved in their daily lives in a limited way. Their everyday masters were the three priests who seemed determined to erase their cultural identity and make Spaniards of them all. And if one was recalcitrant, then on occasion the whip had to be used. But at least they received more food and better shelter than the African slaves who did the heavy field work upon the plantation.

In the beginning after his return from Spain, Francisco reached out to his people, but they were resentful towards him. He had become too much like the Spanish. It was not useful to their relationship that he was now allowed to reside in the home of Lucas. He tried to convince them that they must persevere if they wanted to be returned to their homes, and that such a return lay not too far in the future. But they remained unconvinced until the day they were actually put on board a ship where they were neither chained nor tied down with ropes. Only then did they know that Francisco had spoken words of wisdom and their old feelings of respect for him returned, except for Touppa. He still held a grudge against him that would smolder until at some future date it would become a raging hatred.

On the second week at home, Lucas went to the docks at Santo Domingo to search out the availability of a captain and crew to return the Indians to the place along the river from which they had been taken captive. He also decided to send another ship on the expedition. He heard reports that very day that one in the harbor might be for sale. In a tavern along the docks he found Quexos who was anxious to find employment as a captain. Seated at the same table drinking a mug of rum with Quexos was Captain Gomez, the same man who had commanded the ship that brought Lucas and Ana to the island from Spain after their marriage.

"Judge, I have heard that you are looking for two captains and crews to sail back to the land of Chicora," Quexos said when Lucas passed near their table.

"Matienzo and you caused me a lot of problems when you convinced Gordillo to disobey my orders on the last expedition I sent out."

"I am no longer in his employment. He has not even paid me all the wages I was entitled too. And he has threatened me with the authorities if I try to collect what is due. So as you can see there is no love lost between us."

"How can I trust you to follow my orders if I hire you?" Lucas asked as he sat down at the table and motioned for the proprietor to bring over a bottle of rum.

"I followed his orders and got into trouble. Would I do less for an honest man like yourself?"

"I am not part of this conflict between you two men," Gomez said. "I just need a ship. You know my skill at sailing and my ability to command a crew. If the wages are good, I will sign on with you."

"What do you know of the ship, *Santa Cathalina*?"

"She is a sturdy one that has weathered many storms crossing the Atlantic. Though she was built years ago, she still has a lot of voyages left in her."

"Come with me. I am going aboard to inspect her. Your good eye would be an advantage to me. And if all goes well you will be her captain."

"What about me, Sir?" Quexos asked.

"I will think it over."

"Remember, I know where those Indians were captured and have in my possession maps of the bay and rivers."

"Have you turned them over to the authorities? You know the law."

"They have value and are my secret unless I'm paid for them. If the authorities ask me about them, they don't exist. Just let them try to discover where I have concealed them."

"Do you know the whereabouts of Sotil the pilot?"

"My cousin is hereabouts."

"Find him and bring the map to my house on the plantation, and I will give you careful consideration to captain the *Choruca*."

'You may just take my maps."

"You said I was an honest man. Now we will find out if those were just empty words spoken to flatter me."

The caravel, *Santa Cathalina*, was a two-mast ship. It was neither the largest type of caravel nor the smallest. Her builders had compromised and built her somewhere in between. After Captain Gomez spent time inspecting her from bow to stern, he could find no defect in her. Now that Lucas knew the vessel was sturdy, his next problem was dealing with the trustee of the owner's estate, a man who might not let go of such a valuable piece of property if he thought he could extend his commissions by leasing her out to carry cargo. But this obstacle did not turn out to present a problem. The man was happy to dispose of the asset, for he was engaged to marry the widow of the merchant who had owned the *Santa Cathalina*. He preferred a sum certain rather than the chance the ship might be lost at sea while still under the ownership of the estate.

* * *

"I can't believe he has filed another lawsuit," Lucas said to Ana. "We have time restraints under the terms of the charter. This will only delay our settlement expedition to the new world."

"What are you going to do about it?"

"See if we can compromise."

"How?"

"I will suggest to Matienzo the withdrawal of his suit claiming an equal right to the lands discovered by my expedition under Captain Gordillo in exchange for my dropping my claim against him for the cost of maintenance on the Indians and their return."

"But that is not fair. He agreed that if you won the appeal to the king, he would pay costs."

"It is not about fairness, but about the time constraints. Everyday I am delayed puts the whole venture at risk."

"When are you going to submit this proposal to him?"

"I will leave for Santo Domingo tomorrow. He is there for the next several weeks and I do not want to wait until he comes back to Puerto de la Plato."

"I will see that the servants have your things packed and that the horse and carriage are made ready. Is there any way that the children and

I could go with you? I miss our lovely home overlooking the water at Santo Domingo."

"I would dearly love you to go, but I need you here overseeing the plantation and sugar mill."

"Are you taking Francisco with you?"

"No, I am leaving him here. He has learned a lot about the operation of my businesses."

"You are right, and he will be a great help to me while you are away."

When Lucas had left the room, Ana went out on the back veranda and looked across the field at the banana trees whose branches were blowing in the breeze. This had a soothing effect but did not totally eradicate the anger that burned within her. An image of Matienzo flashed through her mind. She hated him and all he stood for on this island. She believed the reason for the lawsuit filed against her husband was vindictiveness for her rejection of his advances. He had kept coming by the plantation until at last he had caught her alone. His aggressiveness had only been stopped that day by a sharp paring knife she secretly carried on her person. When he had put his arms around her in a forceful embrace on that day, he quickly found a blade against his throat. She pressed it hard enough to bring a small flow of blood. He finally got the message of how far she was willing to go to be faithful to her husband. He had never returned to the plantation. She told no one about the incident. Not even Lucas. In her male-dominated society everyone, including even the women, would have thought it her fault. They would have believed she led him on. So the best thing for her reputation and to prevent Lucas from calling Matienzo out as a matter of honor was to remain silent.

Matienzo looked at the man who sat across from him at his place of business in Santo Domingo. He enjoyed having such a powerful man on the island at a disadvantage. He held the keys in his hands to the man's ability to comply with the king's charter. He could have been gracious and accepted the compromise that was offered, he chose not too. He enjoyed the humiliation suffered by Lucas. But this was nothing compared to the pleasure it gave him at the thought of the anger which would arise in Ana when her husband delivered the news of his failure. Her rejection of him and the memory of that sharp knife against his throat left him with no pity for them.

Lucas was furious, but he was not a man to let those feelings control his actions. When he left Matienzo, he went directly to the bars that lined the wharf. He had made a decision. He would send the *Choruca* and the *Santa Cathalina* to return the Indians to their home. He would have the captains of his ships explore the best location for his settlement. In the meantime a request would be made to the Royal Council of the Indies to expedite a hearing on Matienzo's claim. In return for this request being granted, he would drop his suit against Matienzo knowing an appeal would follow a favorable decision; he would send a correspondence to Stephen in Seville apprising him of the situation in Hispaniola and have him ready to secure a hearing before the king on any appeal filed by Matienzo with the royal court. These things would all be taken care of tomorrow. Today he must find Captain Quexos and Captain Gomez and inform them of his decision. Preparation needed to be made immediately to prepare the two caravels for the voyage and a competent crew recruited. He had sufficient funds in an account at the Bank of the Indies to offer good wages so that securing a crew and supplies for the expedition would not delay his plan.

It was not an easy decision for Francisco to make. He knew it would further strain the relationship he had with his tribesmen. They already felt he had forsaken their people and adopted the ways of their captors, but he knew it was the right decision. To do otherwise would have filled him with a sense of disloyalty to his benefactor. The bond formed in Spain had grown even stronger since his return to Hispaniola and now extended to Ana and the children. He felt it his duty to remain and not go on the caravels with the others back to Chicora. Instead, he would put his faith in the judge that the settlement expedition would sail by spring. He knew that his benefactor would need his help in establishing the settlement. Looking into the future, he understood that his own people would need his guidance in order to prevent them from being destroyed as the indigenous inhabitants of this island had been decimated by a civilization they could not resist. Somehow an accommodation must be had between these two worlds, and he believed the gods had chosen him as the one person who could bridge this gap.

* * *

In the month of February in the year 1524, the caravels set sail for the land of Chicora. Other then suffering from the cold weather, it was an uneventful journey. Since they did not run into storms, the ships were not blown off course by the winds. In early March during a high tide the two ships sailed directly into the bay named Saint John the Baptist and straight up to the river, Gualdape, where the Winyah Indian village was located. Late in the evening they dropped anchor near a high bluff that provided easy access to the forest and lands beyond. The Indians who had suffered from sea sickness could not be persuaded to wait until morning. So, as the sun was setting, the Winyah Indians who had survived their capture were ferried by row boats to the bank of the river and released. In their possession were many parting gifts. These had been pressed upon them by the captains who hoped to establish friendly relation with their tribe. As soon as the Indians' feet hit the ground they disappeared into the woods. The sailors waited until darkness hoping the released ones would return with their kinsmen. When they failed to return, the sailors became nervous and rowed back to the ship.

The excitement in the village was on a level never experienced by the tribe. At first the appearance out of the woods of figures that approached their night campfires were thought to be spirits of the dead. It took a while for these figures to coach their kindred out of their longhouses back into their presence. When they finally came out, they were overjoyed to discover these were not spirits at all, but those who were taken from them many seasons ago. There was much celebration. Some deer in the enclosure were slaughtered, and cornbread was baked for the tribe rejoiced that their warriors had returned. The gifts brought from the ship were passed out to the chief and his councilors who were much taken with the strange items brought from across the sea. In the back of their minds they coveted more and dreamed of ways they could obtain them. The chief decided that he would go down to the river bank the next day and meet these strangers who had returned their braves.

It was almost noon when a sailor posted on watch cried out, his voice trembling with excitement at seeing a large number of Indians gathered on the river bank. The sailors recognized many of the warriors who had traveled back to this place from the island, even though they had once again assumed their native dress of deerskin breeches. Before Quexos could consider sending a rowboat ashore, several canoes were launched. Aboard were some of the freed warriors. They paddled to the *Choruca* with their chief and his councilors and brought with them animal skins, a bushel of pearls, and silver bracelets. The chief hoped to exchange them for some of the Spanish goods aboard the ship that his tribesmen had told him about. The Indians seemed unafraid despite events of the past. Captain Gomez came over from the *Santa Cathalina*. The two captains sat down upon the deck of the ship and worked out an exchange of goods. The dealing was made easy by the fact that the freed Indians spoke Spanish which they had learned while living on the island. At the end of the morning before the chief left, Quexos was able to obtain permission to establish an encampment near the village.

After the Indians were back on shore, the captains discussed their goals for the next few weeks.

"We must load our ship with as much trade goods as possible," Gomez said.

"And explore the area for gold," Quexos added.

"I am as interested as you are about gold," Gomez said. "We all dream of finding wealth like Cortez. But silver is also a valuable commodity. I would like to know the source of their silver. I do not believe their story of it coming from across the sea in a chest long ago."

"Certainly it must have been mined in the same mountains where they obtained the small quantity of gold they have in their possession," Quexos said.

"The judge wanted us to find a suitable site for a settlement in this land," Gomez said. "We will explore for the best location, but I suspect none will be better than this place. This large river, Gualdape, gives ships access to the sea."

"And it may well be the one that flows through this land to an ocean that will lead us to China and India," Quexos said.

"We should explore this river for some distance from the mouth and see where it leads us," Gomez said.

"But we can't delay very long for the judge expects us to be back in Hispaniola soon to lead the fleet to this land," Ouexos said.

For the three weeks which they had allotted themselves, the two leaders of the expedition explored the landscape. They even took the *Choruca* up the Gualdape and spent two day on the largest fresh-water island they had ever seen. They wanted to go farther upstream, but they simply did not have the time. That would have to wait until they returned with the fleet. Their search had been in vain to find the source of any gold or silver in the streams that flowed into the bay. The wealth of this country they decided lay in its rich soil, the abundance of game, and the quantity of seafood that could be harvested from its marshes. It could be a paradise if one were not constantly seeking mineral wealth. They had a strong feeling that this stream in which their ships were anchored might be the one that flowed into a body of water that led to China and India. If that proved to be true, this Bay of Saint John the Baptist could become the center of trade with the Far East which was awash with not only gold and silver but also with spices, a valuable commodity in their own right.

The last few days of their stay, Quexos tried to convince some of the freed Indians to return with him so they could act as interpreters when the settlement fleet landed. Three of these former captives agreed to return to Hispaniola along with five new Indians who were enticed by the stories of Hispaniola.

On the final day there was a big celebration in the village. The Spanish promised the chief they would come back before the summer season and bring his son, Francisco, with them. In return for this promise, the chief agreed his tribe would clear an area on a high piece of ground near the river. This location that lay a short distance from the village was chosen by Quexos as the place he would encourage Lucas to locate his settlement. The area had a stand of hardwood trees that could be used for constructing buildings, and the soil was fertile enough to raise crops.

* * *

The weather was fair when the two ships left the Bay of Saint John and entered the ocean for their long journey. The captains expected to run into some storms on the way home but were pleasantly surprised to find the weather reasonable. Quexos made a note in his log that future voyages should be made in late winter or early spring instead of the summer and fall when storms seemed to be more intense.

The two caravels arrived at the port of Santo Domingo in July 1525. They found Lucas still frustrated by delays in the civil proceedings. The council had issued judgment in his favor and against Matienzo. They had found that since Matienzo's craft had sailed without authorization and for a purpose in contravention of a decree of the council, that he had no lawful claim to lands discovered. As expected an appeal was sent to the king. Lucas now awaited word from Stephen at the king's court in Seville.

The decree of the king finally arrived in May in the year 1526. Having received a favorable ruling, Lucas rushed the last-minute preparations because the season of storms was fast approaching.

The delay had almost driven Lucas into bankruptcy. He had secured additional ships, and the island had been scrounged for available supplies. Many of the working men had signed on for a handful of gold coins and for the chance of a better future. A hundred Spaniards with combat experience who landed on a ship from Florida signed up for the promise of land. He knew he must sail soon before his funds ran out so he issued orders that in seven days the fleet would weigh anchor.

THE
AFRICANS

In a grass hut in the middle of the village that lay close to a river that flowed into the sea, lay Gomo and his first wife, Sepo. Now in the fourth year of living together, he still loved to look upon her beautiful young body as she slept naked beside him. The nipples on her breasts were taut even at this early hour. He breathed in the cool morning air. Soon the sun would rise and cast its rays upon his home, and the heat would drive his family from this enclosure to the trees that lined the avenues that ran to a meadow nearby where herds of cattle grazed. His happiness was at its height this morning, for his father, the chief of this tribe, expected the Arab merchants to arrive sometime before noon. There would be much trading to do with these strangers who traveled far to bring them items that were absent from their culture. There would be a large feast. The tribe would cook the meat of several slaughtered bulls and pots of beer would be served to all. When the celebrating was over that evening, they would all enjoy a good nights rest. The next day would be restricted to serious trading. The warehouses built of mud and straw were bursting with ivory and tanned animal skins. In an enclosure on the outskirts of the village was a commodity greatly prized by the Arabs: war slaves recently captured on a night raid into the land of the Yakongo. They were all fit for travel, and the Arabs would pay a high price for them.

Everyone in the village lay on mats in their huts until late that morning, for last night there had been much celebration over the defeat of their enemy who lived nearby. Much food had been consumed and they had danced around the campfire until late in the evening. While the villagers slept, so did the five guards who were always posted on the jungle's edge where heavy foliage hid the movement of life from one's view.

Through the foliage crept the warriors of the Kango tribe. They had trailed the merchants for days and now they were a great distance from their home village. The lure of riches drove them, for their tribe was small and resources scant. But there among them had arisen a chief who was both brave and intelligent. In a short time he had welded these men into a fierce group of fighters. They watched the village throughout the day, and when the sun set, no fires were lit by his men. When the celebration in the village had stopped and the inhabitants lay in a deep slumber, his men traveled in the darkness to an assigned position. As the sun rose the next morning, their weapons of war were ready. Still they waited, though their stomachs were empty. Finally the merchants appeared and were met with great fanfare. The guards, awakened by the noise, deserted their post and went to the center of the village where all the tribe had gathered.

The attackers did not scream when they left the foliage but simply ran toward their objective. Gomo was the first to notice and let out a war cry, but it was too late. Their enemy was upon them. A club struck him across the back of the head, and he fell unconscious to the ground. When he awoke, he wore an iron collar around his neck. The collar had a chain through it which connected him with a man in front and one in back. Around each leg was a shackle also connected by chains. He looked around and saw the bodies of many who were dead from having their heads bashed in by the clubs. A few minutes later, he passed out again. He awoke a second time when someone kicked him in the ribs. He did not understand what the enemy was saying but he knew what the words meant. He was forced to his feet and began a march down the trail, a pathway that led to a settlement on the sea where white men had built a fort made of mud and which was visited by large boats with sails.

When they stopped for the night beside the trail, word was passed to Gomo that Sepo was alive. She was chained with other women near the back of the line. He could do nothing right now to rescue her, but he took an oath to his gods that he would free her from the chains at the first opportunity. The next morning the march continued. They had been given some water but no food and some collapsed. Their shackles were removed and the guards beat them to death with clubs. The others seeing this knew what to expect if they fell down. No mercy could be expected. On the evening of the second full day the smell of the ocean was in the air, and Gomo realized they would reach their destination the next morning.

* * *

The fort was small and its walls were made from a mixture of mud and straw. It was not occupied most of year. Its only use was to protect the slave ships that came in the early spring. Men with weapons of war would be off-loaded and placed within the fort. These sailors would keep a watch for the chained members of humanity that would eventually be brought from the jungle to this area on the beach. Some of those chained were captured in war, and others had been sold into slavery by their own chiefs.

Occasionally a rival would be taken during the night and delivered to the beach never to see his home again. The Spanish had not been at this business long. They had depended upon the Portuguese, who were the first Europeans to exploit the trade thereby breaking the monopoly of the Arabs who had been in the business for centuries. But after the Indian slave revolt in Hispaniola in 1522 and the decimation of Indians in that part of the world from disease, African laborers became much in demand on the islands that were in Spain's possession.

From the deck of his ship, the captain saw the group arriving. It looked like about a hundred and they were mostly men.

"See that food and water are taken to them immediately," he said to his second in command.

It was not out of compassion that he issued the order. Keeping slaves in good physical shape was simply a good business decision.

* * *

The water flowed down Gomo's parched throat. Then gruel was served. It was like a paste and tasteless, but it filled the emptiness in his stomach. After the feeding, slaves were placed in a circle. For the first time since their capture, he saw Sepo. Even in her chains, she was a thing of beauty. He could see that she had not given into despair. Her eyes glowed with hatred, and when those eyes fell upon him, her determination gave him renewed strength. She cast her eyes upon the ship anchored nearby. He read her thoughts. They must escape before being placed there. He nodded his head in acknowledgement, and she was able to read his lips: "tonight." The message was passed and all waited for the signal.

Their captors had received their bounty and departed. Only a few sailors were now about, and the rum they had consumed had dulled their senses. Gomo spied the one with the keys. He understood what this instrument was used for because he had watched as the slaves the white man rejected had had their bonds loosened with it. Those poor creatures would now be taken back to their captor's village for human sacrifices to the gods.

At midnight the word was passed. Each separately chained group moved forward toward the sailors closest to them. The key was soon in Gomo's hand and he quickly freed several others, but it was not enough. The men at the fort nearby heard the guards' dying cries, and they attacked and laid low many of those who had been freed. The rest, bewildered and still bound, fell to the ground and begged for mercy. But Gomo and Sepo fought on until the clubs were slammed against their heads. The next morning when they awoke the two were in the cargo space of the ship chained to its wall along with many others. Now for the first time since their capture, despair appeared in the pair's eyes.

* * *

At the start of the voyage, ninety men and ten women were tightly packed in a small space. Down into this dark hole twice a day came the key holder and two other sailors who brought them their rations of water and food. The only daylight seen was by the slaves chosen to carry up the buckets of human waste each day. Even with this disposal system, the confined area began to smell so bad that the offensive odor reached the deck of the ship and caused the captain to make a decision. It was not one he took lightly. But it was a necessary one. He ordered the slaves brought up ten at a time. When Gomo reached the deck he was with four men and five women. They stood on the deck blinded by the sunlight while buckets of cold sea water were poured over their bodies. Then they were handed bars of a harsh soap. When they were returned to the hole, two of the women were kept on deck. They did not return until the next day. Their bodies were bruised. They told the others how the men lined up and took them, one after another, until the sailors' desires were satisfied. The next day Sepo went up from the bowels of the ship with nine others.

Captain Narvez had seen the slender young female slave when she was brought on deck. He continued to observe as water was poured over her body and then she was forced to scrub with the harsh soap. He had joined his men yesterday in their activities with the two women slaves. Today he felt lust rise again within his loins as he observed her clean naked body glistening in the noon sun and saw the defiance in her eyes. I will enjoy breaking this one, he thought.

"That one I want you to save for me," he said to his first mate. "Be sure you dry her before she is brought to my cabin."

Sepo knew from other women tales what was to be expected. First the captain, then the first mate, and soon all the others would enjoy that which she gave freely only to Gomo. A desire for vengeance against those who had slaughtered her children swelled within her heart. But she could not have that revenge, for those warriors were far away. So she would have her vengeance upon those who now sought to rape her.

The captain was in a state of partial undress when she was delivered.

"That will be all," he said.

"I will be right outside the door if you should need me, Sir."

She stood before him, a picture of black beauty that he had not seen before. His mind fantasized for a moment of keeping her for his own, but he knew that was not possible. Already the men were waiting to be next in line after the first mate. No, he would have to be satisfied with exercising the captain's right of being the first one.

"Come here," he said.

Though Sepo did not speak his language, she understood from his hand motion what he meant. Out of the corner of her eye she had already spotted a sharp tool on the small desk in the corner. She had no way of knowing that it was a steel letter opener. All she knew was its sharpness. She pretended to want to please him. He fell for the deception as men are apt to do regardless of the circumstances. As he lay there naked and ready to penetrate her, she showed discomfort and motioned to the piss pot in the corner of the cabin. He nodded his consent. She crawled out of the bed and stepped toward it. As she passed the small desk, her hand reached out. In a flash her hand was upon the letter opener and like a leopard she pounced upon him stabbing him in the areas where she knew his heart beat. The captain screamed out for help, but it was too late. The instrument had punctured his heart with the first blow. The first mate charged into the captain quarters and with the help of another sailor subdued her. The crew was outraged by what she had done. In their moral indignation, they strapped Sepo down with heavy chain and cast her overboard thinking they were delivering her into the hands of Lucifer. Her cries before she hit the water were drowned out by the winds of a gale which had come up suddenly. Soon thoughts of the captain's fate became secondary as the men fought to keep the ship from being swallowed by the waves.

* * *

The slave ship sailed into Santo Domingo two weeks before Lucas' fleet was scheduled to depart from its base at Puerto de la Plata. The first mate told the authorities a harrowing tale of the voyage: a captain murdered and a ship battered by a three-day storm. After those disasters, a sickness had swept the crew and spread to the slaves below deck. The loss of life was substantial.

The ship's owners were a group of merchants from Seville, but they had an agent in Santo Domingo who could act on their behalf. He was a person of low birth who had risen from the bottom of society by his knowledge of numbers and by having a good head for business. The agent saw both a disaster and an opportunity. He needed to get rid of the ship and slaves. No plantation owner would want to buy the slaves for fear they carried disease that might spread to their own field hands. The ship would have low value for the same reason. Disease in this part of the world spread quickly and was frequently fatal. He went to see Lucas who wanted African slaves for his planned settlement to clear the ground for farms. The agent offered to sell both for a reasonable price. When Lucas declared he did not have the funds available at that moment, the agent offered to extend a line of credit secured by the gold mine, plantation, and sugar mill. Lucas accepted provided that only the gold mine and plantation were encumbered, with it being declared in writing that no right was reserved to seize the homes in Santo Domingo and Puerto de la Plata, nor the sugar mill. It was the best the agent could squeeze out of Lucas so he agreed. He had that day done a great benefit for his benefactors in Seville and for himself. A large commission on the sale was due him upon the payment of the sum owed, and he was relieved of the headache of holding the ship and slaves for an unknown period.

The ship with the slaves sailed that very day into Puerto de la Plata. Because the ship was viewed unlucky, Lucas tried to change this perception by renaming her the *Bretorn*. Men were set to work cleaning her and the slaves were taken to the plantation where they were kept separate from the field hands. Lucas saw that they were fed well and treated by a doctor. This man of medicine pronounced them free of disease and fit to sail to Chicora. When they boarded the ship the day of departure they numbered forty and among their number was Gomo.

VOYAGE TO
THE BAY OF
SAINT JOHN

It was the middle of July in the year 1526 when the fleet sailed from
Puerto de la Plata. Ana and her children looked at the departing fleet
from her home, a place built on an elevated piece of earth near a grove of
banana trees on their plantation. She repeated to her children the names
of the ships that would take their father and his settlers across the sea to
a new land. The largest ship purchased last year and given her maiden
name of *Becerra* was in front. Its cargo included most of the food provisions and eighty-nine horses. There was a skeleton crew on board and no
passengers. Following the *Becerra* out of the harbor were three caravels:
Choruca, Santa Cathalina, and *Breton*. A small tender was attached to the
Bretorn to be used to carry messages and supplies between the other ships.

For this reason, Lucas had chosen the *Bretorn* as his headquarters ship. He sailed on her with his close associates, Francisco and Father Montesinos. Also with him were the three Indian interpreters who had returned with Quexos from his last trip to the Gualdape River that flowed into the Bay of Saint John the Baptist. Though Montesinos was aboard the *Bretorn,* the other ships were not without their own spiritual advisors. Father Antonio de Cervantes was on the *Santa Cathalina*, Brother Pedro de Estrada on the *Choruca*, and Brother Agustin Endez on the *Becerra*.

Ana pointed out to her children the figures of those aboard who were looking back toward the port and waving good-bye. She explained to them that five hundred men were on board as well as fifty women, ten children, and forty slaves. But of course they could not see the slaves who were chained in the bottom of the *Santa Cathalina*. An hour after the ships passed from view, she took the children back into the house and immediately began giving orders to her household staff, which included five Indians from the Gualdape. They had come to Hispaniola to learn Spanish, so they could act as interpreters at a later date for the settlement. They had no way of knowing that they would never see their tribe again but would live out their lives on the island. Later that afternoon Ana visited the fields and observed that the overseers were getting sufficient labor out of the African slaves. Tomorrow she would go to the gold mine and inspect the production, and the next day would find her at the sugar mill. Keeping busy was her way of dealing with the loneliness she knew would overwhelm her with Lucas absent from her life.

* * *

Lucas had done everything within his power to leave the island earlier in the season. Delayed by matters beyond his control, he was now sailing during the period when storms visited the waters of the Caribbean. But he had no choice. His liquid funds were exhausted by the costs of supporting those who had signed on. Not only were gold coins paid them in advance, but once they were under contract, he was legally responsible for feeding and housing them. So he could not afford to wait beyond the storm season to depart. He prayed for fair weather and also had his priests pray, but God chose not to give him a favorable reply.

One moment the sun was shining that morning and the waves were normal. The next moment conditions had drastically changed. First dark clouds appeared on the horizon. This was followed by a heavy rain. The wind had a sudden burst of energy. At first this was intermittent, but soon it became a gale. As the size of the waves mounted, attempts to keep the fleet intact became more difficult. Lucas soon realized this was not just a passing storm, but one of those phenomena that had recently been given the name *hurricane*. It bore down upon them with increasing ferocity. Before the storm, they were within reach of their destination, but the wind, waves, and current swept them on a new course not of their choosing. To the north along the coast they were taken. Then catastrophe fell upon them. The *Becerra* took on so much water that she began to founder in the waves, and Lucas lost hope that she could be saved.

On board the *Becerra,* the crew knew the ship was not going to survive. They had been short on crew members when they had set sail. In the midst of this storm, this shortage was fatal. When it appeared they were only minutes from disaster, the captain gave orders to release the horses, thinking perhaps they would provide a way to get to an island he had spotted a short distance away. Just as the order was carried out the ship sank. Everyone struggled to find any item that would float and support a seaman's weight. The horses had been the first into the water and somehow they sensed that land lay a few hundred yards away. They swam toward the island. Most of the horses were swept out to sea, as were all of the sailors. But twenty horses reached the shore. They would survive the storm, and many years later, English and French explorers would write about these Spanish horses that inhabited the islands off the coast of North Carolina. Even into the modern era, their origin would continue to be a mystery.

Lucas and the captains of the other ships saw the *Becerra* in distress, but it was not within their power to come to her aid. Nor were they able to assist the sailors in the water. They watched helplessly as the men tried desperately to reach an island before being seized by the current and dragged out to sea.

The storm continued for hours, and then there was a lull, which seamen with experience in this part of the world understood was temporary. It was during this lull that Quexos saw in the distance a harbor that might provide a haven when the storm resumed its ferocity. He steered for it and the other ships followed. The water was deep, and a swift current was running into the bay from the ocean. The ships were swept along by this current for a considerable distance. When the current stopped and the ships were being drawn back toward the sea, the captains gave orders to drop anchor. Despite the strength of the current that was now flowing back into the sea and taking all kinds of debris with it, the anchors held and the ships remained in place. After what seemed to be an eternity to those on board, the wind died down and the rain stopped. By that time darkness had settled upon the earth. Those on board the surviving ships slept, while the men posted on watch waited for the rising sun.

* * *

On shore the storm had caused devastation. but it wasn't the kind of damage that modern society would suffer. It was relegated to uprooted trees that would in a short time provide homes for all species of small animals. They would find a safe haven from their natural predators and multiply. This would provide a secure food source for the Waccamaw Indians who lived in the area. Having seen this effect in the past, the local shaman did not look at these storms which visited his area as a bad omen. Instead, he viewed them as a blessing from the gods, who, through the use of nature, replenished their food supply. The longhouses which were made of logs and built in a rectangular shape rarely suffered damage. The only negative effect was the destruction of the corn crop which could have created a devastating effect on their food supply if it had not been for the fact that there always existed corn cribs with ample supplies. So when the Indians awoke the next morning they expected no ill effects from the storm that had swept their village yesterday. What they did not expect to see were ships anchored in their bay.

* * *

The ship carrying the provisions having been lost at sea, the Spanish woke up the next morning faced with the immediate problem of securing food to prevent starvation. There was some food stored on each ship, but it was insufficient to feed them for more than two weeks. To make matters worse, they were not anchored in waters where they had planned the settlement. However, everything was not bad news. Captain Gordillo had visited this location on a prior expedition, and Francisco assured the judge that this place was inhabited by the Waccamaw, a tribe that belonged to the Sioux confederation. He proposed that the tender boat be used to approached land and seek help from the tribe whose village lay a short distance away. But before the tender could be launched, canoes appeared. The Waccamaws had discovered their presence and were anxious to make contact. As with all the tribes along the coast, they had developed a taste for European trade goods, and were always willing to put their lives and civilization on the line in order to obtain them. Unfortunately, this would be their undoing in the long term, leaving their villages destroyed either by death inflicted by the force of arms or by disease.

Lucas was on the *Santa Cathalina* having been transported there on the tender when the canoes appeared. He was in conversation with Sotil who broke out with a big smile when he recognized the tall Indian in the first boat. It was Neus, the chief with whom he had built a relationship with when he and Gordillo had spent some time here on a previous journey. He waved and called out his name. Upon hearing his voice, Neus motioned for the other canoes to follow him as his boat was paddled toward the *Santa Cathalina*. Soon all the Indians were on board. The civilians on the ship were initially frightened of these creatures, but in a short time they grew accustomed to their presence. Francisco was able to act as an interpreter. Soon negotiations were in progress for Lucas and his men to go ashore and visit the tribe's village. Before the canoes left they were loaded with trade goods to encourage a warm reception for Lucas and his entourage.

That afternoon, after a meeting with his captains, it was agreed that Lucas would take Sotil, Francisco, and ten other men to the shore. Once they were at the village, an attempt would be made to secure food for the ships. After this was done, Lucas wanted to immediately set sail for the Bay of Saint John the Baptist. He was aware from Sotil of prior trouble with Neus' warriors, and he could not afford to overstay his visit and rekindle any animosity that might still linger among some of the tribesmen.

Sotil, upon arriving at the village, found the storm had done little damage, but he noticed that the fields of corn nearby had been leveled. He immediately recognized that the overabundance of food available on his last trip would not be available this time, regardless of the trade goods offered.

A week later the food situation had barely improved. The fresh meat, vegetables, and corn had been a welcome relief, but they had not increased substantially the provisions on board.

"We must leave soon," Lucas said to Quexos and Gomez.

"I suggest we take the able-bodied men and African slaves down the coast to the land of the Winyahs," Quexos said. "You and the others could follow the shoreline. The distance is not that great, and you should have no problem finding the site where the settlement will be planted. You have a copy of my charts, and it would be impossible for us to get separated as long as you enter the bay."

Lucas thought on this proposition for a few moments. Francisco had suggested the same idea last night. It was the best of all the alternatives. This tribe did not have the resources to sustain them much longer and soon conflicts were bound to arise between the Indians and his men. The soldiers were already getting a little hard to control with their usual short-sighted thirst for gold, plunder, and women. There were two comrades-in-arms whose insubordination had been brought to his attention. Ginez Doncel and Pedro de Bacan's reputations for violence and rape had even appalled their former leader, Juan Navarrete, during an expedition to Florida. That was how they had ended up in Hispaniola. He had put them on a ship to the island just to get rid of them. Besides all the other issues that confronted Lucas, sickness had now raised its ugly head on board the ships. No one knew the cause, but the illness was spreading. Separating the healthy ones and allowing them to travel by a land route where they could subsist on the land while the sick traveled by sea seemed the most viable option. He wanted to keep Francisco with him on board the *Bretorn*, but he knew the expedition would be better served if Francisco traveled overland, for the other interpreters would listen to him. If he were not present they might desert the Spaniards.

* * *

The first week in August the fleet sailed from the river they called Jordan, which was later named Cape Fear. The men were led by Quexos who had temporarily given up the command of his ship at Lucas' request to lead the land expedition. It would not be difficult, for there were paths that for centuries had been used as a highway for trade. The route had no natural barriers, except shallow streams that were easily forded. The path, as it grew closer to their destination, followed an area that ran along the high ground behind marshes. On the other side were wetlands and strips of sand with high sand dunes which hid a view of the ocean that lay beyond. Though they could not see the waters of the Atlantic, when the wind blew in their direction, the smell of salt air filled their nostrils. On the march, the ability to feed the men was made more difficult because the feet of so many marching through the wilderness scared away the wildlife. But foraging parties were able to kill enough wild game each day to keep starvation away.

One morning when the group awoke, they discovered that all the interpreters except Francisco had left them during the night. At first Quexos and his men thought the ungrateful savages had deserted them. But Francisco explained they were but two days from the lands of the

Winyah and the men had only gone ahead to alert the village. Pacified, the group continued their journey. The next day they awoke to the sound of Francisco's voice talking in the dialect of the Sioux near the edge of their encampment. Several warriors and the interpreters were in conversation with Francisco. Quexos and the others were afraid the warriors were plotting with Francisco against them, until he explained their presence.

"They have been sent ahead to guide us to food that awaits us at the river," Francisco said. "After we have eaten, we will go to my village."

The march continued with the Spanish following Francisco and the others. An hour later they smelled the smoke of campfires and soon arrived at a clearing in view of the Gualdape. More than forty women were busy cooking food. The smell of it stirred the appetites of the travelers who for several days had fed off unsalted game cooked over poorly made fires. Now they proceeded to gorge themselves on a variety of seafood and cornbread. The food was salted heavily, but this did not present a problem because the fresh water of the nearby river was availabl to wash it down. Afterward, they made their way to the village. Quexos was glad to see that the heavy storm that had visited the River Jordan region had not made an appearance on the Gualdape.

The Winyah homes in the village were long houses built from the timber of a nearby hardwood forest. Moss mixed with mud was used to seal the cracks between the logs. The men in the village slept separately from the women in lodges that were spaced a great distance apart.

One thing had changed since their last visit. The chief they had dealt with on prior occasions had died. Upon meeting the new leader of the tribe, Quexos was not confident that this man would be as close an ally as Francisco's father had been during their prior visit. Another thing that made him feel uneasy was that one of the new chief's councilors was an Indian named Touppa. He was one of the tribesmen who had been captured and then returned. Quexos noticed the look of hatred in his eyes every time he looked into the faces of his guests. This was not a good omen.

Touppa was livid that his chief had welcomed the Spanish. But he understood the majority of his tribesmen were inclined to treat these strangers with hospitality because not only were they fascinated by them, they desired the trade goods these strangers brought from across the water. He would bide his time until the Spaniards' actions caused the people to turn against them. When that time came his fingers would clutch a tomahawk and he would spill the blood of these strangers upon the ground. Knowing his enemy as he did, Touppa knew he would not have long to wait.

The sailors were not surprised to see children in the arms of the women they had slept with on their last journey to this river. They felt no attachment or responsibility for these offsprings. To them it had simply been a matter of lust and opportunity. Now their eyes moved to other maidens who showed an interest by their body language.

When the Spaniards awoke the next morning, they were led a mile down a path to where the project of clearing land for the Spanish settlement had begun. The underbrush had been removed over a five-acre piece of land. The standing trees were dead, having been killed by cutting a circle in their trunks a few inches from the ground and then burned by stacking dried brush against the trunks. Quexos knew that when the judge arrived with the fleet they would use the axes to cut and remove the trees so they could start building a town.

That evening Quexos excused himself after eating and returned to the lodge assigned to him. As he lay upon mats made of marsh reeds, he wondered if this grand dream of the judge would come to fruition. Many of the free men who had traveled overland with him were soldiers. Generally this type of individual was not good at manual labor. Their only skill was in the manual of arms. The rest of the males were composed of a mixture from every level of society. Even in this group there were few farmers, and that was a necessary ingredient for the success of this settlement. He knew the judge was depending on the forty zoo slaves to clear ground for planting. He wasn't sure how that would work out. They were straight from the jungles of Africa and had not undergone even the rudimentary domestication. That is why the name *zoo slaves* was attached to them. They had either been shackled or kept in a cage since their capture. There was the additional problem that they came from the same tribe, and thus they could communicate among themselves without the overseers understanding their spoken words. That would make it easier for them to revolt or even escape into the wilderness. Only the fear of the Indians might keep them from exercising that second option.

* * *

When the second violent storm struck the fleet as it sailed down the coast, Lucas was not surprised. He had grown to expect the sudden appearance of such bad weather. His pilot spied the entrance to the harbor some distance away just as the storm began to increase in its velocity. They made it to the entrance of Saint John the Baptist. The Spanish arrival was just before the height of the storm struck. However, none of the ships was able to enter the channel because it was low tide. And despite the waves kicked up by the wind, the channel was still too shallow. The ships sailed back out to sea where they rode out the storm while they waited for a change in the tide.

The bad weather proved to be of short duration and soon the *Bretorn* led the way through the channel. The *Choruca* was bringing up the rear. She had taken in water during the storm, and it was questionable whether her bottom would clear the channel entrance. She never got the chance to find out. When she was a few hundred yards away she began to sink. The settlers and crew took to the water as she disappeared beneath the waves. Great effort by the sailors on the other ships saved most of those who had been on board. However, many materials needed for the colony were lost forever.

Though they were close to their objective, Lucas chose to wait just inside the channel. With night coming on, he had the ships drop anchor. Father Montesinos held services and gave thanks to God that he had delivered them safety to this new land, and he asked His blessing upon this endeavor. The priest on the other ship followed suit. That night by candle light, Lucas wrote in his journal about the events of the day as he did every evening. He looked toward the sea and noted the land near where he was anchored was the upper lip to an estuary. This land that jutted out where he entered from the north he named San Roman because it was San Romanus' day when they arrived. He made a note of the date as August 24, 1526.

The loss of both the *Becerra* and the *Choruca* was not a good sign for the success of his colony. But Lucas had not lost hope. If Quexos and his party had made it safely, and assuming he could locate them, then there was still a chance his colony could survive.

The next morning Lucas was filled with renewed optimism as he sailed up the Saint John. He was impressed by the wealth of wildlife that flourished everywhere. He realized in the marshes and creeks there was such an abundance of seafood that no one should ever starve in this land. He passed a muddy creek on his left that apparently was fed by a small stream. Soon thereafter he entered a part of the bay that had several rivers whose waters poured into it. There was no question on which river Quexos waited for him. As the *Bretorn* entered the mouth of the Gualdape, a wave of excitement swept through him and the passengers. The river was broad and deep. It allowed the fleet to move upstream unhindered at high tide. A crewman on the *Bretorn* was the first to recognize the flag of Spain fluttering in the breeze from a rampart built on the bank of a bluff. Soon they could see others of their own kind gathered there. In a few minutes, the sounds of their distant voices would be heard as they shouted their greeting to those on board the fleet.

The arrival could not have come at a better time. The provisions on board the ships were exhausted, and a town must be built so that the settlers would have shelters before the coming winter season. Most of the seeds and plants brought for planting were lost on the *Becerra*. Besides, the planting season was over because it was the middle of August and the temperatures would drop in this region by the end of September. The Indians had their winter crops of squash and pumpkins. However, there would not be enough to share since the winter season was a time when food was scarce. Already the chief had foolishly allowed some of the corn reserve to be eaten in exchange for the Spanish trade goods. Any wise man would have known that both groups were heading for a season where stomachs would frequently not have enough food in them to stop the gnawing pains of hunger.

THE
SETTLEMENT

Lucas noted in his journal the first night on the banks of the Gualdape that the current population of his settlement, after taking into account those lost to the sea and disease, was four hundred men, thirty women, five children and forty slaves. The women were wives of the men who had sailed with the fleet, though a few had become widows during the voyage. Most of these women were whites who had originally been brought to Hispaniola as prisoners. The others were Indian maidens who were chosen because they were the most attractive of their lot among the enslaved indigenous population on the island. Both groups were thankful, for their present position at the settlement was vastly superior to their former status. They would be faithful to their husbands. Otherwise, under the law, they might find themselves relegated to their former status.

As the last entry in his journal before he went to bed that night, Lucas wrote the name he had given the new settlement. It was to be called

Saint Michael on the Gualdape. He envisioned the town he would build becoming a flourishing center of Spanish commerce, a place where he and his successors would be its leading citizens.

* * *

Francisco spent the first few days grieving the loss of his father, who had been the chief of the Winyahs. When this period of mourning was over he took stock of what was going on around him. The town was being laid out under the watchful eye of Quexos who was entrusted with the project. Captain Gomez was named as acting mayor and was granted authority over the civil administration. General Gonzalo Velasco was put in command of the garrison and quickly used his officer's skills to take the thirty men assigned to his command and organize them into a garrison troop that would protect the colony from any hostilities. Father Montesinos was insistent that a place of worship be given top priority. As always, he had his way. The settlers lived in makeshift shelters that were not much better than sleeping under the trees while the church, the city hall, and a warehouse were built. Many continued to make the ships their home during this period. Finally in the first week of October as the weather began to turn cold, construction of the homes began in earnest.

While the town was beginning to take shape, Lucas started exploring the rivers in the tender, but he soon found that this boat was not conducive for his purpose. So after inquiring about the men who were busy building structures for the town, he discovered some had knowledge of shipbuilding. Despite the protest of Father Montesinos and Quexos, he pulled them off the projects they were working on and had them spend days on the construction of a craft that could be used in the bay, rivers, and tributaries. It was the first craft built by European in what was later to become the United States. It had one mast, but most of the time paddles were used to reach destinations Lucas wanted to explore.

* * *

Every trip on the new craft, *Toledo*, Lucas had Francisco accompany him along with four others. They went up the Gualdape and spent the night on the large island that lay in the center of the river. The next two days they went farther upriver until Lucas decided this body of water would not lead them to the Orient. Later they explored the other rivers that emptied into the Saint John. One of the reasons for these trips was that Lucas knew under the terms of the charter, he could lay claim to all lands he had explored. At the same time he fulfilled its requirement that he search the area for a water route to India and China. On returning to Saint Michael, he found that during the two weeks he was away, things had not gone well at the settlement.

"It was Ginez Doncel and Pedro de Bacan," Quexos said. "They raped some young Indians maidens when they were walking back to their village. No food has been brought to us since the incident happened four days ago. And yesterday some of our men who were out hunting were shot at by Winyah warriors. We are afraid to leave our town site. Food supplies will run out tomorrow."

"I will go and meet with their chief. Francisco will go with me."

"No Judge, I should go alone," Francisco said. "If it is as Quexos says, you will be in danger."

"What about you?"

"I am still a Winyah warrior and the son of their last chief."

"That may not be enough. I will go with General Velasco and some of his men. That will intimidate them."

"You do not know my people well. They will see that as an act of war and they will call upon the Sioux of Chicora to come to their aid. Then there will be no peace until you have been destroyed."

"I will listen to your words of wisdom. I will also have Father Montesinos pray for your safety."

The next morning when the sun rose, Francisco left Saint Michael and walked along the path to his village. When he drew near, he could feel the eyes of warriors hidden in the forest upon him.

When he entered the village no one came out of the lodges to greet him as was customary. He did see some women and children staring from the lodges that he passed. Their demeanor was sullen. He kept walking until he reached the lodge of the chief that was built upon an earthen mound and stood at a height above all others. The chief's first wife came out.

"Why have you come to us?"

"I must see the chief."

"He is ill. The shaman is with him now."

The chief recognizing Francisco's voice, called out. When he entered, the look of fever was on the man who lay upon the soft mats.

"How long has he been ill?" he asked the shaman.

"Two moons ago."

The chief motioned him closer.

"I know why you have come. There is nothing I can do to help your friends. You must tell them to leave this place and return to their own country. And you must go with them."

"But I am a Winyah, and my place is here with my tribe."

"The one called Touppa has turned the people against you. If you remain he will have you killed."

"I am not afraid of him."

"The elders will elect him chief, and the tribe will do what he tells them. You must go for even now your life is in danger. I will have the shaman send word to those who have taken to the forest that they shall not touch you until my soul has been taken by the spirits."

Francisco left the lodge. When he passed the first wife, she gave him a blank stare. At that moment, he knew he was dead to his tribe. And yet he also knew he would never be accepted by those he had lived among for the last five years. When he returned to the Spanish town he would tell the interpreters they must return to their people. For once hostility broke into open warfare, they would be treated as the enemy. They still had options that were not available to him.

Lucas, upon receiving the report from Francisco, called a meeting with Quexos, Gomez, and General Velasco.

"I will double the men under your command," he said to General Velasco. "I want some type of stockade built around the structures that have been completed.

"Quexos, I shall put you in charge of securing provisions for the settlement. Perhaps you could take the tender and the *Toledo* up the rivers and hunt in those areas. It will not be as dangerous as hunting game so close to their village."

"Gomez, we will have to stop work on other homes. All work must be centered on building a palisade. Until this wooden enclosure is completed many of our settlers must continue to live on the ships."

"I will keep order on the ships and be sure no one decides to mutiny and take the vessels back to Hispaniola," Gomez said.

"This hostility with the Indians will soon blow over. We will keep the two guilty men in the stockade until we can send them back to Hispaniola," General Velasco said.

* * *

Staying busy building and cutting timber in the forest had made life bearable for the slaves. Even Gomo, who had no love for his captors, had settled into the routine. The meaning of many Spanish words had now entered their vocabulary. But this sense of being semi-free came to an end when they were restricted to camp. The food that had been sufficient before became scant as the judge imposed rations on everyone. Gomo and his fellow tribesmen soon became restless. The Spanish sensed this, and they dealt even more harshly with the slaves.

When it seemed that the situation had finally stabilized, three events occurred that would decide the destiny of the colony. The chief of the Winyahs died. Word of this was brought to Francisco by one of the interpreters who had returned to live with the tribe. Then a second tragedy struck. A fever swept the town. It left many either dying or incapacitated in its wake.

On Saint Luke's Day, Father Montesinos came to see Francisco about a third tragedy.

"The judge has the fever."

"How long has he had it?"

"It came upon him two days ago."

"Why wasn't I told?"

"He gave orders to tell no one. He was afraid it would cause the people to lose heart."

"Why are you telling me now?"

"He is dying and has sent for you, Francisco. You must hurry for he will not be of this world much longer. I have already given him last rites."

In his private lodge, Lucas lay upon the bed that a carpenter had made for him. He was pale and his breathing was strained.

Francisco leaned over him, for barely a whisper came from his lips.

"Francisco, you are like the brother I never had. I am about to go meet my maker, but before my spirit leaves this body, I must ask for your forgiveness. It was wrong for me to keep you from your people for over five years while I pursed my selfish ambitions."

"Do not waste your words. You have treated me kindly and opened up a world that I would never have known."

As these words fell from Francisco's lips, Lucas soul passed from his body. It was the 18th day of October 1526. As word of his death spread through the town, many fell on their knees and prayed while others plotted.

* * *

The death of the judge provided an opportunity for Doncel and Bacan. With the settlement short of able- bodied men, they had been released to help work on the palisade which was almost complete. It did not take long for Doncel, the dominant of the two, to sow dissention among the garrison troops. Their commander was a disciplinary type, and his strictness had already pushed the men under his control to near mutiny. In Doncel they found someone willing to listen to their grievances, both real and imagined. When the men were ordered to assist the African slaves in completing the last portion of the palisade, they rebelled. Doncel quickly took command and with the help of Bacan and the others, they staged a coup d'etat. The commander, General Velasco, was seized and hanged, while Gomaz and Quexos were imprisoned in the stockade. The only thing that saved Francisco was that he fled to the church where he received the protection of Father Montesinos and the other priests. Even Doncel did not dare challenge the priests, for he knew his fellow mutineers would resist such a command.

One of the first acts of Doncel was to lead an expedition into Indian country. They attacked the Winyah village at dawn. The people fled into the woods. Those warriors who chose to stand and fight were slaughtered. The Spanish stole anything edible, including the stored corn. They arrived back in town to a hero's welcome, but their popularity was short-lived.

The Winyahs had been taken by surprise. Part of this weakness was because no new chief had been chosen. The attack brought a resolution. Touppa was chosen and he immediately started a campaign of attacking the Spanish at every opportunity. Not only were their movements restricted around the town, but any hunting trips upstream also came under attack. The spoils of war that had brought the coup leaders temporary popularity were soon exhausted, and everyone was put on rations again.

In the slave lodge, people were getting desperate. While Lucas had been a fairly benevolent master, Doncel and his lieutenant Bacan were brutal. Slaves were whipped for the slightest infraction. Two were hanged when they were caught stealing food. The slaves' anger reached a boiling point.

In times of crisis an individual will frequently be chosen to lead. In their midst was one who commanded such respect. Gomo was a person in whose veins ran the blood of a chief. He quickly filled the power vacuum in the group. Soon he was plotting rebellion with four men he had chosen as his lieutenants. He was smart enough to know there was no way they could subdue the entire town. There simply were not enough of them to accomplish that. Their numbers had been reduced to thirty men and some of these were not well. He could count on twenty who were still strong physically and eager to lash out against their tormentor. But Gomo planned more than vengeance. He was under no illusion they would ever be able to return home. He soon helped to dispel any such notions from the thoughts of his fellow slaves. He then presented them with a vision of creating a new tribe in the wildness. Over time the men accepted this vision as the final plans were made to escape.

The keeper of the slave lodge entrance opened it late one evening. He followed the other two soldiers inside where the slaves waited for their evening meal. Their arrival was like clockwork every day; an hour before dark after everyone else in Saint Michael had received their rations. The two carrying the pots were easily tripped, and rags were quickly stuffed into their mouths. While they struggled against the many hands which held them, chains were wrapped around their necks and their larynxes were crushed. In the meantime, Gomo had reached up and grabbed the doorkeeper by the rope belt that held the keys to the door and to their shackles. In one swift jerk he forced the man to the ground. His large black hands were around the Spaniard's throat before any scream could leave his mouth. He struggled for only a moment as those hands crushed everything they touched. The keys were removed and the door unlocked. According to plan everyone remained inside except the two who had been chosen to create a diversion. These slaves managed to make it to the lodge where Doncel and Bacan lived. This time of day the self-appointed leaders of the colony were always drunk on rum. This evening was no different. Using embers from a fire nearby, the two slaves set fire to a stack of dry pine straw and threw it on top of the roof made from marsh grass. This combustible material caught fire quickly and the fire spread across the roof while the slaves hurried back to the slave quarters.

Gomo had been watching and knew the first part of the plan was a success. When the two men returned, everyone slipped out of the lodge and ran into the darkness toward the part of town where the palisade was not yet completed. They killed the six soldiers who were standing guard. After taking the weapons off the bodies, Gomo and his men fled into the woods. Along the way they grabbed the wives of two settlers who happened to be in their path. The screams of the women were heard by the Spanish who had gathered around the burning lodge attempting to douse the flames. By the time they reacted, the Africans and their captive women had disappeared into the woods. By morning after severe beatings and multiple rapes, the women stopped their resistance and became subdued. Their screaming was replaced by silence. That night, Gomo and two of his lieutenants were able to swim in the darkness and steal the craft made by the settlers and christened the *Toledo*. The next day they used it to make several trips to a nearby river whose color was black from the organic matter that washed into the stream from the surrounding vegetation every time the rain fell. There Gomo made contact with a tribe called the Hooks. After giving the chief items they had found on the boat, they were granted permission to settle near the tribe's village. Some of the Indian maidens, attracted by these strange men, found reason to visit their settlement. In the years ahead there would be born children that carried African and Hook traits. The wives of the settlers knew they would never be returned, and after a while, some of their captors claimed their permanent attention and children were born. Thus more genes were added to the pool. After a generation they became a sub-tribe within the Hook family tree. They were never fully accepted nor never completely rejected. Their first chief was Gomo, and after that, his descendants who followed him as chief were known far and wide for their prowess in battle.

* * *

During the disruption of the fire, Francisco and Father Montesinos went to the stockade. Only one man was guarding it. The Catholic priest demanded that he release those held within its wall. When the guard hesitated, Montesinos threatened to bring the wrath of God down upon his head. No one could withstand the priest when he sounded like the prophet of the Almighty. He handed the keys to Francisco who released the prisoners. There were others besides Quexos and Gomez incarcerated, and all were eager to follow the lead of the legitimate authority.

While Doncel and Bacan were standing outside their burning lodge with the rest of the crowd, Quexos and the others approached. Doncel ordered his soldiers to arrest them, but his reign of terror had removed their loyalty. When Quexos countermanded the order and directed the soldiers to arrest Doncel and Bacan, they were immediately seized and put in irons. The crowd cheered, and the two men were placed in the stockade.

Now that proper authority had been restored, the people were united once again. A trial of the usurpers was held. They were found guilty of many crimes besides the charge of mutiny. The sentence was death. The two men were beheaded in a courtyard beside city hall. The next day Quexos sent for Francisco.

"I want you to go on a dangerous mission."

"What is it?"

"Take the heads of Doncel and Bacan to your village and present them to the chief. Tell them nothing of the mutiny and other crimes committed by these scoundrels. Instead, tell them we have punished these men for the rapes of the Indian women."

"I will go though it may not be enough to end hostility."

"Let me send twelve of my best armed men with you."

"That would only ensure my death as well as theirs. No, I must go alone. If I do not return within three days, that will mean I have been killed."

"May God go with you."

After placing the two heads in a large leather bag, Francisco went to see Father Montesinos.

"I have come for your blessing."

It was an acknowledgement by Francisco that he had at last gone from pretending to a real acceptance of the Christian faith. It was only natural that he should do so for he had already crossed a great cultural divide.

"Kneel my son."

The priest placed his hand upon Francisco's head and raised the other toward the heavens. Then he prayed to his god on behalf of the man who knelt before him. When it was over, he placed a silver cross around Francisco's neck. It was the one that had been given to him by his mentor at the abbey where he studied for the priesthood.

On the way to the village, one of Francisco's hands clutched the leather bag, while the other touched the silver cross suspended on a chain around his neck. He hoped the power in the gift from the priest would safeguard him against the evil spirit that controlled the thoughts of Touppa.

The avenues between the lodges were empty of people. The smell of death permeated the camp. An old woman came out of a lodge and approached him.

"What happened here?"

"An evil has visited our people, and the shaman has not had the power to expel it."

"Where is your chief?"

"His spirit has departed him and his bones lie in a mass grave with his warriors."

"Who has authority to speak for the tribe?"

"No one has been chosen."

"Where is the shaman?"

She pointed to a lodge set far apart from all the others. He went directly to it. The shaman was outside stirring a pot of boiling water into which he had placed every herb of which he had knowledge. So far this treatment had been ineffective in stopping the fever which had taken many lives. But he continued, even though he had lost faith in its healing power. If he stopped, then the people would have nothing to place their faith in, and that was unacceptable. He looked up when Francisco approached.

"I have come with the heads of the evil ones."

He dumped the heads from the satchel onto the ground.

"Why do you bring these to me?" the shaman asked, as he stared at the heads whose eyes seemed to stare back at him.

"There is no one else in authority to give them to."

Suddenly a wise thought crossed the shaman's mind.

"Wait here," he said.

He picked up the two heads by their hair and then disappeared into the forest. It was late afternoon before he returned, and with him came twenty warriors. Francisco at first thought they meant him harm, but this was soon dispelled when the leader of the group spoke.

"The shaman has communicated with the spirits. They said the cause of our sickness was the evil allowed into our lives by the men whose heads you have brought us, and also by an evil spirit that dwelt in Touppa. Now they are all dead and the evil is buried. The shaman has told us that a chief must be selected or the evil will rise out of the ground and strike us again. We have chosen you. Your father was a chief with a clean spirit within him. During his time, we prospered and mutiplied. The blood that runs in the Datha veins also runs in yours. Like him, you are a descendant of the god, Baldar. The good spirits will be pleased with our choice."

Francisco thought of the blessing of Father Montesinos. Surely this must be the Christian God's answer.

"I will accept. But we must move our village to the land where our ancestors went when they faced a crisis. When we have completely healed, we shall return to our ancestral home."

The next morning he sent to the town one of the interpreters to inform Quexos what had occurred. The interpreter took with him a skin filled with corn as a sign that the hostility between them was ended. Quexos was elated with the news. His men could now hunt in the areas outside the town without fear. However, his expectations that the Indians would furnish him with sufficient corn and meat to get through the winter were dashed when Francisco sent him word that any food he sent would be out of the mouths of his own people. And this he could not do. This bad news was compounded when a hunting party brought him news that the village was deserted and no traces of the Indians were found. Without the craft constructed by the settlers, he did not have the ability to search the areas they may have moved too.

* * *

It was the coldest winter in a century. Although the Winyah camp was free of the fever, they were constantly on the verge of starvation. There was no corn reserve and the animals had disappeared deep into the forest. But somehow with the food from the marshes, ducks from the air, and the occasional deer the group survived.

Unlike the Indians, the settlers were without the skills necessary to endure the cold period. The ships could not be warmed and there were not enough lodges in town to accommodate everyone. A council was held and it was decided to abandon the town. Even though it was the middle of February, an attempt must be made to reach Hispaniola. Every possible source of food was collected. When it was loaded onto the *Santa Cathalina* and *Bretorn*, the gruesome task of digging up the body of Lucas was completed. The council, at Father Montesinos' urging, had made the decision to return his remains to his wife. It was loaded onto the tender, which was attached by ropes to the *Bretorn*. It was snowing when the ships sailed out into the bay and then into the ocean.

A warrior brought word of sails in the bay. From the edge of the woods near where their camp lay, Francisco and his people watched the ships enter the ocean. Although it was freezing, they remained there until the ships disappeared from view.

* * *

The passengers were sick and discouraged. Ice covered the deck and people froze to death during the night. On the third day at sea a storm came upon them and the ropes that held the tender to the ship snapped. The passengers watched in horror as it was swallowed up by the sea. They were helpless to save it and the body of Lucas Vazquez de Ayllon. Two days later the *Bretorn* began taking on water. The passengers and crew were transferred to the *Santa Cathalina*. They watched as the *Bretorn* was also claimed by the ocean's floor.

There were no ships on the horizon until they were three days from Santo Domingo. A passing merchant ship gave them a small quantity of food and water before sailing on to its destination. The supplies filled their stomachs, if only for a day. But the real change was in the morale. They now knew that soon their ship would be in a safe harbor.

* * *

Word reached Ana at her home in Puerto de la Plata that the *Santa Cathalina* had returned. She had her carriage made ready, and then she gathered the children. Within an hour they were on their way to Santo Domingo. By the time she arrived, the excitement created by the ship's return had receded, and there were no longer spectators milling around. But there was an officer of the court waiting to serve a writ upon her for the seizure of the ship, the plantation, and the gold mine. The agent had wasted no time when he discovered the *Santa Cathalina* in the harbor and heard the story of Lucas Vazquez de Ayllon's death. He was not a man without a conscience, but in his mind there was no place for sentimentality in business affairs.

After being served with the legal process, Ana had the driver take her and the children to their home that overlooked the port in Santa Domingo. It had been some time since she had stayed there and no servants were about. They would not arrive from the plantation until later that day. She took her children out onto the veranda. With her arms around them, she explained their father would not be coming home. Afterwards, she sent the driver into town to find someone from the ship to come and speak with her. He returned with Quexos and Gomez.

"Spare no details," she said to them.

It was difficult for them to describe the last days of her husband's life and what had happened to his body. As they were finishing their conversation, Father Montesinos appeared. Ana broke down for a moment, then regained her composure. The captains took their leave, and Ana once again broke into tears.

'We can be sure that the judge's soul is with our savior," Montesinos said.

These words seemed to bring her some comfort. She showed him the legal process that had been served upon her when she arrived at the docks. Montesinos initially went into a rage, but soon realized this only made the situation worse for the widow. After he departed, several servants from the plantation arrived. Soon the house was filled with the sounds of life as rooms were dusted and linens washed. The smell of food from the kitchen filled the house. The children, too young to understand what death really meant, went to the back yard and played. Ana sat on the veranda for an hour. She wanted to be alone to grieve for a longer period, but she would have to do that later. Right now she must send for the family lawyer and find out what steps could be taken to preserve the family assets from creditors.

Inside the house, the servants had their own worries. Most were African slaves, and they knew what happened when a master died. Slaves were sometimes sold. They were now in a suspended state until the estate was settled. Although their worries were different from their mistress, both were centered on what would happen when the creditors came knocking on the door.

The lawyer arrived the next morning. He joined Ana on the veranda for a cup of Spanish coffee and a piece of toast with molasses.

"It could have been worse," he said. "Thank goodness, your husband was very concerned about having his affairs in order before he sailed."

He handed her a legal document. Not being learned in the law, she was dependent upon the lawyer to explain what the terms in it meant.

"Everything was left to the children. You and I are named as trustees."

"What does that mean?"

"The unsecured creditor can't touch the property."

"What about the legal papers served on me yesterday?"

"They are against property that was secured by a legal instrument. It gives that particular creditor a lien against the plantation, gold mine, and the ship that survived the venture. But the agent for the creditor specially waived any right to the home here and the one in Puerto de la Plata. He also waived any claim to the sugar mill. The unsecured creditors of course will try to place liens against those assets, but they will not be successful. During the term of this trusteeship, which will last until the youngest child reaches twenty-one, you have the right to all rents and profits."

Her mind was calculating how much that would mean. It would not be a huge sum, but it would be sufficient to care for her children and maintain her status in society.

"Thank you for coming on such short notice."

"I considered Lucas to be more than a client. He was a personal friend. I will answer any legal process. You do not need to worry about the judges. Lucas was well respected by them all."

After the lawyer left, Ana went into her bedroom and collapsed. A doctor was called. He gave her a potion to make her sleep. She stayed in bed for three days. Then one morning she shook off the covers, ordered the servants to pour her a bath, and made plans to return to the family home in Puerto de la Plata. The time for mourning had passed. She must get back and oversee the production at the sugar mill. This was the asset that could produce a steady income to support her family. The idea of finding another husband of means for support did not cross her mind. No one would ever share her bed again. Her virtue as a widow would remain intact until her death many years later after her son had become a successful businessman and the Mayor of Puerto de la Plata. Her daughter would marry into the aristocratic society on the island. Neither would ever see the land of their parents' birth, nor the place where their father died trying to plant a settlement upon a terrain near a bay: a beautiful estuary that lay along the eastern seaboard upon which one day a great civilization would rise.

THE
AFTERMATH

It was the year 1540, and to the south of Francisco's people, the Spanish conquistador, Hernando De Soto, was making his way across the landscape near a region where the English would later establish a settlement named Charles Town. He found the land sparsely populated. Many sites where villages once stood were vacant. Items shown him during his travels in this region by the few Indians residing there were a cross, dagger, beads, and some goods made by the natives that were imitations of things that could be found in Spain. These, a De Soto chronicler wrote, must have come from Lucas Vazques de Ayllon's settlement that the Indians said was two days travel to the north along the coast. The writer wrote down that De Soto believed the emptiness of the land was caused from malaria spread by African slaves brought by the Spanish settlers to Saint Michael on the Gualdape near the Bay of Saint John the Baptist. De Soto sent a small contingent of men to explore the site of Lucas's town, but they were turned back by heavy rains when they reached the rivers of the Santee tribe. On their return the officer in charge reported contact with some Indians who spoke Spanish. The warriors said they were from the Winyah tribe. They attempted to seize the Indians to bring them before De Soto, but they fled into the woods and evaded capture.

* * *

On the banks of the Gualdape, Francisco received word about the presence of the Spanish explorer to the south of Sioux territory. He advised his people to avoid them. He knew his tribe was weak and could not resist any encroachment. He remembered when the settlers had sailed away from the bay many years ago and left behind a disease that ravished the land. It even reached the Datha in Duhare. The ruler and many of his people had succumbed. By the time the sickness left the land, the confederation was destroyed. But his people had survived on the land near the beaches where they sustained themselves on foods readily available from the marsh. Finally they had grown strong enough to return to the site of their ancestral home near the settlement the Spanish called Saint Michael. Recently they had moved once again. This time they established a village on the Sampas River. The region was empty because the Sampas people had migrated farther south years earlier in an attempt to avoid the sickness of the Spanish settlement. Shortly after his people established their new base, their old habitat became the home of the Waccamaws who had fled from their territory in the north because of pressure from a more warlike tribe. The Waccamaws called their new home Hobcaw, which, in their language, meant "the land between the waters."

Sometimes at night Francisco would dream of the things he had seen when in Hispaniola and Spain. But he did not mention this to his wife or ten children. They would not have been able to comprehend any of it. As the years had progressed, the thin layer of civilization was peeled away and almost completely disappeared. He did not remember the things Father Montesinos taught him. The silver cross he traded long ago to a tribe that lived to the south of the Bay of Saint John. He did not have regrets. His lodge was full of grandchildren now and there was once again sufficient food for everyone.

On the first day of spring in the year 1550, Francisco died at the ripe old age of fifty. He had no way of knowing how his short stay in Spain had altered the gene pool of the royal families of Europe. The countess' child would wear a crown. Unknown to this king, the neighboring ruler would be a half brother, for although Isabel died in childbirth, the infant had survived.

The Winyahs continued over the years to have some contact with Europeans. In 1561 Admiral Villafone sailed into the Bay of Saint John and then up the Gualdape where he anchored near the old site of Saint Michael. He had settlers on board. He stayed for a few days. Then he decided that the heirs of Lucas might still have a claim to the area, so he sailed away. In later years the French occasionally sailed into the Bay of Saint John and up the Gualdape. Their visits were always short and their trade goods limited. Eventually both Spanish and French captains would use San Roman, the land that lay at the north entrance of the bay, as a site to repair their ships. They also ventured into the bay on occasion and up the river to trade with the Waccamaws. But no one attempted to settle the area until the British decided to expand their colony at Charleston to areas farther north.

THE
BRITISH

Jacques Marshall's name reflected his mixed cultural roots. In his blood ran the traits of two great nations. He was born of a mother whose noble family fled France during the reign of terror against the Huguenots and settled in Belfast, Ireland. Her father, though destitute having lost his estate in Bordeaux, was able to obtain a position at the university. With the stipend paid by this center of learning, he had purchased a modest home where he lived alone with his three daughters, the mother of the girls having passed away before the flight from France. Unable to provide a dowry for his daughters, he was forced to seek husbands for them from the local merchant class.

When Jacques mother, Felicia, reached the age of sixteen, arrangements were made for a marriage contract with the Marshalls, a Scotch-Irish family who owned an export business. Their oldest son, Kinsey, an industrious lad was good at business, and that is how it came to be that the young pair married. Shortly afterwards, Kinsey's father died and the responsibility for the business fell upon him. Within nine months the additional responsibility of a son was added. They named him Jacques after his French grandfather.

Jacques was a child who loved his letters and soon surpassed all the children of his age in the neighborhood. His father's attempts to interest him in the export business came to no avail as his heart was set upon going to the university. Through the effort of his grandfather, the young man was admitted at the age of fifteen. Everything seemed bright for his future until the plague struck.

The plague started in the workhouses operated by his father. It spread until many citizens of the town had either died, or suffered the loss of family members. The disease was unusually harsh to Jacques. The reaper swept away his mother and then his father. Before the plague had run its course, his grandfather and aunts were placed beneath the sod. Without family or money he was overnight almost destitute. He sold the few assets of the estate that were awarded to him and booked passage on a ship. The vessel was sailing for a British settlement named Charles Town on the coast of a province called Carolina. There he hoped to carve out a new life for himself and leave behind the pain and suffering that had scarred his young soul.

* * *

The ship entered the harbor at Charles Town on a beautiful bright spring morning in the year 1679. When the anchor dropped, Jacques was rowed to shore with several other passengers. Once he placed his feet on the wharf, his lungs breathed in air that had a quality about it different from the old world. It wasn't the smell of the marsh or even the ocean that caught his immediate attention, but the smell of excitement. People scurried about as if there weren't enough hours in the day to complete whatever task they had set for themselves. It was a type of energy he had never encountered in Europe. He knew the right choice had been made in coming to this new world.

After finding a boarding house, he stored his baggage, and placed his valuables, which included a leather pouch of gold coins, in the proprietor's safe. Then he went back to the commercial district that lay along the harbor to look for a position. Never having been employed, he was not sure how to approach the matter. The first establishment to catch his attention was a warehouse near the docks. There seemed to be a lot of activity there. Perhaps they were looking to hire. When he entered the front area of the building, he observed an elderly man shouting orders, using words that were a mixture of French and English.

"Excuse me, Sir," he said as he approached the man. "I am looking for employment. Do you have a position available?"

The man had an expression that looked like someone had just slapped him across the face. He just stood there and gawked at Jacques. Perhaps he did not speak English well. Jacques repeated his question in French. The man broke out in a smile.

"I am Richie Beza, the owner of this establishment," he said. "Where are you from?"

"Belfast."

"How did you learn to speak French?"

"My mother was from France."

Before he could contain his tongue, Jacques was telling the man about his family. The old man did not seem to mind. He listened to every word for a substantial amount of time before finally interrupting him.

"Can you write your letters, and do you know numbers?"

When Jacques answered in the affirmative, he was hired on the spot. The old man took him back into his office and showed him some ledgers, then handed him several bills of goods. After explaining what he wanted him to do with this information, he went back out onto the floor of the warehouse where he started barking orders to his other employees.

* * *

On the seventh week after his arrival in Charles Town, Jacques saw her. She had accompanied her family's housekeeper to the business. They brought a basket of food for her father. It was his birthday and the basket was filled with his favorite treats. She was the most beautiful thing he had ever seen. Standing several inches over five feet, she was taller than most women. She had color in her complexion instead of the milky appearance he had encountered in the young ladies of Belfast. Watching her smile at her father from a distance, he noticed how her lips parted just enough to show an attractive mouth. She must have felt his presence, for during her conversation with her father she suddenly turned and looked in his direction. Then she turned her attention back to her father. He hoped the father would bring her into the office and introduce them, but she departed without even glancing back in his direction. When Beza returned, he brought the basket which he shared with Jacques, but for some reason he never mentioned his daughter.

* * *

"Mama, please send father a note telling him to invite that young man he has hired as a scribe to the dinner party tonight," Camille said.

Constance looked at her daughter. She was fifteen and this was the first time she had expressed an interest in any man. It was about time, for most girls living in this speck of civilization that clung to the coast were married by sixteen. She had already learned about the young man and his history from her husband. Several weeks ago he had come home and announced that he had hired a scribe to assist him. He said Jacques would be a great help. The paper work was requiring too much of his time and diverting his attention from more important matters. Their discussion in the privacy of their bedroom extended to the issue of whether this young man was an acceptable mate for their daughter, Camille. Although Constance knew Jacques was educated, he had no wealth, nor prospects of an inheritance. There were other suitors available who were men of property that had an interest in Camille. But she had not given them the slightest encouragement. Constance was exasperated that her oldest daughter seemed unconcerned that time was slipping away and with it the opportunity to find a proper husband.

When Beza received the note he read it and then placed the piece of paper in his coat pocket. Among the guest invited to the dinner party was a widower: a merchant who had lost his wife only last year and who needed a new mate. He also had three young children that needed a mother. At twenty-six, he was a little old for Camille. But because of his wealth, Constance and Beza had overlooked the age difference, and the fact that he had a reputation as a hard drinker. Now Beza faced a dilemma. If he invited Jacques, Camille's attention might be diverted from Richard. And one of the prime reasons for the birthday dinner was to place Camille and Richard together in a social setting. But if he ignored the note, which he knew Camille had instigated, then she would pout all night. That certainly would not make a good impression on Richard. After weighing the matter, he extended the invitation to Jacques.

Beza could tell by the expression on Jacques' face that he was excited at the prospect. He suspected why the young man wanted to come, for he had noticed him staring at his daughter the day she had visited the warehouse. He saw a conflict with his wife on the horizon, for although he was amenable to this lad as a son-in-law, he knew Constance was focused on marrying their daughter to someone with assets.

Granted permission to leave work early, Jacques went straight to the boarding house. There he paid the owner a few coins to bring a tin bath tub to his room and fill it with hot soapy water. He bathed in it for sometime to remove the dirt and sweat from his body. Personal hygiene was not something that was given a lot of attention in this new colony. In fact, Jacques had fallen into the practice of bathing only when the scent of his body became too much for even him to stand. He located some proper clothing in his trunk and had the servant downstairs press it with an iron heated in the fireplace. The owner, caught up in the mood of the moment, did a fair job with a pair of steel scissors in trimming his hair to an acceptable length and giving him a shave. Afterwards, Jacques looked in the mirror downstairs and was satisfied that his appearance was acceptable.

* * *

Beza's home was a two-story house on King Street. It had a large veranda encircling three quarters of the bottom structure that was covered by a large balcony. Jacques was met at the entrance by a doorman who was an African recently purchased at the slave market. As Jacques stepped into the parlor, he encountered Beza who introduced him to Constance. Later, he was introduced to the merchants, their wives and the only persons in the room unattached, Richard and Melinda.

Melinda was the sixteen year-old daughter of a merchant at the party. Of English origin, she had an aristocratic air about her. Immediately upon being introduced, she engaged Jacques in conversation about topics that were above the intellectual level of the other guests but not beyond his grasp. It was while they were so engaged that Camille stepped into the room. Although she pretended not to notice Jacques, in fact she was furious. She did not like Melinda whom she found to be pretentious. Like a good French Huguenot, she felt culturally superior to this English woman. It did not matter that the wealth of Melinda's family far exceeded her own. Eventually, Camille's father took her by the hand and guided her in Jacques direction.

"Jacques, I want you to meet my daughter," Beza said. "Camille, this is Jacques Marshall, the new clerk I have mentioned."

Though in fact the name had never been the topic in conversations between the two, she tried to think of a proper response. Camille responded with a lie.

"My father has had some very kind words to say about you," she said in French thereby attempting to exclude Melinda from the conversation.

"I am sure he has exaggerated my attributes," he replied in French.

Melinda not to be isolated quickly broke into the conversation using her English in a way that sent a message to both that implied conversations should be conducted in the official language of the colony. Jacques had no experience with women other than family. However, even he could recognize that these two did not like each another. But he did not have the slightest clue that the present disturbance between them was over who would have his attention this night.

The table arrangements had Jacques seated across from Melinda and her father. Camille was seated across from Richard at the other end of the table. Though Camille and Jacques were on opposite ends of the table, eye contact was still possible between the two.

Camille showered attention on Richard and kept glancing to see if Jacques noticed. And he did. However, this feminine device, though it inspired the jealously intended, had a negative effect on her objective. Jacques assumed that Richard was where Camille's interest lay and any attention by him toward her would be a waste of time. Melinda showered Jacques with her attentiveness, but it was not because she had any long-term interest in him. She had set her sights on marrying Richard, who was presently enjoying playing the field. Meanwhile, at the other end of the table, the cleavage that Richard was forced to look upon across the table inspired him to consider a deflowering of Camille as he had many other young ladies in the colony, even before the death of his wife.

Melinda's father became part of a lively conversation on the prospects of accumulating wealth from the expansion of the Indian trade. He believed now was the time to send traders into other regions along the coast. He pointed out that constant expansion was necessary. The tribes around Charles Town had suffered depopulation as a result of pestilence and from the fact that many had been sold as slaves to the West Indies.

"Besides," he said, "trading with Indians is better than enslaving them. We have learn from experience that attempts to keep the Indians as slaves on our plantations has only resulted in disaster. At every opportunity, they flee into the woods,and are adopted into those tribes that have not yet come under British domination."

Soon the other merchants became involved in the conversation about trading versus enslavement. Jacques listened closely to the words that were being spoken. Sometime during the evening an idea occurred to him about ways to accumulate his own fortune. The idea continued to grow in his mind, until several weeks later he was ready to act upon it.

* * *

The business proposition was a sound one, though Beza found it surprising that a lad of only seventeen could have come up with it, and have the daring to propose it to him. He was impressed with the lad. Jacques was willing to put forth the necessary capital for his share that under the terms of the agreement would be an equal partnership. He had not realized Jacques had such funds available to him. Constance would be happy to learn that the boy was not a pauper. This agreement provided that Jacques would go north and establish trade with the Indians. He would take with him a quantity of trade goods and return a few months later with items that could be transported for sale in Europe. The venture was not without risks. Part was economic, and part was a matter of personal safety. But if successful, it could establish a permanent flow of wealth into the pockets of both men.

Once the legal documents were signed, steps were taken for securing the merchandise, as well as supplies to survive during this perilous journey into the unknown. It was not a place that had never had a European footprint. The Spanish and French had landed in the area long ago, but they had never established a permanent presence.

* * *

Jacques was excited about the maps. He could not believe his luck. A ship captain whose vessel lay in the harbor had allowed him to copy three maps of the region where he planned to establish an outpost for trade with the

Indians. There had also been copies of journals. Some of the journals were in Spanish and others in French. He had no trouble with the French ones, but he could not decipher the Spanish ones. Luck was again with him for he found a Spaniard living within the township. It had cost him a couple of gold coins to get a translation but it was a wise investment. He spent every night studying the materials. When the time arrived for his departure, he was well versed about the region.

Camille did not go to the docks to tell him good-bye. In fact, she had not seen him since the dinner party two months ago. During that same time, Richard had pursued her. She was not sure he had marriage on his mind. Of course, during his courtship she was always protected by having a chaperone present.

Standing in the widow's watch, Camille had a clear view of the harbor, and the vessel upon which Jacques would sail. As she watched the ship depart the harbor, her heart ached, a feeling she had not experienced before. She now wished she had swallowed her pride and gone down to the dock to wish him good-bye. But she had not, and the expectation that she would see him from her perch on the roof did not materialize. The distance was too great for her to distinguish him from the other figures boarding. She could place part of the blame on her mother, who had discouraged her from going to the dock–though this provided little comfort.

Now back in her room, she took the Huguenot Bible off the dresser. Holding in her hands this sacred text, she prayed for Jacques' safe return. She would continue this prayer everyday until he was once again in her presence.

* * *

The method of departure had been discussed many times between Beza and Jacques. What route should he take to get to their objective. Should he proceed overland or by sea. This decision was made easier when an outbreak of hostilities commenced between the Sampas Tribe and the British that September on the outskirts of Charles Town. It just so happened that at the same time there was a scheduled departure of a ship for Jamestown. Passage was booked on the vessel. It would enter the bay in the North Channel where it would discharge Jacques and his supplies along with the two canoes stored on the ship.

Unfortunately for Jacques, the ship arrived at the Bay of Saint John at low tide. The captain, having been paid in full, had no desire to delay his trip to Jamestown by waiting for high tide. So over the protest of Jacques, he had his crew place the canoes in the water. After packing the vessels with the trade goods, he watched his former passenger paddle to the northern lip of the estuary in his canoe with the second craft tied to it. Jacques almost capsized twice, but he was finally able to land his boats. Although they were heavily loaded, after a struggle he pulled them far enough onto the sandy beach to prevent them from being taken out to sea by the approaching high tide. Since it was getting late in the afternoon, Jacques decided to build a fire and wait until morning before entering the bay.

As he sat by the fire that evening, he studied his maps. The place where he beached the canoes was noted on the charts as San Roman. He decided that the old Spanish name did not fit the present British era. He took out his writing tool and started sketching a new map. The Spanish designation was replaced with the name North Island, a name that would forever after be used even when the adventures of Jacques faded from human memory. The name San Roman would continue to have vitality in the region, however. The term Cape Romain, sometimes spelled Romania, would be attached to an area farther south and cause great confusion later for historians of the region.

* * *

Stalmar's village sat upon high ground across the bay from Hobcaw. The terrain on which his people lived was the same area that many years earlier had been the land of the Sampas. But his tribe, the Winyahs, had been in possession now for over a hundred years. The Sampas still maintained contact with the area through trade and frequently visited the river where they believed the spirits of their ancestors lived. The Winyahs feared the Sampas would one day return to claim the land, for this fellow Sioux tribe still treated the Winyahs as only guests upon their river.

The excited utterances in the village square woke Stalmar even before a warrior entered his lodge with news that a white man was camped upon the sand at the entrance to the bay. He arose and with the arrogance that his people expected in their chief, strode to where they had gathered.

"It is one of them," said the warrior who had spotted the campfire during the early morning hours. "I crept up from the sand dunes and watched him as he slept. He brought many trade goods which he has stored in two canoes. My fellow warriors wanted to kill him and take the goods, but I knew that you would be angry if we acted without your permission."

Stalmar let this information soak into his brain and as it was processed, he thought of what action he should direct his people to take. Should they attack the man and take his goods, or should they extend the hand of friendship in hope that others would follow. At present, the tribe was dependent on the Sampas to bring European items up the trail from a settlement called Charles Town. They always required many cured skins in exchange for things the Winyahs desired, such as axes. Perhaps it was best to welcome this stranger, for the hand of friendship could always be withdrawn.

"We shall go to the mouth of the bay and meet this white man," he said. "And we shall bring him to our village before our Sioux brethren, the Waccamaws, discover his presence."

An hour later, four of the tribe's largest canoes were launched from the mouth of the Sampas River. In the boats were seated Stalmar and his most fiercest warriors. He did not bring goods for trade because it was important that he convince this trader to return with him. As his canoes sped toward their destination, he thought about the place the stranger had chosen to spend the night. Once white men from many different tribes had visited that site and repaired their ships there. The Winyahs had always used these opportunities to trade with them. Sometimes the strangers had even sailed up the river of the Waccamaws. He only knew this from the stories his grandfather had told him, for it had been three generations since the last ship was seen at the entrance to the bay. No one knew why they stopped coming, but they had.

Jacques was still sitting by the campfire eating breakfast that September morning and pondering his next step of contacting the Indians when he saw the canoes approaching. He instinctively reached for his musket, then released his hand from the comfort of the cold steel barrel. If they were hostile, the firing of one shot would only serve to enrage them. He stood beside the fire and waited.

After the canoes had been beached next to the ones that belonged to the white man, Stalmar led his warriors toward the campfire. As he approached, he saw a flicker of fear in the man's eyes, but he also saw determination. He was surprised at the stranger's youth. He had expected a much older person to be in charge of canoes loaded with such valuable articles.

Jacques held out two frying pans filled with hot biscuits and sliced ham. The Indians accepted this peace offering and sat down at the campfire with him. Soon Stalmar and Jacques were communicating in sign language. The chief was able to make Jacques understand what he wanted. It didn't take long for Jacques to pack his personal gear. The fleet of canoes was paddled down the deep channel until they reached a small peninsula that jutted into the water at a spot where the mouth of a small river emptied into the bay. There, upon high ground, sat the village. He was greeted with great fanfare, and was taken to an empty lodge where the warriors deposited his goods. While the Indians watched, he unpacked his merchandise. Later, intense bargaining began. Jacques knew his goods were limited, but the resources of the Indians were inexhaustible. So he set the price high for each item. The warriors were soon scouting the woods for the animals whose skins he required, while the women were digging in the ground for sassafras roots, an item in great demand in Europe.

Word of Jacques' presence soon spread, and the Sioux tribes that lived on the other rivers that flowed into the bay began to send delegations to Stalmar's village. Jacques used this opportunity to write extensively about them in his journal.

The Hook tribe lived near the mouth of a river that twisted and curled its way up the landscape into the interior. He was particularly fascinated by a group of them that he called the Black Hooks because they had characteristics that resembled the African slaves he had seen in Charles Town. One day when they were visiting, Jacques accepted an invitation to accompany them back to their village. As they paddled up the river that was the lifeline of their people, Jacques made sketches of it and named it Black River.

Stalmar was glad to see Jacques return from his visit to the Hooks, for he worried they would steal him away from the Winyah. This perceived threat so frightened Stalmar that he laid awake at night thinking about how he could keep this white man in his camp. Then one morning a thought occurred to him. He would give his sister to Jacques.

* * *

Bright Star was a beautiful child who had only ten moons ago turned fifteen, the age at which she could be promised to a warrior. The first man who had stepped forward would not have been her choice. He already had three wives, whom he was known to beat on occasion. Bright Star knew this to be true for her older sister was one of them. When her brother spoke to her of marrying the trader, she was not unhappy about such an arrangement. She, along with the other unattached girls, had wondered if the trader would choose a wife from among them. And each had secretly hoped she would be the one. The stranger, being different in appearance from others, acted as a magnet to the women. And of course, they dreamed of possessing the goods that his lodge contained.

The day Jacques turned eighteen, Stalmar offered his sister to him as a wife. Jacques was at a loss for words for he had no inkling that such a proposal would be forthcoming. As the chief watched him, Jacques pondered what consequences would follow rejecting the offer. He tried to delay, but the chief pressed him for an answer.

Bright Star received the news from her brother. She was pleased and knew all her friends would be filled with envy. The time was set only three days away, for her brother was anxious to cement the bonds between his tribe and the trader.

Now that the decision was made, Jacques thoughts turned to the chief's sister. He had noticed her his first day in the village. She had stood out from the others because her features were in sharp contrast to the other women. Her hair held a reddish tint and her eyes were hazel.

* * *

Jacques felt like a pagan standing before the chief and receiving his blessing. Then the shaman danced around the couple shaking gourds filled with beans, which made an awful noise. The blood of animals was spread upon his bare chest, after which he was separated from his bride and taken to the lodge where he was told to wait. Alone, he washed the blood which smelled awful from his body. He lay upon the primitive bed that was composed of animal skins on a dirt floor. In the corner of the lodge a smoking fire blazed, driving away the chill of the evening.

While Jacques waited, Bright Star was being scrubbed by the older women of her village. When they had completed that task, they rubbed her body with the scents of the forest and the peeling of wild fruit that grew nearby. Afterwards, they dressed her in the skin of a white doe as a symbol of her purity.

It was dark by the time they left her at the opening to the lodge. Bright Star entered ready to shed her innocence. She had been given no instruction from the women, but she had observed the animals and thought a man would act no different. She saw his figure lying upon the skins near the fire. She lay down beside him and covered them with the furry skin of a black bear. In the darkness they touched, at first hesitantly, then more aggressively until the desire of each was kindled. She slipped out of the doeskin garment and then helped him to remove his clothing. Soon the passions of youth overcame their nervousness and inexperience.

* * *

It was time to go. The first frost of winter had fallen last night and Jacques knew he must reach Charles Town before the weather turned too cold for travel. His trade goods were gone and had been replaced by stacks of tanned skins and mounds of sassafras roots. There was also a small quantity of gold and silver that tribesmen had relinquished to him in exchange for colored beads and other trinkets. Stalmar had agreed to furnish four Winyah canoes and men to help him take his goods to Charles Town.

Bright Star was distraught that he was leaving. The child she carried within her had just begun to show through the skin garments. Although she would soon be a mother, her emotions were that of a fifteen-year-old who was not yet sure of her man. She worried that when he returned to his world, he would not come back to hers. In this worry she was not without a reason, for she often saw that faraway look in his eyes. She instinctively knew that another woman existed in his world whom he was anxious to see.

It wasn't that Jacques didn't have feelings for Bright Star. But she was from a primitive tribe and he could never introduce her into his culture. While that might seem cold to some viewing it from a distance, it was the way society operated. In his mind, the fact that he had undergone a pagan ritual to solidify his trade with the Indians did not mean that he was really married to her. He knew that the child she carried would never be accepted outside her tribe. None of this meant that he did not plan to return. He wanted to open up a permanent trading post near the bay with the profits from this adventure. In time he planned to expand his business into the interior where the resources had not been touched by traders. The genes of Jacques' father for business, which had been buried deep within him, had now come to the forefront of his brain. These genes for business would, for the rest of his life, dominate his every move.

An unbelievable blessing occurred. Only a few hours after they started their journey on the open sea, a British ship sailing toward Charles Town spotted the canoes. It changed course and the captain granted Jacques' request to take him and his cargo aboard. With a friendly farewell,

Jacques sent the Indian braves back to their village after he had secured his own canoes on deck. The expression on the Indians' faces showed they were happy to return home for the waves of the oceans had clearly frightened them.

* * *

At first, Beza did not recognize Jacques when he stepped into the warehouse. It was only when Jacques spoke a greeting in French that the sweet quality of his words and the tone of his voice caused Beza to call out his name.

"Jacques, you have returned."

"I have and with much success."

Beza, a man with much business experience, was taken aback by the richness of the cargo that now lay on the floor of his warehouse. He was amazed by how this newly acquired wealth had been accumulated in such a short span of time.

Camille was busy helping her mother, Constance, decorate the downstairs for a Christmas party the family was having that evening when a boy delivered a note from Beza. Constance read the message out loud.

"So the lad has returned," Constance said before leaving the room.

Camille remained alone in the parlor. Her emotions were torn between the excitement of Jacques' return, and a fear that he might not desire her. She knew his success would spread quickly and prominent families would immediately push their eligible daughters toward him. Available, educated, and prosperous men were in short supply in the settlement.

It was rare that Constance would admit that she had exercised an error of judgment, but this was one of those occasions. She had not recognized the ambitious nature of Jacques that lay just beneath the surface. Nor had she listened to her husband's advice on the boy's character. She had allowed herself to be blinded by the prospects of Richard marrying Camille. Now that possibility had disappeared with the man's marriage to Melinda. There were no other eligible men in the colony whom she would consider suitable for her daughter. So she must scheme to get Jacques' proposal before her friends secured it for their own daughters. Unfortunately, there were several eligible girls who would be at the party tonight. She wished they had not been invited. There was no use in wasting her energy worrying over that now. It was impossible to withdraw the invitations. Instead, she must see that Camille was the most attractive. Despite the fact that she was a strong Huguenot in her faith, this would not prevent her from using her daughter's budding sexuality to ensnare Jacques.

The proprietor was glad to see Jacques return to his boarding house. The largest and most expensive room was available. He had his servant take up the tin tub and fill it with hot water. It did not take long for the harsh lye soap to remove the months of accumulated dirt and grim from his body. It took a little longer to get the caked soil from beneath his fingernails and out of his hair. When this was finished, the proprietor clipped his hair and trimmed his beard. The local tailor came with new articles of clothing. By that evening, when Jacques looked into the mirror, he was pleased with his image. He realized for the first time that he had left a boy and returned a man, not just emotionally but also physically.

Constance had her personal servant help her with Camille. They worked most of the day remaking a dress and styling her hair. When the task was completed, Constance was satisfied that no other young female could compare with her daughter.

Camille was confident when she looked into the mirror. It was good, that mother and I are in agreement on the goal for tonight.

Jacques was the last guest to arrive. When he was announced by the doorman, all eyes turned to apprise the young man who was the object of conversation throughout Charles Town. The young ladies almost swooned at his appearance. He had an air of confidence that had not been present the last time he entered this house. Even Melinda, who was heavy with child, wondered if she had made a mistake in not pursuing him. When Camille's eyes fell upon Jacques and then saw the reaction from the guests, her earlier confidence dissolved. She wanted to flee from the room, but she saw the stern look in her mother's face and knew she could not.

"You remember my daughter, Camille," Beza said.

"Yes, of course," replied Jacques, who was suddenly intimidated by a woman who was more beautiful then he remembered.

"I heard you had returned from living with the Indians," she said in French, fighting to find words that would hold his interest. "Perhaps you could find time to dine with us tomorrow evening and give my family a first-hand account of your adventures in the wilderness."

"I would be delighted to do so. I hope you won't find my stories too boring."

"I am sure that my family will be greatly entertained by news of the savages that live along the coast."

As he tried to keep up his side of the conversation, he could not help but be distracted by the breasts that were partially exposed by Camille's surprisingly low-cut gown.

Elsewhere in the room, the other mothers were quietly making disparaging remarks about how outrageous the gown was, while secretly wishing they had dressed their own daughters in a similar fashion.

That night after the guests departed, Camille lay in bed with her Bible pressed against her chest. She prayed to her god, making promises that no mortal could keep, if he would grant her the man she wanted.

At the boarding house, Jacques could not sleep as his thoughts were centered on Camille. He knew that she was within his grasp. Thoughts of Bright Star were pushed back into the recesses of his mind, as was the child she carried.

The next day, Constance spared no expense in the dinner that was set for their guest. Afterwards, they all retired to the parlor where Jacques enthralled them with stories of his trip to the Bay of Saint John the Baptist, which he had made a sketch of and renamed Winyah Bay after the Indians who resided on its shore. Before he left, Constance invited him to come over the next day and bring the other sketches he had discussed, so that the family could see them.

Jacques was surprised when he arrived the next day at twelve o'clock to be taken by the doorman through the house to the back garden and seated at a small table that was set for only two.

The doorman served him tea and then disappeared. A few minutes later, Camille appeared.

"I am sorry but Father could not be here. He had problems that needed his urgent attention at the warehouse. And Mother, with the other family members, went out to visit a relative who unexpectedly became ill. I am afraid you shall be bored today, since I am your only audience. But I do so want to see the sketches and the people you have met on your journey there."

Jacques felt a little uncomfortable at first because it was highly unusual for an unmarried lady to be alone with a man who was not a member of her family. But as he showed her his drawings, explaining what they were and adding stories to each of them, his uncomfortable feeling disappeared. That was until she spied a sketch of Bright Star.

"And who is this lovely creature?" she asked.

"She is the daughter of the chief, Stalmar."

"Is she married?"

"Yes," he answered without hesitation. "To a warrior, and when I left she was with child."

Camille changed the subject, but somehow she knew there was more to that story. She chose not to confront him about it. Did she really expect him to come to her wedding bed a virgin, inexperienced in matters of the bedroom. Besides, she could not believe that a savage would be any competition for her. Despite these thoughts, she still was not comfortable that Jacques would be spending many months each year living with the Indians along the bay.

It was time for Jacques to leave. He had exhausted his sketches and stories. Yet he sensed that she did not want him to depart. They took a walk through the garden which was not particularly beautiful this time of year. When that was completed, there was no longer any excuse they could find to keep him there.

"I must go, for I know that I have outstayed my welcome.'

"You will never over stay your welcome with me."

They were near an old live oak tree when these words were spoken. She reached out and pulled him behind its large trunk where no spying eyes could see them. Her lips found his and her breasts pressed hard against his chest. Then she pulled away and walked toward the house.

"The doorman will show you out," she said without turning back to give him so much as a parting glance.

Jacques just stood there for a moment trying to figure out what had just happened and what it all meant. Despite his mental confusion, he knew for certain that she was the one he wanted to marry. What he did not know was that Camille also felt the same toward him.

As Camille walked toward her room, she thought about the Indian girl.

"After that kiss Jacques, you can compare what I have to offer against what that savage can give you," she muttered to herself.

She was confident which one he would choose.

* * *

That early spring, the wedding was the social event of the season. Everyone commented on how beautiful the bride looked in her flowing white gown. All the women looked on with envy when the Jacques took Camille by the hand and accepted the oath of marriage. A reception at the father's house followed. Then the couple departed to a small country estate called Medo, where they would live until next fall when Jacques once again would depart for Winyah Bay.

The house was owned by Camille's father and was the center of a small agricultural enterprise that concentrated on raising livestock to provide local inhabitants in Charles Town with fresh meat and to supply the ships returning to Europe. It was operated by an overseer and two slaves. They lived in a cabin on the far end of the plantation.

Before the newlyweds arrived, the overseer had seen to it that a fire blazed in the chimney and a pork roast and cooked vegetables were ready for his master's daughter and her new husband. Candles, in the windows, cast a light in the room sufficient to drive away the darkness.

"I will prepare the table," Camille said, after their baggage had been stored temporarily in a corner of the room. Jacques sat at the table while she located two dinner plates, a carving knife and eating utensils.

After they finished their meal, she reached into one of her trunks and removed a bottle of wine.

"It was given to me by my father."

"What is it?"

"It is the last bottle of wine from my father's estate, Medo, in France. He owned a vineyard before he was forced to escape in the middle of the night from the Catholics who wanted to spill his blood. This plantation carries the same name as that estate. He hopes to get some cuttings someday and once again plant a vineyard. But so far it has been difficult to obtain them."

"We share a common tragedy. That is why I have removed the names that the Spanish Catholics placed upon the land of the Winyahs. Soon my charts will be used by others and then all that remains of their influence will be removed from the region."

"That is as it should be. Protestant names for a Protestant colony."

The cork was pulled and glasses poured.

"It has turned to vinegar," he said as he removed the glass from his lips.

She too realized what had happened to this once precious bottle that had been so closely guarded by her father for many years. Tears began to flow, though she tried to hold them back.

"I hope it is not a sign," she said.

"It only means that a bottle of wine has gone bad and nothing more."

"I shall go and prepare myself for bed," she said, tears still streaming down her cheeks that had by now turned red.

Camille got up from the table and went into the bedroom at the end of a hallway. Jacques remained seated, thinking that he should give her some time to calm herself. He was sure that after a tiring day, her nerves must be unsettled. He went to the cupboard where he located a bottle of rum. He warmed some of it in a pot. Then poured a shot of it into a wooden mug for her. This will calm her nerves, he thought.

Only with great effort had Camille managed to stop the tears. She rummaged through the trunk in the room until she located the nightgown that she knew her mother had placed there last week. It was a simple one-piece pull-over made for this special night when her childhood would be taken from her. After slipping it on, she curled up in bed and waited for him.

Jacques came through the door with a mug in his hand.

"I have prepared you some hot rum. Take a drink, it will make you feel better."

He handed the mug to her. As the warm fluid flowed down her throat, she began to relax. Now that she was able to compose herself, she waited quietly while he undressed. His silhouette was visible to her from the the candlelight in the window. When he had stripped, he slipped beneath the covers beside her. He spoke to her in French. They were simple sentences of love. Soon she was in his arms. She could feel his naked body through her thin cotton nightgown, which she soon helped him remove. His hands immediately were upon her breasts, which filled her with excitement. Instinctively, she let her legs part as his hand began to explore there.

Jacques proceeded cautiously at first because he knew she had never been touched. He did not want her to think him a brute. Then he sensed a little impatience. So he quickly entered her as he had Bright Star. Unlike the Indian girl, Camille clung to him as they made love, until she finally cried out with joy and then relaxed against him. Afterward, she curled up in his arms and stayed there until the morning sun light poured through the shutter of their bedroom window.

* * *

Jacques and Camille had planned to stay at the plantation until he had to leave for Winyah Bay, but their plans were interrupted by an unforeseen event, one that would forever be seared into their memory.

Jacques was walking down a forest trail to the overseer's cabin one morning when he heard the war cry of Indian braves in the distance.

He quickly stepped off the path and made his way through a clump of bushes until he had a clear view of the cabin, for that was the direction he thought the war chants were coming from. To his horror, he saw a dozen Sampas Indians standing over the overseer and two slaves. They were in the process of stripping the lifeless bodies of their clothing. He turned and quietly made his way back to the trail. When he reached it, he began to run toward the house. Fear gripped him as he thought about the fact that the Indians might already be there. When he broke through the forest onto the clearing, he was relieved to see Camille in the yard tending flowers. He waited until he was near before he spoke, for he did not know how close Indians might be to the house.

"Get inside. There are Indians about and they are on the warpath."

Camille just stood there as if in a trance, until Jacques reached out and grabbed her arm. Then he dragged her into the house.

"What are you talking about?" she cried out when they were safely inside.

"The overseer and the slaves are dead. They were killed by Sampas Indians. I saw them stripping the bodies. They will be here any moment. Quick, we must load the guns."

There were three muskets, powder, and shot in the house.

"Do you know how to load them?" he asked.

She shook her head.

"Watch me and then follow my example."

She watched him load the first musket and then she loaded the second.

"Now load the third."

She did so without looking up to him for direction.

"Good. Now when they appear, you must load as I fire. I will not have time to guide you. Do you understand?"

"Yes."

"Let's secure the doors and the wooden shutters. We'll fire from the upstairs windows. It's our only hope of survival."

After securing everything downstairs, they went up and waited. Camille was afraid, but Jacques' courage gave her strength. They did not have long to wait. She saw a movement near the edge of the forest. Soon the Indians left the protection of the trees and began to slowly move across the open fields that surrounded the house. Jacques waited until he was sure they were within firing distance before he aimed for the one that appeared to be their leader. His shot was true as it stuck the Indian in his chest. As the man fell to the ground, the other Indians seemed to freeze in place. Jacques took advantage of their moment of indecision to fire the second musket and bring down another warrior. They fled back to the safety of the woods but not before a third shot rang out and killed a warrior who was slow in his retreat.

"Where did you learn to shoot so well?" she asked.

"My grandfather."

"But wasn't he a man of letters?"

"Yes, but as a young man, he was an officer in the King's Guards. That was before they excluded Protestants."

The warriors waited for over an hour before they mustered enough courage to try another assault on the house. During this time Jacques showed Camille how to operate the mechanism on the musket in case their situation became so desperate that she must fire it. He also had her bring upstairs the big carving knife from the kitchen.

This time the Indians came at a run. Jacques struck down two before they reached the house. Now they were on the porch and around the sides where he could not get a clear shot. They heard the Indians trying to force the doors open but they were solid and would not give. The shutters were a different story.

"Take this," Jacques said, as he handed Camille a loaded musket. "I must go downstairs. You stay here."

Jacques grabbed the other two muskets and started down the stairs. When he was almost to the last step, a shutter finally gave way. He killed the first Indian as he attempted to climb through. When another shutter gave way he retreated upstairs. He stopped near the top step, where he handed the empty musket to Camille to reload and then turned and fired a shot through the heart of a brave who was charging up the steps. The dead man's body fell backward with such force that it knocked down the warriors behind him. He had time to take the reloaded musket from Camille's hand and fire one last shot into the mass of Indians as they charged up the stairs. They were upon him and he used the musket as a club and struck several blows until he was finally overwhelmed. They were on top of him, and he couldn't get free. He could feel hands upon his throat choking off his air passages. He heard a musket go off and felt the fingers release their grip on him. He struggled from beneath them as blood from a slashed artery sprayed upon him. Camille had hit her first target and then charged into the mass slashing with the carving knife until Jacques was released from their hands. Now, together they fled into a room. They knew the end was only moments away, and they were prepared to face it together. Suddenly, they heard the sound of several muskets firing and the hooves of horses charging about. They looked out the window and saw the militia from Charles Town giving chase across the cleared ground to the Indians who were in a state of flight. The next day they returned to the safety of Charles Town. The terror they had endured was a thing of the past. But it had forever changed their relationship. The battle made them more mature than others their age, and the conflict bonded them in a way that years of marriage could not have.

* * *

At the end of September with cool weather having returned, the swarming insects were now reduced to the point that Jacques felt it was safe to sail to the bay. This time Beza and he had purchased a two-mast caravel which they loaded with trade goods. The plan was to build a permanent trading post near the mouth of a river that flowed into the bay. Jacques would choose the site.

Camille hated to see him leave. The child within her was already beginning to kick and she feared he would not be back in time for the birth.

As she lay in his arms that night, she made one last attempt to sway him.

"Must you go?"

"Camille, we have been through this conversation many times. You know that I must. Your father is depending on me."

'What about me and your child? Aren't we as important?"

"You are. But if we are to prosper, I must establish myself in the Indian trade before others take advantage of the opportunity."

Then she used the last weapon she had in her arsenal.

"What if I die in childbirth like Melinda did? You won't even be here."

He chose not to respond to that question, for there was no good answer. He simply held her tight in his arms.

She knew by his silence that her last attempt had failed. He would sail tomorrow.

* * *

Thoughts of Bright Star had been buried in the deep recesses of Jacques' mind while he was in Charles Town with Camille. But once the voyage was under way, his feelings changed. As he began to focus on the bay and the wealth it could provide, his thoughts also turned to his Indian wife and the child that by now had been born.

As the caravel sailed into the river beside the peninsula, Jacques saw his friend Chief Stalmar and a group of warriors racing toward him in canoes. On an elevated area near the village a woman stood with a child in her arms. She waved at him as the ship dropped anchor. Though the woman was too far away to see her facial features, he knew it was Bright Star.

The village had been awakened that morning by a group of warriors returning from a hunting trip on the land between the waters. They were full of excitement, for their eyes had spotted a large boat coming down the channel toward the village. It was the first time in several generations that such a large ship had entered this broad expanse of water.

When she heard the news, Bright Star felt certain it was Jacques. She hurried to prepare herself. A woman of the village held her baby while she scrubbed her body and put on a new deerskin pullover. She went into the forest and picked some wild flowers that she knew had a sweet fragrance and rubbed her body with them. Afterwards, she took her child to a high bluff that had been cleared many years ago for use as a vegetable plot. From there she could see a great distance down the bay. As soon as she arrived at this spot, there appeared in the distance two large white sails. Though she had no logical way of knowing if it was Jacques, or even if the ship was from his nation, she could feel his presence. She remembered many in the village said he would never return. She too had doubts whether she would ever see him again. But they had all been wrong. He had come home.

* * *

"Greetings my brother," Stalmar said from the bow of his canoe. "I am glad to see you."

"I have brought many trade goods. We shall need to build a great lodge to store them."

"We shall start tomorrow building it, but today we shall have a feast to celebrate your return."

After stepping on shore, Jacques glanced toward the bluff, hoping to catch a glimpse of his wife and child, but they was no longer there.

Stalmar saw the disappointment on his friend's face.

"She has probably gone to her lodge. It is located on the east side of the village. We built it for her after you went away."

Jacques left and went to seek her. Thoughts of his wife in Charles Town were no longer paramount in his mind. Instead, he was focused on his Indian wife and child. He found her outside the lodge under the branches of a live oak tree. When she looked up and saw him, she did not get up and run to meet him as he had expected. Instead, she picked up the child and turned her back to him. Without so much as a word of greeting, she walked into the lodge. He followed her inside. She still had her back to him and was in the process of placing the child into a crudely made cradle when the first words fell from her lips.

"You were gone a long time."

"It was necessary," he said.

"The child is a boy. I have called him Chicora. It is an ancient name handed down from my ancestors."

He recognized the word from a Spanish journal he had translated.

"It is a beautiful name," he said.

She turned for the first time and faced him. He had forgotten how beautiful she was. The birth of the child had caused her body to mature. Her breasts were more filled out and her face was no longer that of a young girl, but of a striking young woman. He walked hesitantly toward her, unsure how she would react. She stood there and watched his movement but gave no sign of her feeling toward him until they were less than three feet apart. He reached out and she rushed into his arms where she nestled her face against his chest. She began to sob, a trait that was unusual for a Winyah woman. His heart began to melt and he reached down and lifted up her chin. His lips pressed against her mouth. She pulled him toward the corner where several animal skins on the dirt floor served as a bed. She stripped his clothes off, and then removed her own garment. After he lay down upon the soft skins, she remained standing above him for a few moments to give him a full view of her naked body.

Although he had not long been without intimacy, at that moment he felt as if he had not slept with a woman in a long time. When she lay down beside him, her naked body pressed against his. The smell of her incited his lust and drove him to take her quickly. And then he took her again.

The next morning, Bright Star awoke with renewed confidence. She knew there was another woman in Charles Town, but believed Jacques' desire for her and his love for Chicora would always bring him back to the bay.

* * *

The lodge having been completed, the trade goods stored, and the caravel having left for the return voyage to Charles Town, Jacques was now ready to explore the surrounding rivers for a permanent trading post.

"I want to go to the ancestral grounds of my people on the Wacca-maw's river," Bright Star said to Jacques one morning.

"What are you talking about?"

"In another age, the Winyahs resided at a place upon the banks of this big river, and it is still where the spirits of my tribe dwell."

It was the first time he had heard this story. Perhaps he would discover more about the history of her tribe now that his wife was learning to speak English.

They filled a large canoe with supplies and two braves accompanied them to help with the arduous task of paddling upstream. The day was unusually warm for the middle of October and this made for a pleasant journey. Bright Star placed Chicora upon a blanket in the bottom of the canoe. It wasn't long before he was crying to be fed. He still enjoyed the abundance of milk that his mother's breasts held. Soon the time for nursing would end, and his diet would consist of soft corn meal until he reached an age when he could chew.

As they entered the mouth of the Waccamaw River, a name that Jacques had placed on a sketch he was busy drawing that morning, Bright Star pointed out a bluff not far upriver.

"That is where my people lived during the days when we were a powerful tribe and long before the Waccamaws moved down from the north and seized the region from us."

It was an easy area to reach, for at low tide, a sandy beach allowed Jacques and the braves to land and pull the canoe out of the water onto the land. As a safety precaution, Jacques secured the boat by using a rope to tie it to a small cypress tree growing out of the bank. They trudged up the slope without much difficulty. Bright Star had the child securely strapped to her back. When they reached the top, they saw that the bluff was densely forested. It had been so long without human habitation that one could easily believe that no man had ever set foot upon this terrain. The braves helped Jacques build a lean-to structure that would protect the party from rain and wind. After this was completed, nightfall was near so they built a fire and cooked some fresh meat that they had packed for the trip. To this was added cornbread which was a staple of the tribe. After the braves retired to their blankets under the trees, Bright Star and Jacques continued to sit by the fire and huddle together for the night had turned cold. The child was in the lean-to shelter nearby, and he was soundly asleep between a blanket and bear skin.

"Tell me about this place?"

"I know very little, but a few stories that have been handed down. There was once a race of people whose complexion resembled the color of your tribe. We call them the ancient ones. There are some among us who are their descendants. You can often see it in those who have different hair and eye color. You have often commented about those traits in me. That is the only knowledge we have of those ancestors. At a later time the Spanish came and built a town on this very spot, but they were wiped out by disease. They left this fever among us and there was great death. The Winyahs became weak in numbers and we were driven from our homes by other tribes. All the other history of my people is forever lost in time."

"I would like to build a trading post here for it is an excellent spot."

"The Waccamaws would probably grant you permission, but I would be greatly saddened if you disturbed this site."

They returned the next afternoon to the village to find great turmoil. The other two Winyah villages upriver had been attacked by the Sampas who had just migrated back from Charles Town region after their defeat at the hands of the colonists. Now these Winyahs had fled and claimed the protection of Stalmar.

Within the next five days the number of Winyahs who straggled into camp numbered more than two hundred. That was all that remained after the attacks. The rest had been killed or taken as slaves. Stalmar's village was now the last remaining settlement of his tribe. Most of the refugees were women and children. Their arrival put a tremendous strain on the food supply, so Jacques joined the others in hunting the surrounding area to supply fresh meat. He also supervised the construction of a palisade, which would provide some protection if the Sampas attacked. In addition, he gave Stalmar ten muskets and taught the braves how to use them. The defense preparations left Jacques little time to spare, so the building of a trading post on the banks of a river was delayed. Then a further complication developed when the caravel arrived unexpectedly. The captain came ashore and Jacques learned the reason the ship had returned so soon.

"I'm sorry to inform you that Beza has died," the captain said. "I have orders to take you back to Charles Town. The family needs you to take control of the warehouse. Your wife, Camille, said the business requires your urgent attention and that if you delay, all might be lost."

He saw the look on Bright Star's face. She was standing next to him when the message was delivered.

"I have a man on board named Silas Johnson, whom the family sent to remain this winter and be responsible for trading with the Indians. You knew his father. He was the overseer who was killed when Medo Plantation was attacked."

"It was such a tragedy. We are also having a problem now in this region with the Sampas tribe. They have seized some Winyah villages on this stream that I have designated as the Sampit River on my maps. It's a rough translation of the Spanish term *Sampas*."

"When will you be ready to leave?"

"Tomorrow at high tide."

EPILOGUE

The Indian trader, Jacques Marshall, returned to Winyah Bay. He built a thriving post on the Waccamaw River at the very spot where many earlier inhabitants had lived. He continued to divide his time between his two families.

The Indian trade was extinguished in the bay area shortly after the appearance of British settlers, who first built their plantations on the Black River and then expanded throughout the area. Many of the local Indians were sold into slavery. Ships departing from Charles Town took them to the West Indies where they died from disease, starvation, and exhaustion.

* * *

HISTORICAL CHARACTERS, PLACES, TRIBES, PEOPLES, RIVERS AND BAYS.

Lucas de Ayllon, Ana de Becerra, Bacan, Francisco Chicora, Datha, Gomez, Gordillo, Madoc, Montesinos, Pre-Clovis People, Quezos, Quexos, Snorr, The Gale, African slaves at San Miguel De Gualdape, White Indians at Winyah Bay, Sioux Indians, Hooks, Black Hooks, Catawba, Pee Dee, Sampas, Santee, Waccamaw, Winyah, Land of Chicora, Land of Duthare, Cape Romain, San Roman, North Island, Santa Elena, Bay of Saint John the Baptist, San Michael De Gualdape, Saint Michael's on the Gualdape, River Jordan, Waccamaw River, Winyah Bay, Sampit River,

Pee Dee River, Pawley's Island, Puerto de la Plata, Santo Domingo, Santa Cathalina, Bretorn, Choruca, and a Tender.

* * *

Winyah Bay is the first book in a trilogy. A second book's expected date of publication is expected in November 2014.

Visit the author's website at **www.dmaring.com** to learn more about his other published novels.

The Serpent's Seed – This is the first thriller in a trilogy about international political intrigue. In the underground library at Timbuktu, Professor William Weston discovers a map describing the location of an ancient city located in Iran. He does not realize his excavation will be interrupted by a confrontation between America and Iran. Weston also does not foresee that he and his assistant, Rachael, will be drawn into a whirlpool of intrigue that may lead to a nuclear Armageddon.

The Mullahs – The second book in the trilogy concerns the original manuscript of the Book of Revelation buried with the Apostle John. During his search for the tomb, Weston is confronted with a geopolitical crisis in the Middle East and Islamic terrorism. A secret society attempts to harness the turmoil and bring about a confrontation between America and Iran.

Carolina Justice – This novel is written in the tradition of such books as *To Kill a Mocking Bird*, and other stories whose settings are in the segregated South. When two white women are murdered, a mob wants to hang the accused who is an African-American war hero. But when the Ku Klux Klan challenges the legal system, the governor activates the state militia.

ACKNOWLEDGMENTS ON WINYAH BAY

I am thankful to the following individuals who contributed to this novel.

My wife, Judy, helped me improve the manuscript with her helpful suggestions.

My daughter, Lorie, gave me help early in my literary career and kept my feet on the right path.

My son, David, read the manuscript and offered constructive criticism which aided me in writing a better manuscript.

My son, Robert, encouraged me to write and came to my aid when I encountered computer problems.

My brother, Waldo, encouragement and comments were helpful in creating a better story.

My friends Bill Craine, Elise Crosby, Cheryl Gause, Jeannie Johnson, Suzanne Fox, Jane Moon, Stacey Rabon, and Sam Rion made comments on the manuscript which were invaluable in improving the final draft.

* * *